CATHERINE FEAR  ʌ

Liverpool, UK. Known

series of crime fiction n

and short fiction has also

As a musician, she is ɛ

and her solo albums are ɛ ...... Blue Spiral Records.

She also plays guitar and keyboards in all-female heavy metal

group Chaos Rising.

Follow Catherine on Twitter @Metalmamawrites

Instagram @catherine_fearns

Website catherine-fearns.com

BOOK ONE IN
THE REPROBATION SERIES

REPROBATION

CATHERINE FEARNS

Northodox Press Ltd
Maiden Greve, Malton,
North Yorkshire, YO17 7BE

This edition 2023

1
First published in Great Britain by
Darkstone 2018

ISBN: 9781915179883

This book is set in Caslon Pro Std

In memory of Joseph Fearns
1929 -2017

Chapter One

Across grey waters, where the river Mersey meets the Irish Sea, wind turbines puncture the dawn horizon like spinning crucifixes. Beyond, tiny lights frame the ghostly shape of an exploratory oil rig guarding this watery Golgotha. On the beach, the smooth sandscape is perforated by the evenly spaced bronze figures of Antony Gormley's art installation, *Another Place*. So many faceless men, some half submerged, gazing out to sea and waiting calmly, expectantly in this liminal space. To the south is the port of Liverpool, where piles of coloured containers and bright blue gantry cranes pierce the landscape, yearning for a prosperity long lost. And to the north, as the beach recedes into sand dunes and forest and piles of war-rubble, here too is a crucifix.

A cross erected in the sand, fashioned from two pieces of builders' timber, supported by sandbags. The cross supports a man, a hand nailed to each end of the horizontal plane. The naked body in between the hands does not hang forlorn and Christ-like, but instead tied and undignified to the rigid vertical plank. Its skin is papery and grey in the early stages of decomposition. His neck is fastened in an eternal throttle with ropes at the intersection of the cross, causing the man's face to tilt up towards the words painted neatly on the wood above his head.

'*Hath not the potter power over the clay?*'

At his feet, the tide has left a pile of razor clams and bladder wrack, an offering to the dead. But no crown of thorns for this martyr; instead, across his forehead, a deep carving in which the blood has long dried, leaving the clear dark outline of an image of an inverted axe with a double blade. And no jeering crowds for this condemned man; only scatterings of oystercatchers and sandpipers that beachcomb for treasures, while gulls and starlings soar vulture-like against the wind. Soon the first dog-walkers and joggers of the day will find their morning pilgrimage tainted forever.

* * *

'What happens when we die?'

Dr Helen Hope looked up at her audience. A decent smattering of first and second years ranged on benches that rose to the top of the windowless basement lecture theatre. Nowadays, she always enjoyed this first rhetorical question of the trimester, this easy and rather theatrical provocation. The stage fright and spiritual terror that had crippled her at the beginning of her lectureship had dissipated, and she was spurred by the popularity of this course she had designed. Since Eschatology had been offered as a course, there had been a run on applications, both from within and outside of the Theology department.

'What happens when we die?' she repeated, shrugging expectantly. It appeared to be a shy group and no one today was going to play along and venture an answer, so she continued.

'This is surely the central question that all religions and philosophies try to answer, and that's why it must be the central question of any Theology degree. Perhaps you chose this course because you are looking for that answer. Perhaps you just needed another credit and thought it sounded cool. Perhaps you heard there was a hot nun in a habit who teaches it.'

There was a ripple of laughter and she felt the tension in the room lift instantly; this always got them and she had perfected her deadpan reaction. But she still loathed herself for saying it and imagined herself in thirty years' time, still here, with the wording of her joke changed to 'crazy old nun.'

'Perhaps you don't even know what eschatology means, and you're not sure why you are here. Eschatology is the study of death, judgement, and the ultimate destiny of the soul and of humankind. Pretty important, right? Eschatologies vary as to their degree of optimism or pessimism about the future. Each religion, each philosophy, each individual, all have their own interpretation of the hereafter. In this course, we will study eschatological texts in the hope that they will illuminate history, psychology, and what motivates humankind to keep going. You may also use this course as an opportunity to consider your personal belief system.

'And so for your first essay, using the reading list which should be in front of you, I'd like you to consider that simple question. What Happens When We Die? You can be as creative as you like with it really, but make sure you use at least one of the set texts and carefully consider the structure of your essays. Now if anyone needs help with essay planning…'

She stopped when she noticed that someone had put up their hand to ask a question. A man leant back in his seat, legs outstretched, twirling a pen and looking wry. He was older than the rest, perhaps a mature student.

'Yes - please go ahead?' she nodded towards him.

'What do *you* think happens when we die, Dr Hope?'

Ah, there's always one, thought Helen. *The cynic, the wise guy. He's already gone there. And why not - it livens things up.* A hush fell over the room, and those who had been making moves to leave now stopped and took notice.

'That's an excellent question, er… sorry, I don't know your name yet?'

'Paul.'

'Paul. That's a very good question, and I was planning to

cover it during our first proper lecture next week, but perhaps I should have introduced myself more fully at the beginning. Now the first thing to say, before I answer, is that none of you should feel obliged to reveal your personal beliefs, either inside this room or in the pub afterwards. That's not what this course is about. But since you asked so nicely,' she smiled and bowed her head, 'I will tell you just briefly about the belief system in which I operate. I am a Calvinist nun. Calvinist, referring to John Calvin, the theologian who played a prominent role in the sixteenth century Reformation. Calvinist Christians, or reformed Christians, believe in Heaven and Hell, of course, but they also believe in-'

'The tulip, right?' the young man interrupted.

'Well, that's right, the TULIP is sometimes known as the five pillars of Calvinism. T for Total Depravity, U for Unconditional Election, L for Limited Atonement, I for Irresistible Grace, P for Perseverance of the Saints.'

As she said this, he was nodding knowingly, which she couldn't help but find irritating. 'We'll have to leave discussion for another time,' she continued, 'but the essential idea is that of predestination; God has already decided who will be saved and who will be damned. Some say it's a cruel doctrine, but it's actually a clear interpretation of the Bible. And it leaves us with the enormous challenge of how to know a god we cannot understand. I suppose I dedicate my life to solving the ultimate paradox of the two divine wills.'

She was losing their attention since the session had run over into lunchtime, so she decided to wrap things up.

'That question in itself is worthy of multiple PhDs, so I hope it gives you a sense of how broad this course is.' She packed up her own things, indicating that the students could do the same and raising her voice over the commotion. 'As I say, it doesn't have to be Christian or religious at all. Some of you may want to focus on futurism, climate change, or terrorism, for example.

I hope you enjoy your first assignment. Please don't worry about anything and email me if you have any questions. Thank you. Oh, and remember, ladies and gentlemen - no Wikipedia. I will know if you cut and paste!'

Students filed out, switching on phones and chatting. Dr Hope made her way out of the lecture theatre, avoiding eye contact with Paul as she went; along corridors and upstairs until she emerged from the university building onto Hope Street. The two cathedrals of Liverpool framed either end of the vista, both these monoliths shrouded in a fine drizzly mist on this grey October day. Closest to her was the modern Catholic cathedral, known affectionately as Paddy's wigwam due to its unique modernist structure. The spiked cylindrical tower splayed down to a truncated conical body supported by flying buttresses, giving it a tent-like appearance. The quirky architectural design and multi-coloured stained-glass conferred a scouse character and made this, the Metropolitan Cathedral of Christ the King, the 'fun' cathedral. Therefore, despite this Catholic cathedral's unusual look, and the traditional dominance of Catholicism in Liverpool, it was the traditional-looking and austere Anglican cathedral, a lonely brick castle on its plateau opposite, which looked down over the city in judgement.

Today Helen had been lucky and secured a parking space right outside the lecture hall, and as she fumbled with her car keys, she was aware of amused whisperings from a group of students hanging around nearby. It was to be expected; a nun climbing into a bright green Volkswagen Beetle was an odd sight to behold. Helen's religious order made no concessions to modernity with their uniform. Her habit consisted of a floor-length grey tunic, belted at the waist with a traditional rope cincture. Over this was a white scapula and guimpe, while a white coif fitted around her head, ensured that her hair couldn't be seen underneath the black veil crowing everything. A large wooden cross on a long string of wooden beads was her permanent accessory.

Helen started the engine and waved to the students whom she knew were still talking about her, admitting to herself that somewhere deep inside she enjoyed this little notoriety. The ancient Volkswagen was the Order's shared car, known cosily by the Sisters as the 'pootler', a term that had made her cringe once but that now, she noticed with dismay, she was beginning to use herself. Apart from Helen, only one other Sister had a driving license, and so for the most part the car was effectively hers alone.

She drove back towards Formby contented, enjoying the mild exhilaration and relief of having completed this week's public performance. The dock road always provided an evocative drive; the romance of industry, empty warehouses, broken windows, faded signs for businesses and pubs long closed. Liverpool was scattered with abandoned churches; some converted into apartments or climbing walls; others left to rot and crumble with graffiti, weeds growing in cracks, the whispering of angry ghosts. Here and there were businesses still thriving poignantly - a workman's café, a sex shop, and a Chinese supermarket - amongst the wreckage of the past. This was all changing, of course. The regeneration of Liverpool had been underway for ten years, ever since being awarded the European City of Culture in 2008, and now parts of the city centre sparkled with modernity. Container ships and car ferries easing into Liverpool Bay would still see the famous skyline of the Liver birds, the Seventies-style Radio City Tower and the two cathedrals, but these landmarks now mingled with futuristic skyscrapers, chrome and glass.

Meanwhile, the crumbling warehouses along the docks were gradually being transformed into luxury apartments, hotels, and live-work complexes. While she was glad for the city, Helen couldn't help feeling a quixotic wistfulness for the nostalgia of industrial dereliction; the histories that lay behind each broken factory window, each faded shop sign.

She never allowed herself to listen to music, in the car or anywhere else, but today perhaps a little radio news was in order, and she turned on City FM to hear a soft scouse accent announcing the headlines.

'There is a police incident underway today on Crosby beach; reports are of a body being found, the area has been cordoned off for investigation. No further details at this time, but we'll keep you updated.'

Her ears pricked up at the mention of Crosby beach; the Order was only a couple of miles up the coast from there in the Formby pinewoods, and her walks along the dunes took her down to Crosby almost daily. She imagined a drowning, perhaps the mud flats or a rip tide, and shuddered at unnameable ghosts.

Soon docks became suburbs became farmland and autumnal forest, as Helen approached the affluent residential area of Formby. She wound her familiar way down the long driveway of Argarmeols Hall, home of the Order of the Sisters of Grace. Argarmeols Hall comprised a rambling and somewhat crumbling Victorian mansion flanked by a small church, which was in rather better condition. Both hidden from the road and surrounded by forest - the huge sweeping coastal pinewoods of Formby and Freshfields, the last stronghold of the natterjack toad, and protected reserve for England's dwindling population of red squirrels. Fortunate walkers would see them darting up and down the tree trunks.

The Sisters of Grace was the only Calvinist Order, male or female, in the northwest of England, the mansion and adjoining church donated by an eccentric benefactor early in the last century. In a city of kindness, warmth and Catholic forgiveness, Argarmeols Hall stood fast as a fortress of severity, and for the ten years since she had taken the veil, it had been Helen's home, providing the mercilessness that she craved.

The crunch of gravel beneath her tyres was always her familiar welcome, followed by the scent of damp pine as she opened the car door. But today, as she pulled into Argarmeols, the first thing she saw was a police car, and then Sister Mary, waiting anxiously in the doorway. Mary came waddling hurriedly down the steps towards her, picking up her skirts clumsily.

'Sister Helen, there are two detectives here to see you. They want to ask you some questions about a body?' Sister Mary looked nervous, but also a little excited. She lived for the promise of rare moments of drama like these, and Helen often wondered how on earth she could stand to live the life they had chosen.

'We put them in the living room with a cup of tea, but you should go straight in. I think they're in a hurry.'

'OK, thank you, Sister Mary.'

'God bless you, Helen. Let me know how it goes, won't you?'

'I will,' Helen smiled as she went opened the door.

* * *

A young man and woman stood up as she entered the room and reached forward to shake hands. They didn't look hostile at all, causing Helen to instantly relax. In fact, they looked out of their depth in more ways than one, eyeing their ascetic surroundings uncertainly. He was wearing a somewhat ill-fitting suit, with shoes that appeared to be running trainers. He was tall and handsome in that wiry, scouse fashion, with an earnest frown and deep-set eyes that gleamed with sarcasm. But he rubbed frequently at his designer stubble and gave the impression that he would rather wear the same uniform as his colleague. Over her regulation white shirt and tie, this small and neat young woman wore an intimidating dark blue flak waistcoat, which displayed the Merseyside Police logo, along with its radio, weapon, and other threatening paraphernalia of law enforcement. Her hair was conservatively tied back under her policewoman's hat, but she wore full make-up. She and Helen nodded almost imperceptibly at each other in knowing amusement at the incongruity of their respective female uniforms.

The man spoke with a deep Liverpudlian accent.

'Dr Hope?'

'Sister Helen, please,' she smiled. 'I'm only "Doctor" when I'm at the University.'

'Right, Sister. I'm Detective Inspector Darren Swift, and this is Detective Constable Colette Quinn. Nothing to worry about at all, and we'll try not to take up too much of your time. We were just hoping for some guidance from you, really.'

'Guidance? You mean spiritual guidance, detective?' Helen said with an arched eyebrow as they sat down. The detectives looked unamused, and she instantly regretted the moment of uncharacteristic insolence; what on earth was she thinking? Perhaps that student Paul had somehow rattled her today. Detective Inspector Swift continued.

'Unfortunately, a body was found in the early hours of this morning on Crosby beach, up at the north end, so very close to here.'

'Yes, I know.'

'How..?' Both detectives were taken aback, and glanced at each other.

'I heard it on the radio on the way here.'

'Oh, oh right.'

'I didn't hear it from God, if that's what you were wondering.' She smiled. *Back in the game, that one worked.*

But she had set the detectives on edge, and they seemed irritable now. 'So anyway,' said Swift, 'we haven't identified the body yet, and we're checking missing persons, but unfortunately, it is going to be a murder investigation. Whoever did this appears to have covered their tracks very well, and the tide has also been in and out, so we're working with the evidence we have while we wait for forensics to identify the body. It's likely to be drugs-related.'

'Ah, I see.' Helen nodded expectantly as Swift went on.

'The reason we're here is that there was some writing at the crime scene, and it's some sort of religious quote. Obviously, we looked it up, and it's from the Bible, the Book of Romans, it says. Anyway, we just went into the nearest vicarage in Crosby and they sent us here to see you, because apparently, you're an expert on religious texts. We're just looking for some context and whether it could give us any clues. It says here,' he read from his notes, 'you're an eschatologist - what does that mean exactly?'

'Yes, I'm a lecturer in the Theology Department at the University, and eschatology is just a course I've been teaching for the past couple of years. It's about death, the end of the world, fun stuff like that. So - what's the quotation?'

'Right, yes. It's...' he read from his notes, '*Hath not the potter power over the clay?*'

With that said, Helen was momentarily lost to the room, drawn into private thoughts, and DC Quinn leaned forward and coughed to nudge her back into the conversation.

'Do you know it, then?' Quinn asked. 'If you can't remember, we can show you where we looked it up online, or there must be plenty of Bibles here.' She gestured to the bookshelves around the room.

'Sorry, yes, sorry.' Helen shook herself back into the conversation. 'Of course I know it. *Hath not the potter power over the clay, of the same lump to make one vessel unto honour, and another unto dishonour*? It's from Romans, chapter nine verse twenty-one, if I'm not mistaken. I was just startled because it's so very relevant to our...'

She paused, lost in thought, and the detectives waited restlessly for her to continue.

'It's one of the many passages in the Bible that refers to the concept of divine will, or God's power over the fate of mankind; and in particular, the idea of predestination. That is, God in his wisdom chooses certain individuals who will be saved and certain who will be sinners, condemned to Hell.'

At this, Swift and Quinn both made the same facial expression, mouths turned down at the edges in unwilling acknowledgement of her elucidation.

Swift said, 'Predestination... and that can't be changed? Seems a bit depressing. Why on earth would you choose to believe that?'

Helen smiled benignly. This was the usual reaction to Calvinism. 'It's not so much what we choose to believe. More important than the doctrine itself is the way it causes us to live our lives.'

'And are we supposed to know who these saved and sinners are?'

'Oh no. Can you imagine a world in which we knew? All we can do is our best.'

Swift looked at his watch, then at Quinn, saying, 'We should get back. That crime scene needs to be moved before the next tide comes in.' Then he looked directly at Helen. 'If you don't mind me asking, how does this place stay afloat?'

'Well, we receive grants from English Heritage thanks to the history of the buildings, and funds from the United Reformed Church, since we act as an unofficial care home for very old or infirm nuns. One of our Sisters once trained as a doctor, so we have a degree of medical expertise here to take care of them. Then of course, my lecturer salary goes to the Order, plus the Deaconess works as a schoolteacher part-time. Other than that, we need very little, really.'

'Do you get many visitors to the convent? Has anyone unusual come here recently?'

'We do get visitors, yes. Although Calvinism is a very conservative form of Christianity, we try to play some role in the community. There are the public church services on Sundays and Wednesdays. We get a few locals in for that, and then the food bank on Fridays. And we try to be an open door to people in need - we act as a women's refuge, for example.'

'Not really an area of great need around here is it, Formby footballer belt...' mused Swift. 'Anyone taking refuge here at the moment?'

Quinn shifted uncomfortably, visibly bristling at her colleague's harshness, but the nun seemed unoffended.

'No, not at the moment,' Helen replied. 'Of course, we use our country retreat for that anyway, and that's in a secret location for obvious reasons.'

'Well,' said Swift, straightening up to leave, 'it's impossible to tie any of that to a murder motive at this stage, but thank you for your time and we'll come back to you if we find any more… religious clues, let's say. It's very likely to be drugs-related.'

'Or maybe a disgruntled potter,' ventured Helen. They realised she was making a joke, a terrible one, and were unamused. She told herself off again. What was she thinking, making light of something like this? She could feel herself becoming a bore, long before her time, gradually turning into one of the old dears at thirty-two. A faint spark of something, perhaps desperation, was kindling somewhere within her and beginning to somehow alter her behaviour. Swift was getting up to leave when Quinn touched his arm and whispered.

'What about the marking on the body? It might be linked…'

Swift sighed; irritated she had brought it up but conceding and sitting down again. 'There is something else, as Detective Constable Quinn said out loud; there was a marking on the body. If you're not too squeamish… we can show you on the iPad. This is confidential, of course, not for the press or social media.'

'I'm a nun. I don't know what social media is.' *And now a pointless lie. What am I doing?*

Swift placed the iPad in front of her, and she suddenly recoiled and gasped. They hadn't prepared her, and yet again, she was taken from the room, lost in the private horror of another time she had seen a body.

'*A crucifixion?*'

'No, not exactly. He didn't die like that. Looks like he died a while ago and this elaborate set-up was constructed last night for people to find. Sorry, should have told you more before we showed you the photo. The carving on the body - it's an axe, right? Does it mean anything, religious-wise?'

Again, Sister Helen was very silent and still, and the detectives were about to give up, wishing they hadn't shown her. Then she spoke.

'It's a double-headed axe, and it does have a meaning, yes. Several meanings. Sometimes known as a Labrys, it is originally from Crete and is one of the oldest symbols of Greek civilisation. It was often associated with female deities, a symbol of Greek fascism. But… and the reason I know about this symbol, since it relates to my eschatological study, is that it is also a symbol of death. It symbolises duality in a similar way to the Tau Cross. In ancient Athens, those prisoners sentenced to death had the lower case 't' tattooed on their foreheads and if the prisoner was fortunate to be found innocent, he would have an upper case 'T' in the form of the Tau, which is the symbol of life, tattooed on their forehead.'

'Symbol of death, OK.' Swift tried again to leave, but Helen wasn't finished.

'But detective, this axe is inverted, which means something else again. An inverted axe means anti-justice or rebellion. Rebelling against God. The work of Satan. So, I suppose what the writing and the symbol are saying together is that this person has rebelled against God and is going to Hell… no matter what. Of course, that is horrible and unknowable. How terribly sad for his family. Who was he? He looks very young…'

But Swift had stood up and moved towards the door. 'We're not releasing any more details at this stage. Once the body is identified and the family notified, you'll no doubt hear about it in the local press.'

* * *

Helen saw them out and watched from the doorway as they made their way across the gravel to the police car. Once they were out of her earshot, Quinn looked at Swift across the car doors. They had only known each other for a few hours, and she was still trying to get the measure of this mysterious detective who had been sent over from the Murder Squad in the city centre. According to the lads back at Crosby station, he was some career-ladder hotshot, but Quinn was beginning to wonder whether his brooding manner might, in fact, be shyness.

'You seemed on edge in there, like you couldn't wait to get out.' she said. 'What are you thinking?'

'I was thinking we should get back to identifying bodies and looking for witnesses, not messing about with nuns and riddles like it's *The Da Vinci Code*.'

'What a place, though. Like it's been frozen in time. And those old nuns who opened the door were so cute.' She decided to test the waters for banter. 'I was a convent school girl myself, d'you reckon it did me any harm?'

'Debatable.' he said as they drove away. 'Religion and me, we have a history, and not a good one. Anyway, this is Liverpool; football is our religion, and Anfield is our church.'

'Goodison Park, you mean.'

'Oh, don't tell me you're a fucking blue.'

'Does that mean we're incompatible, then?'

Quinn smiled sidelong at him, but Swift didn't take the bait.

'Anyway,' he said, 'what sort of young, nice-looking girl becomes a nun? It's attention seeking if you ask me. Dead weird.'

'Ah, that was it. You fancied her.'

'Fuck off.'

Insults traded, they relaxed into their working relationship, and Quinn had a good feeling about it.

'Coincidence, wasn't it?' she said as they pulled onto the bypass that headed back towards the city. 'That quotation being so… Calvinist or whatever.'

'The quote, the axe, the crucifixion - that entire crime scene was a message, a warning. There are plenty of local drug-lords with mansions around here. It has to be gang-related somehow. Detective school 101 - there are no coincidences.'

'What does that mean?'

'I don't know. I'm just messing. To be perfectly honest with you, Colette, this is my first case on the Murder Squad. I started last week, passed me exams and switched from Vice. I was only sent down the beach this morning because I live the nearest. Trust me to get a weird one for my first case, eh?'

'A horrible one as well. Where d'you live?'

'Waterloo. By the docks, right at the other end of the beach. Just moved there. Anyway, they haven't taken the case off me yet, but it's only been a few hours.'

'It was only by chance I was the Duty Officer this morning. We get the odd body in Crosby, but it's usually a domestic. You'll be sound, boss. With me behind you, what could go wrong, eh?'

'Nice one. Let's check in with the CSIs on the beach, then head back to Crosby to set up an Incident Room and put the team together.'

'They're a good bunch in Crosby, rowdy like, but they'll get stuck in to this. A lot of them seemed to know you.'

'Yeah, I grew up there; in fact, I started at Crosby station ten years ago. It's good to be back.'

'Not one of the lads anymore though, are you?'

* * *

Helen was still standing on the doorstep, lost in a reverie, when the Deaconess came up behind her quietly, startling her. The Deaconess always stood a little too close, and Helen could smell her sophisticated scent, which was possibly Chanel, one of her few indulgences being not to wash with the rough, pungent carbolic soap that the other Sisters used.

'Everything alright, Helen? We haven't had police here since the time Sister Josephine bought those marijuana plants by mistake. What have you been up to, you naughty girl?'

'Yes, yes, Margaret, everything's fine. Very odd, though. Terrible, really. They found a body on Crosby beach.' For some reason Helen didn't feel like sharing the detail about the crucifix. 'There was a religious quotation with the body, and they wanted someone to explain it. Turned out it was rather Calvinist, actually.'

'Ah, then they came to the best person to analyse it, of course. Our very own little scholar. You know,' she straightened Helen's veil as she spoke; 'I rather miss those chats we used to have. You've been so busy with all that university work. We're very proud of you, of course. But we miss you. Why don't you come and see me later in my room? We could have a glass of wine together after dinner.'

The Deaconess turned Helen around by her shoulders and looked into her eyes, in a way that Helen had used to find so powerful, but now she found slightly patronising. Deaconess Margaret Mills was statuesque in middle age, still the second youngest in the Order after Helen, and she ruled her little dictatorship with a benevolence constantly tinged with threat. The moment was interrupted by Sister Mary eagerly shuffling down the corridor.

'Come on now, Helen, there's time before chapel. Tell us everything!' Margaret released Helen, who linked arms with Mary and was bustled away.

* * *

That evening after dinner and prayers, Helen sat at her desk in pyjamas and dressing gown, to mark the latest batch of essays and prepare for next week's tutorials. However, she was unable to concentrate, so shaken by the day's events, and her spartan little room provided no comfort or distraction, so she decided to go and work in the convent's library. She crept along the Hall's silent corridor and down the main staircase without really knowing why she was creeping, since there was nothing forbidden or surreptitious about leaving her room at night. But there was an unofficial curfew at the convent in the evenings, the mostly elderly women tired after the rigours of the day's prayer schedule.

Alone under the lamplight and surrounded by books, Helen felt cocooned, and she decided to use the convent's one computer to look up the local news website and see if there had been any developments. There was a video clip with Detective Inspector Swift giving a statement from Crosby beach. He was standing on the sand with the bronze figures of 'Another Place' ranged out behind him into the grey water. The wind had whipped up, sending whistling spindrift along the sand and causing his anorak to flap.

'The body of an unidentified man was found here in the early hours of this morning. We are currently looking through missing persons and asking for any witnesses to come forward.'

The reporter from behind the camera asked, 'Can you confirm reports that the body was hung up on a cross?'

'At this time, we cannot divulge any more details about the crime scene. But I can confirm that we are treating this as a murder investigation.'

Helen clicked on a couple of other news stories and then, absent-mindedly and absurdly looking over her shoulder before she did it, typed 'double-headed axe' into the search engine.

There was the Wikipedia entry detailing the Cretan axe, which she had explained, almost word for word, to the detectives. Below it were listings for computer games, fancy dress websites, and historical blogs. She clicked on the 'Images' tab; so thrown had she been by the image on the body, she had an urge to see more of these axes. As she scrolled through, one picture caught her eye, since not only was it inverted, but also it looked exactly the same design as the axe on the body.

She clicked on it and was suddenly confronted with a double-headed axe flashing on a black screen, plus an infernal guitar noise blasting through the computer's speakers. She quickly turned down the volume and, again looking over her shoulder, clicked on the flashing axe that implored her to enter. She found herself on the website of some sort of rock band; five bearded men stood in a forest staring at her, almost comical in the intensity of their expressions. She smiled to herself. She had heard of these heavy metal bands that use religious or satanic imagery for shock value, and she felt it was all harmless enough. Two things kept her on the webpage. First, the band's name was Total Depravity, an inherently Calvinist notion of sin affecting all parts of man. A flashing button implored her to buy their new album, which was called *Irresistible Grace* - another one of the five pillars of the Tulip. Irresistible Grace. *Whatever God decrees to happen will inevitably happen, and those whom He elects for salvation will inevitably be saved.*

Helen clicked on the band's 'Bio' tab and established that they were a Norwegian group who were apparently 'melodic death metal masters.' Whatever that was, she thought it sounded rather beautiful. They were in the middle of a European tour and had already played a concert in Liverpool; just the other night, in fact, and tomorrow they would be in Manchester. *They are here.* A nameless fear, tinged with excitement, stirred in the pit of her stomach.

The lyrics were composed by lead vocalist and guitarist Mikko Kristensen, who claimed to 'rail against the tyranny of religion and the lies of belief. If you worship God, you also worship Satan!' However, for someone who professed to hate religion, he seemed to be obsessed with exploring its ideas. When Helen clicked on the band's 'Discography' tab, she saw immediately that this Kristensen had a deep interest in Calvinist notions. One album, which advertised itself as a 'concept album', was entitled *Satan's Progress* and appeared to be a version of John Bunyan's Pilgrim's Progress, except with the protagonist aiming to get to Hell. There were plenty of other satanic references, too; another album was called *Demoness*, with each song title the name of a female demon: Lilith, Succubus, Empusa, Lamia, and Hantu Kopek.

The record covers abounded with religious imagery, but the overriding theme was always that of a dark figure holding a double-headed axe in front of a wrought-iron gate. She looked up some of the lyrics, which were peppered with expletives and sexual references, but also with quotations from the Bible, from St. Augustine, even from the Canons of Dort. This person had done a lot of theological research, focusing particularly on Calvinist doctrine. *How fascinating*, she thought. *Why is God drawing me towards this?* Today there had been too many signs and wonders, and she was overwhelmed. It was long past midnight now, so Helen shut down the web browser and, without really knowing why, she cleared her browser history before turning off the computer and the lights and going back to bed.

She was still unable to settle, the images of the day flashing past her closed eyelids like an old movie projector; a crucifix, a symbol carved in blood, that expression of unimaginable horror and sadness on the corpse's face, despite his closed eyes. The detectives and their odd manner; the Deaconess at her shoulder, touching her arm; the band members staring out at her with their heavily charcoaled eyes that attempted to bore into her soul. And then other images, the ones for which her whole life was a penance.

This would be one of those nights, she knew, when sleep would not come. She had learned to accept it. It was always this time of the month, when she was never quite dry down below, and she would writhe and yearn and her hands would slip down towards her thighs. But she would stop herself; her fingers gripping the sheets and she would pray and wait in patient frustration for the dawn light.

Chapter Two

The next morning, Crosby police station was alive with the buzz of hushed urgency as Detective Inspector Darren Swift came striding in, take-away coffee, bacon sandwich, and files in hand. Things were moving, and he had a new sense of purpose; perhaps he wasn't going to screw up his first murder investigation after all. DC Colette Quinn followed him through the desks to the front of the room with her facial expression steeled against the inevitable jocular whispers of 'Go 'ed Colette!' She stood next to Darren as he faced his new handful of staff, mustering as much confident authority as he could.

'Right, can I have everyone's attention, please? Lads? Right, as you know, we have a category B homicide on Crosby beach. Merseyside Police want to keep things in the area for now, so the murder investigation is going to happen from here. You can basically treat this whole station as the incident room.' There were murmurs and mutterings and a few arms raised, but he put his hands up to quell any questions and continued.

'I'll be the Senior Investigative Officer on this case. For those of you who don't know me, my name is DI Darren Swift; I grew up in Crosby and started off at this station ten years ago, so I recognise a few faces.' He nodded and smiled awkwardly as a few hands waved at him. 'Alright Dazza. Nice to have you back, Swifty.'

'I was down at the Met for a while, and more recently on Vice at Canning Place. DC Quinn here will be my deputy-'

At this, there were more murmurings of 'Wahey, nice one, Colette.'

'…and we'll continue assigning tasks at the end of this meeting, but thanks everyone for a great start.' The general atmosphere of support inwardly buoyed Swift, but behind the banter, he knew everyone felt the seriousness of the situation.

'Lads, this is a murder, bit of respect, OK. We've already made significant progress - Quinn, do you want to fill everyone in on what we know?'

Colette cleared her throat and stepped forward. It was bizarre to hear her own voice speaking out to her peers.

'Right, Forensics and Path were on fire yesterday, so this is what we've got already. Missing Persons brought up a probable ID on the body, which was formally identified last night. The victim's name is Jason Hardman, aged twenty, and lived with his mum and brother in Seaforth. Aged seventeen, he spent a year at Tomlinson Young Offenders Institution for drugs offences, but has been in the clear since and worked as a barman at Zeus. That's the gay club on Seel Street for those of you who don't know. He was reported missing by his family a month ago, and was last seen at work the same day.'

'Anything on social media?' someone asked.

'He had an open Facebook page, but he wasn't very active on it and last posted over a month ago, nothing significant so far. Mobile phone records and other social media will be the next stage.'

'Do we have a cause of death?'

'We do. Cause of death strangulation with no sign of struggle, so it's consistent with him being sedated in some way, although we're still waiting on the toxicology results. There are…' - and here she read carefully from the pathology report - 'significant needle marks on both arms, which do not look consistent with drug use but with medical treatment, since they were carefully rather than crudely done. The carving of an upside-down axe on the forehead was done with a sharp instrument.' As Quinn said this, Swift was putting up photos of the body, and as the team took in the gruesome sight, there were audible shudders and a noticeable darkening of the mood. Swift could feel that Quinn was tiring of her public performance, so he stepped in to help her out.

'Unfortunately, the tide came in between the body being placed and discovered, which has wiped any decent traces of footprints or tyre tracks, and presumably this was intentional. One priority is to figure out how they got the body there. In theory, a car could have driven down the ramp and onto the beach, but it's also feasible that someone strong could have dragged the cross down there from the car park. No fingerprints have been found yet. Whoever they were, was very careful indeed. Right... so there's a lot to go on. Questions? Thoughts? Theories?'

'Could one person have put up that cross, though?' someone asked.

'That's a really good question. Unlikely. It points to a team effort, and at least one male, due to the height involved. We'd need to do a reconstruction at some point, but we can't do that without making a huge show of ourselves. We need to be careful. Actually, that's another point.' As new parameters came exploding to hit him, Swift felt he was making it up as he went along, and hoped that was not coming across too clearly to his team.

'Community and media liaison - Tracey that's you - this needs to be handled really carefully. The CSIs had the site covered by sheeting quickly, but those dog-walkers that discovered the body - you should assume they are going to talk to the *Crosby Herald*, even the *Echo*, may have done so already. So get on to the papers and tell them not to report any details of the crime scene. Then I need you down at the site with the uniforms to answer questions from passers-by.'

'Question... are we not closing the beach?'

'No, that's the worst thing we could do. Keep it on the down low, I've been told. *Another Place* is a big tourist attraction, it's a weird crime, there's no need to panic people.'

'Maybe a stupid question, but why are we not releasing details of… the crucifixion?'

'Same reason – to avoid panic, because whoever put the body there was showing off. Why did they want it revealed? Warnings like that are almost always drug-related, so let's get on to Titan and see if they know about anything going down in Crosby.'

A hand went up, and Swift pointed in its direction. 'Yes. Dave, isn't it?'

'What's Titan?'

'North West Organised Crime Unit. Jesus, how long have you been here?'

'Two weeks.'

'Oh, right. Fair enough. Baptism of fire, eh?' *For both of us*, thought Darren.

'What about the quotation and the carving?' someone asked.

'Could be gang-related, and again, Titan might help. We're going to look into visitors to that Calvinist convent in Formby, because apparently,' here he shrugged, looking unconvinced, 'the Biblical quotation had something to do with Calvinism or whatever. I think it's tangential; I wonder if the locality of the convent may have inspired the killer to use religion to throw us off the scent. Let's focus on facts – all this religious stuff is only relevant if it relates to forensic evidence and motive. Those timber planks for the cross didn't fit in a car. Dave, see if you can find any vans in the area that night. The nearest CCTV will have been at Hall Road Station – let's hope whoever it was drove that way. And then let's contact timber yards. There aren't that many.'

Swift could feel himself becoming vague; it was time to wrap up the meeting and start focusing on the next steps.

'Right, Quinn and I are heading over to Seaforth to search Jason Hardman's house and interview friends and neighbours. HOLMES team carry on, Door-to-Door carry on, and could the rest of you get onto Tinder, or Grindr, or whatever it is, and find out if Jason met anyone recently?'

Swift sighed inwardly as this was met with a barrage of jokes and banter.

'Put Dave on that. He's already got a Grindr account…'

'He's their best customer!'

'Boss?' Dave put up his hand. 'How do we do that?'

'Right, you need to contact Merseyside Police head office and find out who their SPoC is.'

'You what?'

'Single Point of Contact with the CSPs.'

'You what?'

'Communication Service Providers. For fuck's sake. Don't let me down, people.'

Swift was out of his depth like one of the bronze men on the beach, the tide rising to engulf him. But unlike the figures on the beach that stood firm and implacable, he felt an ominous sense of panic. *The blind leading the blind*, he thought. *Come on, you can do this.*

* * *

Jason Hardman's family home was a redbrick terraced house on Curran Street in Seaforth, the vein through which Liverpool's working-class lifeblood had flowed since the eighteenth century. Each of these streets seemed to point towards the docks, where the ghosts of prosperity stalked on blue metal legs. Curran Street ended at the roaring flyover, beyond which the tanks of Seaforth Cornmills, piles of rusty Maersk and Hainan shipping containers and giant yellow gantry cranes crowded the horizon. It was a street where every house looked the same, two windows and a door, and occasionally a shared alleyway. Each dwelling was given character by the level of pride put into the frontispieces and tiny gardens. Some were drug dens, with piles of rubble outside, boarded windows, graffiti. Others were scruffy student houses, wheelie bins overflowing, bicycles optimistically chained to the railings. This one was immaculately kept, a miniature citadel of fierce pride amid dilapidation. In the cramped front room dominated by a faux leather sofa suite and a flat screen TV, every surface was littered with family photos: holy communions, weddings, holidays, and nights out - artefacts of love. Mrs Hardman sat comforted by her other son. Swift and Quinn sat on matching armchairs either side of the fireplace, awkwardly clutching cups of tea. Everything was infused with nicotine, and Mrs Hardman's hand shook as she balanced her cigarette over the ashtray. Above the electric fireplace hung a wooden crucifix, which nobody had yet thought to take down.

Swift began. 'Mrs Hardman, I know this is a terrible time for you, but we need to find who did this as quickly as possible. Did your son have any enemies? Anyone to whom he owed money?'

'No, no, nothing. I mean, I know he got up to some hi-jinks in the past. He was no angel, but he was just a lovely, lovely lad. Especially since he got out of Tomlinson. That place was great for him. He had his whole life ahead, he was saving to go to university…' She broke down and was silently comforted by her son.

'Jason was at Tomlinson Detention Centre for a spell two years ago; did he keep in touch with anyone from there?'

'None of the inmates, no. He wasn't friends with any of them. He really wanted a fresh start when he got out. Absolutely no drugs at all, I'm sure of it.'

'There was that teacher, though,' ventured her son.

Mrs Hardman nodded. 'That's right, yeah.'

'Teacher?'

'He started taking A-levels in there and he really enjoyed the science, you know, he was very taken with the teacher. He wasn't in there long enough to sit the exam, so they kept in touch afterwards. He used to go over for lessons and then he took A-level Biology. Got a B as well.'

'Go over? To the detention centre?'

'No, to the teacher's place.'

'Do you know where that was?'

'No. He was an adult; we didn't keep tabs on him.'

'Did your son have a boyfriend, Mrs Hardman?'

'Not that we knew of. Nobody who came over, but he kept his personal life to himself, really. Working in a nightclub, his hours were, you know, irregular, and he was often out all night.'

Colette's eyes wandered to the mantelpiece above the fireplace. 'That's him in the Communion photo, isn't it? He was so handsome. Was he religious himself, Mrs Hardman?'

Mrs Hardman looked at them, stirred suddenly, and she and her son released each other from their comforting clutch. 'Why do you ask?'

'Well, because of the nature of the crime scene…'

'He had started talking about it. A bit. About Heaven and Hell. About how he needed to change. He wouldn't go into it, but we just couldn't imagine… He's always been so happy with himself, and so were we - weren't we?' She broke down in tears.

'Did he go to a church?' asked Swift. Mrs Hardman just shook her head, buried in her son's embrace.

'I think me mum's had enough for today,' he implored.

Swift wished he was better at this; expressing sympathy didn't come naturally to him, and he was relieved that the newly appointed Family Liaison Officer would soon arrive. He and Quinn left the family to their grief and went to look around Jason's bedroom upstairs with gloved hands. The room still smelled of his aftershave. There was no laptop or phone to be found. Other than the usual young man's paraphernalia - toiletries, dance music magazines, clothes - only two items stood out. On his bedside table, in pride of place, was a navy leather book, embossed in gold with the words 'Holy Bible.' The book was hard-backed but clearly well thumbed.

And in the drawer of this bedside table, amongst packets of paracetamol and Lemsip, keys and nightclub flyers, was a packet of Dexamethasone.

'Dexamethasone?' said Swift. 'That's a steroid, right? Bag that up.'

* * *

'All of us are sinners. All people are conceived in sin and are born children of wrath, unfit for any saving good. Inclined to evil! Dead in their sins! *Slaves* to sin! Without the grace of the regenerating Holy Spirit, they are neither willing nor able to return to God, to reform their distorted nature, or even to expose themselves to such reform. I say again, All of Us Are Sinners!'

This last sentence was said with such venom and volume that several members of the congregation, who were sitting in the front pews, visibly recoiled. Deaconess Margaret Mills always began her Wednesday evening sermons from the pulpit in a gentle voice tinged with a hint of menace. She would build gradually, moving from the pulpit to the floor, a crescendo of portentous threats as her whole body would come into play. She was a natural performer, with eyes widening and narrowing at just the right moments, catching individuals so that they wanted to look away in shame but couldn't. Her voice would range from ominous low to shrieking high, the gentle Northern accent sounding impossibly grand in this part of the world. There was no comfort to be had from her sermons, only the fear of God struck into one's heart, and this was the appeal. For the residents, for the visitors, for Helen. Most of the congregation loved the firebrand thrill of the performance, the horror-film quality of the fear. For Helen, the fear was genuine, visceral. She craved this punishment, this constant, caustic reminder of her sin. After some more fire and brimstone, the Deaconess softened and brought kindness, a sweet manipulation for her audience.

'Yes, all of us are sinners. And nothing brings the beauty of Jesus Christ to sinful people, believers and unbelievers alike, as powerful as God's own Scriptures. The Scriptures are the basis of our teaching, of our Gospel, for the word of God is the only word. And we do not question the word of God. From this comes our happiness.'

She smiled for a moment, then suddenly, spectacularly, turned up the anger again.

'And to those who complain about this grace of an undeserved election and about the severity of a just reprobation, we reply with the words of the apostle.

Who are you, O man, to talk back to God?'

Her eyes were wild now and ranged from one person to the next in fury. St. Michael's Church was small, more of a chapel than a church, having been built originally to serve only the Argarmeols family and their employees. There was no division between the nave and the chancery, and no room for aisles flanking the nave at its edges. Therefore, there was no escaping the Deaconess's wrath as she stalked the pews, allowing herself to be an eager vessel for the bitter rage of the Calvinist God. The majesty of this church interior lay in its exaggerated height; in typical Victorian Gothic style, it had been built to aspire to the sky, drawing the eye upwards and reminding the worshipper how very far above him his God was to be found.

'God's plan cannot be changed; God's promise cannot fail; the calling according to God's purpose cannot be revoked!'

She sighed with theatrical exhaustion, closing her eyes and raising her hands in supplication before wringing them and returning to the pulpit. She was disappointed with her flock, this rabble of hopeless candidates for Heaven. From one face to the next, she looked expectant. The Deaconess taught religious education part-time in a local private school, and Helen, sitting in her usual position on the front pew, sometimes amused herself at the thought of the terror she must instil in those teenagers.

'May God's son, Jesus Christ, who sits at the right hand of God and gives gifts to humanity, sanctify us in the truth, lead to the truth those who err; silence the mouths of those who lay false accusations against sound teaching, and equip faithful ministers of God's Word with a spirit of wisdom and discretion, that all they say may be to the glory of God and the building up of their hearers. Amen.'

At the end of the service, Helen waited as the small congregation filed out in a silent purge, wrapping their coats against the cold autumn evening, all lost in contemplation of their utter insignificance in the universe. When the church was empty, Helen approached Margaret, who was collecting her papers together at the altar.

'Deaconess?'

Margaret spun around. 'Yes, tell me.'

'Would it be OK if I took the car overnight tonight?'

Margaret's eyes and body language betrayed a momentary flicker of disappointment, as if hoping Helen might ask something else.

'I thought I might go and see my mother.'

'Are you sure that's a good idea, Helen? You've tried very hard, but it only seems to upset you every time. Has something happened?'

'No, no, I... just think it's important to keep showing I'm there for her, you know.'

'Of course.' There were those hands on Helen's shoulders again. 'Drive safely and come and see me tomorrow when you return. Let me know how it went.'

'I will, Margaret, thank you. And may I take some money from the kitty? I think we need petrol.'

Chapter Three

As she drove along the M60 that evening on the short journey to Manchester, Helen felt the mild euphoria of escape that she often felt when she was in the car. What an adventure this would be! However, her excitement turned to nervousness as she approached Manchester and reality hit; what had she been thinking, wearing her habit to a rock concert? But then, she hadn't worn normal clothes for seven years, so there was really nothing else she could have worn. Furthermore, what was she doing? Lying, going to a musical event, a musical event that advertised itself as blasphemous? She told herself that this was just research, which she might even be on to something that could help the police.

The place she was heading to was in a warehouse district on the outskirts of the city. The old Beetle had no GPS and Helen did not have a phone, so she had to stop several times and switch on the car light to consult her map. By the time she had found the right area and somewhere to park the car, her stomach was growling, perhaps with nerves, perhaps hunger, although there was no time to find anything to eat now.

She could hear the thump of music as she walked towards a warehouse flanked by a long queue, and a lump of self-consciousness rose in her throat as she wished she could somehow hide her attire - how conspicuous she must be. However, she was astonished to find that her clothing was surprisingly appropriate. The people in the queue were predominantly men, and most were wearing a combination of denim and leather covered in embroidered patches that appeared to be the emblems of rock bands; it was almost a uniform. There were also many people who were dressed strikingly similar to her. These goths, as she believed they might be called, wore long robes, mostly of black, although one or two had grey or white habits like her, and even veils. Unlike her, however, they had accessorised with heavy silver jewellery and some had even painted their faces white, with dramatic black eye makeup.

Helen bought her ticket, allowed herself to be patted down by a female security guard, and then entered to a wall of sound and bodies, blinking in the strobe lights. She realised immediately why her clothes had raised so few eyebrows in the queue. On stage was a band whose members were all dressed as demonic vicars, the lead singer wearing a bishop's mitre. All of them had doused their faces in fake blood. She manoeuvred herself a little closer to the stage, buffeted by bodies that were strangely unhostile.

The Bishop figure stood still most of the time, singing in a deep, affected baritone. But the surrounding musicians around him cavorted and contorted themselves furiously, faces grimacing, heads and necks thrusting. Their hands moved frantically across their instruments, although it was very difficult to decipher any individual sounds. The volume was almost unbearable; Helen noticed many people were absurdly wearing earplugs, and she longed for some herself.

The audience moved as one many-tentacled creature; a thousand-headed hydra that nodded and shook its heads in unison, at times jumping in unison. At one point, the Bishop made a circling motion with his finger and a whirlpool of bodies broke into spontaneous rotation in the middle of the crowd; running in crazed circles, pushing each other, chaotic yet coordinated at the same time. The ripple effect caused her to be buffeted backwards, and she stumbled into the person behind her, causing him to spill his drink. She whirled round and mouthed, 'I'm sorry,' looking up at a tattooed, pierced, and bearded face.

'Alright, miss,' he smiled and helped her back to her feet before resuming his concentrated nodding.

When the song ended, the hydra erupted into cheers and uniformly lifted hands with two fingers - the index and the little finger - pointed in a cultish salute. They looked like horns, she thought, perhaps devil horns. She looked surreptitiously behind her at the tattooed man, and he was doing it as well. Arm outstretched, index and little finger pointed towards the stage. 'Fuck yes!' he shouted at nothing. Helen noticed that, like him, many people seemed to be there on their own. The band, who she had by now ascertained was called Bishop of Satan, had now finished and there was a period of relative and merciful quiet as enormous men in baggy shorts carried equipment on and off stage. The audience dispersed towards the bar, toilets and exits, checking phones, bringing out cigarettes and lighters. She didn't really know what to do with herself, and so, in a moment of rebellion, she went to the bar to order a drink. The Sisters of Grace occasionally allowed themselves a glass of wine, but Helen decided to try to blend in with the concertgoers, so she ordered herself a beer and was given a huge plastic cup full. She grimaced at the taste; she had only tasted beer once, and that had been a long time ago, in another life.

Soon the floor was filling up again, a palpable sense of expectation in the air as people jostled towards the front. The stage had filled with fake smoke, which smelt not unpleasant but was acrid and stung her eyes. As it dissipated, she saw that a huge banner, or rather four pieces of sheeting sewed together to make a banner, had been hung to fill the back of the stage. Wavering slightly on the flimsy material was the image of the inverted double-headed axe, and in the same jagged lettering she had seen on the website, the words "Total Depravity." She couldn't help but smile, because it didn't even feel like blasphemy; it was already clear to her that the members of this audience were not part of some evil satanic cult, but simply had questionable taste in music. The meaning of those words was possibly lost on most of them, although she knew, having read the lyrics, that it was not lost on the band.

Total Depravity came on to the stage to deafening roars and more of those hand signals, and then the music started. Explosions of drumbeats and distorted guitar noise shook her whole body. She focused on the lead singer Mikko Kristensen, who sometimes concentrated on the furious finger movements on his guitar, sometimes stared at the audience with a demonic expression, sometimes pointed a finger, sometimes stuck out his tongue in a bizarre and, she supposed, sexually suggestive gesture. When he finally put his mouth to the microphone, she almost gasped in shocked laughter, because the sound that emerged was unearthly, inhuman. It was completely without pitch, perhaps a shriek, or a growl, as if he had razor blades in his throat. This was not singing of any type she had ever encountered, and it was impossible to discern any of the lyrics she had read in the noises he was making.

Despite the straggling beard and tattoos, there was something androgynous, even feminine, about him. He was much smaller than his hulking bandmates, and his arms were fragile and elfin. He seemed painfully thin, so that his long blonde hair framed sunken cheekbones, and heavily charcoaled eyes. The guitar he played, which instead of being guitar-shaped was a caricature of jagged edges, seemed too big for him, and he grimaced as he wielded it between thin painted arms.

In between songs, he addressed the audience, a series of foulmouthed expletives hurled in English with a Scandinavian accent. How strange to use so many swear words in a language foreign to you, she thought, and how strange to insult your audience

- yet they behaved with adoration. He made that same circular movement with his finger that the Bishop had made, instigating another of those human circles of play fighting. The circles, the hand signals; so many rituals. This was like a religion in itself. She looked around her and marvelled; everything about this was so ridiculous, and she should have been appalled, yet there was something wonderful about it. There was a keyboardist whose cinematic sound softened the guitars, and she was even getting used to those. It had been so long since she had allowed herself to listen to music of any sort, and it made her tearful. She closed her eyes and bathed in the sonic depths that enveloped her. The distortion from the amplifiers saturated the air with sound, and the drumbeats, sometimes syncopated, sometimes relentless and almost indistinguishable from each other, pounded her whole body like an assault. It was cathartic. *Yes, that's what this is*, she thought. *It's a catharsis, like prayer.*

It went on and on until she had finished her beer and a powerful headache had encroached upon her. Surely, they would be finished soon, and it would be time to attempt what she had come here to do. Towards the back of the room, where the crowd thinned, was a hugely fat man with a long grey beard perched on a stool at the end of the bar. He appeared to be responsible for a table selling merchandise - t-shirts, CDs and posters - but he had no customers during the performance and so was focused on his phone. She wondered if perhaps he was the band's manager - bands had managers and things like that, didn't they? She approached him, tapped him on the shoulder to get his attention and leaned in to shout in his ear.

'How do I get to talk to that man?' She pointed towards Kristensen. 'That man there?'

The man chuckled cynically, but not unkindly. 'Join the queue at the stage door!' he shouted back into her ear. On seeing her disappointment and offence, he softened and looked her up and down. This woman was dressed like a proper nun, with no make-up or jewellery or anything.

'If you're a crazed Bishop fan trying to get backstage, you're not doing an excellent job of hiding it.'

'That Bishop man was dreadful. No, I need to talk to Mr Kristensen; I need to ask him about his songs.'

He smiled and shook his head. 'This has got to be a wind-up. But you seem like a nice lady. Here, I've got one of these left. There was a journalist who didn't turn up.' He reached into his jacket pocket and handed her a lanyard, which read '*Total Depravity: VIP*'.

'This will get you through that door.' He pointed to a door at the side of the stage. 'And you can try to speak with… Mr Kristensen, as you so politely call him, after their set. Can't promise anything, though.'

'Thank you very much.'

'Don't do anything I wouldn't back there.' He winked and laughed to himself as she backed away gratefully, fingering the lanyard and looking towards the stage door, which was shielded by a burly security guard. Now that things were in motion, she was nervous again. Standing in the audience of a concert alone and unnoticed was one thing; going to a party full of strange men speaking a foreign language was another, and she treated herself to another drink first. Perhaps she would have some wine after all.

* * *

The city of Liverpool is in the geographical north of England, but it is not the true north. Liverpool constructs itself as something else, something other than the rest of the north. The scouse spirit, indefinable but incorporating friendliness, family, football and fun, sets itself apart in amicable defiance of the rest of the North, and in slightly less amicable defiance of its rival north-western city, Manchester. These conurbations of the northwest recede into the Pennines, where the North proper begins with

Lancashire and Yorkshire, where desolate purple hills form the backbone of England. The bruised moorland becomes a caricature of bleakness. A nothing place, hinting at the idea of north, but still not the true north.

And here is a house, an old grey stone house once a farm, the only building for miles around. It would have been a type of paradise were it not for the invasion of the M6. The house can be seen from the motorway as cars race by, although drivers themselves will miss it. Passengers may dwell on it romantically for a moment; adults will imagine a country bolthole, another life for themselves, and then dismiss this one as too close to the motorway. Children in the back seats may invent a story and ponder it for a few moments longer, before the signs for the Lake District and the grander fells of Cumbria awake them from their reverie.

What is inside this house? Dated but immaculate rooms with a slight but undeniable damp smell. One too many armchairs crowding the living room with mismatched upholstery and wooden feet. Furniture cobbled together from disparate sources. There is a Bible, more than one. Upstairs, one bedroom contained baby paraphernalia. A brand-new crib, still with its price tag; a baby mattress still wrapped in plastic; a pile of Mothercare bags with nappies, clothes, tubs of formula milk powder. Down in the basement, the bare bulb casts a poor light, and so freestanding lamps are placed around the room, which have exposed brick walls and smells of disinfectant. Here there are brushed steel units, a humming refrigerator, and an assortment of laboratory equipment. And there, on the other side of the room, is a hospital bed with shackles attached. In between the shackles, two large hands and one foot squirm intermittently, hopelessly.

Outside, in the crepuscule, this grey stone house is almost camouflaged against the moorland behind. In the dawn light, unkindnesses of ravens will congregate on its roof and chimney. Their cawing will be drowned out by the roar of traffic, as will the screams from within. Above the front door of this cottage is nailed a small wooden crucifix.

* * *

Helen became aware of daylight, movement, the rumbling of an engine, her forehead against glass, her cheek against the rough material of a coach seat. There was a smell of stale smoke and alcohol. She opened her eyes and saw bodies, limbs, and torsos sprawled across seats. Then she noticed the horrendous throbbing in her head. Two people were sitting up and chatting a few seats forward, one of them absent-mindedly strumming a guitar.

She patted at herself. Shoulder bag still there, shoes and tights still on under her cowl. Her habit had gone and her black hair fell long and loose. She grabbed at it self-consciously, trying not to panic. She was on the back seat of a coach. Next to her thigh was a pair of boots, which were attached to a body lying across the rest of the back seats.

Usually, she would awake to a few precious moments of blank before the horror of what she had done, all those years ago, came flooding back, and that was always the worst part of the day. It was almost a relief to have this confusion on which to focus instead; the black hole of the night before.

She sat up. 'Where am I?' Her voice sounded far away, hoarse, her ears blocked and ringing.

The body next to her stirred and looked at her. It was Mikko Kristensen. 'Oh, hey.' He propped himself up gingerly on one elbow, rubbing his face with his other hand. 'Hey, where the fuck are we?' he shouted hazily down the aisle of the coach.

Someone shouted, 'Half way to Birmingham. Go back to sleep.'

'What the fuck, man? Why did we leave? The fucking nun is on the bus. We're gonna get done for kidnapping… again.'

The men began speaking to each other in a language that she supposed was Norwegian.

'I'm sorry,' she interrupted, 'but I don't really remember anything about last night. How did I get on this bus?'

'I mean, it's pretty fucking blurry for me too,' he smiled. Even accounting for his having just woken up, his speech was so laid-back that the words almost rolled into each other, and his monotone, accented drawl was oddly comforting.

'You were pretty wasted, dude. It was pretty fucking cool, to be honest with you. You were like telling me you were a real nun, asking me loads of stuff about my lyrics. We had a friendly talk… it's a shame you don't remember. Those fucking Bishops are not to be trusted and to be honest with you, I think they put something in your drink. So maybe we took you with us for your own safety. I guess.'

What unimaginable idiocy, Helen thought, and then she marvelled at her own risk-taking behaviour - it was faintly exciting.

'Hey can we stop soon?' he yelled down the aisle. 'I need some fucking coffee, man.' He turned to Helen.

'You want breakfast?'

At the word breakfast, her mouth involuntarily filled with saliva, and the feeling of nausea she had been trying to ignore suddenly enveloped her. She retched, catching all of it in a fold of her habit, and then sat with her head bowed in mortification.

'The Nun Has Hurled,' Mikko announced officially, remarkably unperturbed. 'Dudes, pass me one of those tour t-shirts. And some of my spare jeans.'

'So, Sister Helen Hope. My name is Mikko. We were formally introduced last night, but I guess you don't remember.'

Half an hour later, and they were sitting on top of a picnic table on a grassy bank overlooking the M6. In one direction, the morning rush hour traffic crawled along almost at a standstill, while in the other, metal colours flashed past in a Doppler stream of noise. Both of them shivered in the cold autumn air, Mikko smoking a roll-up as if his life depended on it. Helen clutched a black coffee that warmed both hands, wearing a Total Depravity t-shirt, Mikko's spare jeans and jacket, her hair loose. She had bought a toothbrush and toothpaste at the service station, washed her face, and deposited the soiled habit in a rubbish bin, resolving to think of a good explanation for that before she returned to Formby. Looking into the mirror in the ladies' toilets had been like looking into the face of a stranger. She still felt dizzy from the vomiting and motion of the coach, and her eyes were bloodshot and wide with a mix of shame and exhilaration. There were few mirrors at Argarmeols Hall. She pulled at her long black hair, combing her fingers through the tangles and wondering whether to push it back off her face or leave it falling around her cheekbones as a form of protection. In fact, she found it hard to stop looking at herself. Her dilated pupils, pallid skin and that black hair which nobody ever saw gave her an ethereal, wraith-like appearance, which, she had to admit, a part of her liked. She felt the curious chastened clarity that comes with the worst hangovers, and the situation was so surreal that she floated above it without sentiment, as if watching it happen to someone else.

'Thank you for talking to me, Mikko.'

'No problem. I never met a real nun. I mean, I don't know if I even believe you. But you are the first woman to get on the bus and not try to pick me up, so... that's something.'

Helen didn't really know how to respond to that, and she felt the urgency of her mission upon her; the rest of the band and crew had finished their breakfasts and ablutions, and were making their way back to the coach.

'I just needed to ask you about your music. I mean, your lyrics. What was your inspiration?'

'Oh, it's just horror stories, dude. I like horror movies; I like gross stuff - Satan, torture, death. Its death metal, you know? It's the formula.'

'I don't believe you. Those lyrics came from John Bunyan, from the Canons of Dort, from the scriptures. You did a lot of research.'

'Why are you so interested?'

'I'm a lecturer in Eschatology. That means...'

'I know what it means, dude.' Helen blushed, embarrassed at having underestimated him, but he was smiling. 'That's pretty cool. I would definitely take your course.'

'Well, I think you could probably teach it yourself, with all your knowledge and insight,' she said. 'But what drew you to such... Calvinist ideas?'

He stared ahead at the traffic for a long time; he seemed irritated, torn, and she wondered if he was going to get up and leave. She almost told him about the body, but something stopped her. And then he spoke.

'When I was a kid, I had a near-death experience. I saw something. I guess all of my music ever since has been about that moment, about what I saw. Sort of exorcising my demons. I don't really talk about it though, I just write it, play it.'

'What happened?'

He took a long draw on his cigarette. 'I was like nine years old. We were driving up to the lakes for the summer. My brother and me were fighting in the back, you know, playing up. My mother kept turning around to yell at us, then suddenly the car hit a deer, and we swerved and flipped, then hit a car coming the other way. My brother and mother were killed instantly. I woke up in hospital a week later. But before I did... I saw something.'

'What did you see?'

He looked at her and smiled joylessly, using shaky hand movements to try to explain. 'I haven't really talked about this since, well, since ever. I was in a place where half the world was light, half the world was dark, and I was sort of on the line between the two. There was a gate, like an iron gate, with a cockerel on top and a hooded figure standing in front of it.

I saw my brother, and he had already gone through, to the dark side, and I was calling and calling him, but nothing was coming out of my mouth. And I tried to follow him, but I couldn't move, and then the hooded figure raised his hand and pointed behind me. Like I wasn't supposed to go. I had to turn back. I didn't have a choice.'

'What did the figure look like?'

'He didn't have a face. I mean, I couldn't see a face, just a hood.'

He shook himself. 'Anyway, it's such a cliché, right? It's just one of those things people tell themselves. It's stupid. The Grim Reaper. Enter ye in at the strait gate, right? Isn't that what the Bible says? But why was my brother going into the dark and not the light? He was just a little boy. I suppose that's the question I've been trying to answer ever since. That's why I got into the whole predestination, Calvin thing. Because it felt like it had already been decided.'

'It's not stupid. Not at all. I'm sorry about your family.' She shuffled closer, so they were thigh to thigh, and put an arm around him. It wasn't so strange; she had done this many times to comfort people at the church.

'All of these things are familiar. Religions and mythologies the world over contain images of thresholds and gatekeepers. Reports of encountering spiritual beings, and of having to turn back, are well documented, back to the Middle Ages. It's to do with your brain being starved of oxygen, which gives this intense, threshold-like or tunnel-like experience. And then our cultural background comes into the play with the other aspects of the vision. It's very powerful, but it doesn't necessarily mean anything. And if it means something, it's not necessarily what you think it means. Perhaps it's just a way of the brain processing your grief, giving it a narrative structure.'

He nodded in solemn appreciation.

'So why the fuck are you a nun?'

'It's a long story. I…'

But voices were shouting, hands beckoning, from the bus.

'Fuck. We have to get to Birmingham by noon for the sound check.'

He hopped off the bench and ground his cigarette into the grass. 'To be continued. Some time.'

'Thank you,' she said. 'For your story, and for taking care of me.' Mikko made a bashful attempt at a faux-chivalrous bow and winked shyly. As he turned to go, she said suddenly, 'I liked it, by the way.'

'What?'

'Your music! There was something... grotesquely beautiful about it.'

He threw his head back and laughed. 'Why the fuck are you a nun?' He emphasised the word 'fuck' in this sentence by stamping his whole body into the ground with that childish energy he seemed to exude. He walked back to the bus, a half-swagger, half-traipse, and she watched as he was greeted by joshing arms.

Chapter Four

Red marker pen in hand, Swift studied the incident board, which was gradually taking shape, while the team waited expectantly for his update.

'Right, we've got nothing more from social media, except that there's a clear line between Jason Hardman's behaviour before and after prison. Not necessarily anything unusual there. He seemed to turn over a new leaf after he left, but the problem with that is he really kept himself to himself since he got out. Not even phone calls or texts - mobile phone records haven't flagged anything up yet. All we got from his mother is that he was close to a teacher from the detention centre, and that he was undergoing some sort of religious conversion. So, let's check all the churches in Seaforth, find out if he attended any of them, spreading out from there. The only unusual item in his room was that packet of Dexamethasone, which was from a pharmacy on Granby Road. His family had no idea about it.

'Me and Quinn are heading over to Tomlinson to get a name on this teacher and see what else we can find out. Dave, can you and Baz go to Zeus and interview Jason's colleagues?'

Quinn said, 'Boss, we could go there ourselves on the way back from Tomlinson. It's not far.'

Swift wavered for a second. 'No, no, yous two go. We'll focus on this teacher before heading to the Granby Road pharmacy.'

Quinn looked at him strangely, just for a moment, but Dave and Baz were busy high-fiving and bantering about Zeus.

'Nice one. Can we go tonight? DJ Snake is playing.'
'No, you can't, you divvies. Go there now before opening time.'

* * *

Tomlinson Young Offenders' Institute was an Eighties standard institutional complex that sprawled across several one-storey buildings. Red and tan two-tone brickwork, sheet metal sloped roof, Her Majesty's crest next to the entrance, manicured grass and paths. It was minimum security, and the only thing distinguishing it from a regular school was the abnormally high fence ringed with barbed wire. The place was very familiar to both Swift and Quinn, who had had numerous causes to visit inmates over the years. Sally Morton, the prison's director for almost ten years, took them down the main corridor towards her office.

'Just so terrible. I've been very upset about it, I remember him well and had such high hopes for him. I have to admit he was one of my favourite inmates ever. It's a shame most of the other staff don't remember him; since the privatisation we have such a high turnover. As you know.' She gave the police officers a knowing and exasperated look as they sat down in her office; they were all victims of public service budget cuts.

'So, what can you tell us about Jason?' asked Darren.

'Well, he was very unlucky to be here, really. It was a one-off ecstasy dealing offence. He was only just over the personal use limit. So wrong place, wrong time, really, and they made an example of him. Kept his head down, worked hard, and we were really pleased to be able to secure an early release after nine months.'

'Did he make any enemies here? Any drug contacts he might have kept on the outside?'

'Nothing I can think of, no. As I said he was a great lad, and I'd have been surprised to hear if he re-offended.'

Quinn said, 'Jason's family mentioned a teacher he was fond

of here?'

Sally's face fell, and she frowned. 'Ah yes, well, that was unfortunate. Andrew Shepherd. Science teacher. We had to let him go.'

'Go on.'

'It was odd behaviour. He was an excellent teacher, very popular with the students, no suggestion of impropriety, except... Well, religious grooming, I suppose you would call it. It was the prison chaplain who brought it to my attention, and when I questioned Jason and a couple of others about it, well, they said some funny things.'

'Like what?'

'Bible-bashing stuff, you know. And we can't have that here - we have all religions represented, and the chaplain is non-denominational. It's awkward ground, and you can get into all sorts of trouble nowadays. I felt bad because I was the one who hired Dr Shepherd. PhD, Cambridge University. He was a geneticist; prizes, papers, everything. So, to have someone like that teach GCSE and A-level sciences, it was such a catch for us. Total waste of time for the majority of our inmates, as you know, but Jason was different. Obviously, he DBS checked and everything... I'm just glad it wasn't, you know, anything sexual. That we know of.'

'Do you know why Shepherd applied to come and work here?'

'Yes - he said he was disillusioned with academia and wanted to do something for young people. He had also been signed off with depression for a long time. I think he couldn't cope with a full-time job.'

'So, you fired him when?'

'That would have been around June 2016. I can check the exact date in the files.'

'Do you know where he went?'

'No idea, I'm afraid. It was difficult to give him a good reference, really, so I can't see him working with young people again. No employer has come to me asking for a reference check. I seem to remember he lived Toxteth way, near the University, you know. I'll look up his address for you, but obviously he might have moved.'

Swift and Quinn headed back to the car at almost a run, Swift tapping at his phone furiously. This felt like a genuine lead. 'Dave, can you get me an address on an Andrew Shepherd?'

* * *

One hour later, as dusk was falling over the tower blocks of Toxteth, Swift and Quinn raced up the steps to the eleventh floor of Kenilworth House, a particularly grim Seventies council building.

'Fuckin' hell,' he panted, out of breath. 'Wonder how long the elevator has been broken?'

'I wouldn't go in even it was working,' said Quinn. 'Stinks of piss around here.'

Swift had brought two uniformed officers as back-up; he had a hunch about this place, exacerbated by the excitement of his first time getting to potentially catch a killer. They reached a nondescript apartment with a bright blue front door and a window with curtains closed. Swift rang the doorbell, then knocked, then banged. 'Police. Open up, Dr Shepherd. Hello? Police.'

After a minute's silence, he stepped back and scratched his head. 'Fuckin' hell. We'll have to get a warrant now.'

'We don't need one, look,' said Colette, trying the door handle. 'It's open.'

Swift glanced up and down the eleventh floor walkway. A couple of pensioners had opened their doors to observe the commotion, and at the far end a huddle of scallies were smoking, leaning over the balcony and staring in hostile silence at the police. It was only a few degrees above freezing, but none of them wore a coat. 'Go on then,' he said, and they entered.

Swift was always primed for smell; the initial smell of a place often told him a lot about what to expect. Here, the olfactory clues were hard to define. There was disinfectant, a hospital scent; but it was mingled with rotting food, a festering damp, and sweat. And it soon became clear why. This was an apartment with a split personality, of order versus chaos, or Heaven versus Hell. Swift was not sure which side was the Heaven and which the Hell.

'Don't touch anything people,' he yelled as he put on his latex gloves and looked around the kitchen. There was rotting food in the fridge, and dishes with congealed food in the sink. The dustbin smelled rank. Someone had been here fairly recently and left in a hurry.

The living room of the apartment was pristine and had been transformed into a makeshift clinic or laboratory. There was hospital equipment. A treatment bed, drip stand, monitor. In the same room was a laboratory area, with a microscope, a clear box containing empty petri dishes and test tubes, and a large brushed silver unit, which Swift assumed was a fridge or freezer. He opened it, but it was empty, as were the drawers and cupboards. Everything appeared spotlessly clean. There were also two large machines on a wooden dining table which had been pushed against the wall and was bent under their weight. One machine was much larger than the other and looked like a sort of computer with a built-in printer. It displayed the branded logo 'Revelon Sequencer.' The other, smaller piece of equipment looked like a fax machine, and Swift didn't recognise it either. But Quinn came up beside him and pointed to it.

'That's a PCR machine. Or a thermal cycler. For diagnostics.' she said.

'How do you know that?'

'A-level Biology!'

'The place looks as if it's been expertly cleaned, but it's obviously been used. Weird, then, that the kitchen would be such a mess. If we don't find the bloke, forensics are gonna have a field day in here.'

The other half of the apartment was recently lived in. There were two bedrooms; the smaller bedroom had a single mattress and appeared to have been occupied recently by a woman, a young woman. There was a pile of feminine laundry and a make-up mirror on the desk, which was littered with beauty-related paraphernalia. Teenage magazines were scattered on the unmade bed: *Bliss, Cosmo,* plus a Mothercare catalogue. Quinn was looking in at the doorway when Swift, who had been in the other bedroom, came up beside her.

'A teenage girl who also reads baby magazines.' he mused.

'Did Shepherd have a daughter?' asked Quinn.

'We don't know anything about him yet. But he's our fella. Come and look at the state of this.'

He led her to the master bedroom, and as they opened the door, they were confronted with a bizarre sight. The room had a single mattress on the floor, an open rail of clothes, and was dominated by an enormous desk pushed up against the far wall, which was covered in papers, drawings, and scrawlings, as were the other walls. This was the site of an urgent, if chaotic, project.

'Fucking hell. It's all religious. This is him.'

Can the Ethiopian change his skin or the leopard his spots? Then also you can do good who are accustomed to do evil. **Jeremiah 13:23**

As the proverb of the ancients says, 'Out of the wicked comes wickedness. **Samuel 24:13**

A healthy tree cannot bear bad fruit, nor can a diseased tree bear good fruit. **Luke 6:43**

Biblical quotations had been put on the wall in a sort of mind map that had become increasingly frantic. It began with print-outs, then writing and scrawls, diagrams, drawings, furious underlinings. Covering the desk and floor were stacks of literature, a mixture of scientific textbooks and journals, and religious texts. There must have been hundreds of books there, not one on a shelf. Piles and piles of papers, files which had been carefully put together but then torn open; folders, box files, with scientific labels that Swift and Quinn didn't understand. There was barely any floor space left, and they had to step gingerly to reach the desk.

There was one photo; in a silver frame on the desk sat a picture of three men wearing shirts, ties and lab coats, smiling and looking remarkably pleased with themselves. The photo montage said, 'Wellcome Sanger Institute, Cambridge University, 2001.' The frame was tarnished, but it clearly meant something to Shepherd, because it had been given pride of place on his desk, with a small area cleared around it, and unblemished by the desperate, questioning post-it notes that littered the rest of the room.

Swift and Quinn peered at the photo.

'Presumably one of these guys is him.'

'We'll find out.'

'I haven't got a fucking clue what all this religious stuff means, and we can't be messing around googling,' said Swift. 'We need to bring in that nun again.'

Quinn opened her mouth to say something, then stopped herself. He was the boss, after all.

Chapter Five

'The Angel of Death is a figure that appears across religions and cultures. The spirit that extracts one's soul from the body at the moment of death. Michael and Gabriel have acted as Angels of Death in Judeo-Christian religion. Azrael is the Islamic Angel of Death, who sometimes appears as a horrifying spirit with eyes and tongues covering his entire body. But Death isn't always given a terrifying form; sometimes he is kind and friendly. And sometimes Death is female. In Norse mythology, the Valkyries were beautiful young women who served both as Odin's messengers and as escorts to the souls of warriors killed in battle.'

At the mention of Scandinavia, Helen thought of Mikko, that bizarre night and morning, and she smiled at herself and continued.

'So why do we personify Death?'

Helen always tried to mimic Margaret's stage presence, beginning at the lectern before moving around the stage, trying to engage her eyes, her hands. It didn't come naturally to her, but she was improving, and she enjoyed the challenge, the adrenaline rush of performance.

'Why do we personify Death? It is something that humans have done across cultures, in order to make sense of dying and mortality, to give an abstract, terrifying concept a recognisable form. And sometimes an accessible, almost amusing form. It is for similar reasons that we are entertained by horror movies and Halloween - because they allow us to face our greatest fears in an acceptable way.

'It was the European plague, the Black Death, in the fourteenth century that really cemented our Western cultural view of Death. And now we have the ubiquitous Grim Reaper, whose form varies from terrifying to comical.

'So, for this week's assignment, I'd like you to choose one particular religion, or culture, and research that religion or culture's attitude to death. If anyone has trouble with reading lists for this, please email me sooner rather than later. Now, we have a few minutes left if anyone has any questions?'

A hand was raised and there was that young man again - Paul, the same one as last week, leaning back and looking even more cocky and cynical. Helen had a feeling he was going to be asking questions every week, and she tried to tell herself that was a good thing.

'Sorry, Dr Hope, I'm just still struggling with the whole philosophical premise of the course. Trying to find out what happens when we die. Because surely the whole point of life is that we don't know what will happen when we die.'

'Well, the first point, Paul, is that we're not trying to find out what happens when we die here. I think you know that, and you're being a little provocative there. But you have hit the nail on the head in a sense, because yes - human order is because we don't know. Can you imagine if we did?'

She paused and looked around for effect. Blank faces; phones were being switched on, bags packed, and stomachs growling. They were ready for lunch now. But the body on the beach was on her mind.

'There's a word for it, actually. Antinomianism, which literally means "against law", and in Christianity, an antinomian is one who takes the principle of salvation by divine grace to its logical conclusion; that those who are saved are not bound to follow the Laws of Moses. Imagine if you knew you were going to Heaven, no matter what crimes you committed in your life? Or vice versa, to Hell, no matter how well you lived your life? A nightmare in the wrong hands, no? So, thank goodness we don't know who is to be saved.'

As she spoke, the doors opened at the top of the stairs at the back of the lecture theatre, and Helen saw the two detectives who had visited her last week.

'Well, perhaps you'd like to look it up then, Paul, and that could be the basis of your essay for the week. Thank you everyone.'

* * *

Kenilworth House was near to the University; indeed, the huge council tower had housed hundreds of first-year students until their accommodation had been updated with modern blocks nearer the city centre. When the door of the apartment opened, the first thing Helen saw were two people moving around in hazmat suits and masks.

'There isn't a body, is there?' she asked in almost a whisper.

'Did we say anything about a body?' said Swift, unnecessarily bluntly.

Helen noticed the female detective wince at her superior's harshness, and she also noticed that harshness didn't suit him. Perhaps he was new; perhaps he was still feeling around for his detective personality. He really seemed to have it in for her, and yet he was drawn to her, bringing her to a potential crime scene in a way that she couldn't imagine was orthodox. There was definitely some personal history with religion there, and he reminded Helen of that student, Paul; like a moth to a flame drawn towards belief systems he professed to dislike.

She peered into a bright room that looked like a hospital clinic, but before she had managed more than a cursory glance, she was ushered into Shepherd's bedroom. The first thing she noticed was the terrible clutter, the lack of surfaces, the papers, scrawls, piles, but her eye was drawn to something that took her away from the room entirely. A colourful drawing in pencil and crayon, crudely done, perhaps by a child, on white A4 paper. It was pinned to the wall in a prime position, partially obscuring other pinnings, most of which were newspaper cut-outs that seemed to be about near-death experiences. There on the drawing was the black silhouette of a wrought-iron gate, with a cockerel weather vane on top, also silhouetted against a dark yellow/orange sky. Beyond the gate lay a meandering path, and half-way down the path, where it forked, stood a hooded figure. In his hand was a double-headed axe. And beyond the fork in the path, one half of the earth was light, the other dark. It was clichéd, crude, and almost exactly the image that had been described to her by Mikko. This was what he had seen on the brink of death. She gripped her wooden cross tightly and held it to her chest.

'Dr Hope. Dr Hope?'

Helen was shaken from her reverie.

'What can you tell us about these writings?' urged Swift. 'This is a manhunt now, so anything you can give us might be useful.'

Helen realised she had not yet looked at the rest of the items stuck to the wall, and she scanned them carefully; fascinated, horrified. In places there were pages torn from the Bible, passages highlighted and underlined, sometimes underlined furiously, multiple times. Other papers were handwritten, question-marked, stuck to the wall with sellotape or pins, seemingly in great haste.

'Dr Hope?'

As she tried to piece together the different strands of Shepherd's thought, a theme of a very particular spiritual struggle was emerging.

'It's interesting… very interesting,' she began. 'Many of these quotations, these ideas, are in precisely the same vein as the one on the beach, almost as if he has gone through the Bible looking for… well, looking for evidence of predestination.

Look here - *Samuel 24.13: As the proverb of the ancients says, 'Out of the wicked comes wickedness.'* And here - *Matthew 7.18: A healthy tree cannot bear bad fruit, nor can a diseased tree bear good fruit.*

'But there's a difference from the potter quotation on the beach; here he seems to be focused on birth, rebirth, the passing on of sin. All of us are born with sin, and he seems to be struggling with that. But there's a dichotomy; he is also looking at evidence of the opposite.'

'You're losing me, sorry. Is there anything here that suggests which church he might belong to? We need to find him as quickly as possible.'

But Helen was in her element now. 'Look here - *Jeremiah 13.23: Can the Ethiopian change his skin or the leopard his spots? Then also you can do good who are accustomed to do evil.* He is looking for evidence of God's forgiveness, of man's ability to change. This is someone engaged in a fundamental spiritual battle with himself. And it's remarkably appropriate to the study of Calvinism.'

She trailed off, drawn back to the crayon picture of the iron gate, which for some reason she didn't feel inclined to mention to the police.

Swift sighed to himself; this was getting them nowhere. 'Do you recognise these men? Remember, any of them visiting the convent or the church at any point?'

He showed her the photograph of the three geneticists, but she drew a blank. She looked around at the books, the journals. 'He's a scientist, a geneticist? And you think he is the murderer?'

They didn't answer her. She could see that they had all but given up on her being useful to them; Swift was busying himself with his phone, and Quinn began supervising something on the other side of the room. They were then interrupted by a uniformed officer who knocked on the open door.

'Boss - initial door-to-door; no-one has seen him this week. Or her.'

'Her?' Swift and Quinn both looked up.

'Apparently, there's a girl living here as well. No name yet. Sounds like they kept themselves to themselves.'

The police appeared to have forgotten Helen was there, and she took the opportunity to look around the room for more information. The place was spellbinding, terrifying. She saw a partially hidden degree certificate in a cracked frame, with the name 'Andrew Shepherd', and she made a mental note. She also made a mental note of the research institute and date on the photograph they had shown her, resolving to look it up as soon as she got home.

Chapter Six

Toxteth Community Pharmacy was one of the few remaining places of business on Granby Road, amongst boarded up shop fronts and dilapidated red-brick terraced houses, some of which had once been grand. The pharmacy was a forlorn establishment whose main purpose, judging by the barred windows and preponderance of security cameras, was to provide methadone to locals engaged in heroin recovery. Mr Sawhney, the owner, stood behind the counter glass looking sheepish when Swift and Quinn presented him with the box of dexamethasone. The serial number on the box had traced it unmistakeably to his dispensary.

'Ah, yes,' he said, peering at the date. 'February this year. We had an issue with our previous assistant pharmacist, Natalie Curran. I caught her falsifying prescriptions. It's not unusual around here, but this was quite odd, not just because she worked here, but because the drugs she was stealing were not what you would expect.'

'What do you mean?'

'Normally it would be methadone, oxycodone, things like that. Not steroids. Also, she was only taking small amounts, nowhere near enough to sell for that amount of risk. I thought she might have been one of those compulsive thieves, or perhaps had some sort of Munchausen's. Or perhaps something to do with her... her weight... some sort of misplaced self-medication.'

'So, you fired her, but you didn't report her?' Swift looked severe, and the pharmacist panicked.

'I'm sorry. It was such a small amount, and she was very...
vulnerable.'

'Right, OK, Mr Sawhney. We'll get on to... what was her
name again? Natalie Curran.'

'She just lives around the corner, actually.'

* * *

Natalie Curran lived only a couple of blocks away, in a bungalow
on a new-build council estate. Swift and Quinn rang the
doorbell and looked into the camera, and after a long wait, the
door clicked itself open. They heard a voice from inside saying,
'Just let yourselves in.' The bungalow smelt a little fetid, and
they saw a folded wheelchair leaning against the wall. They
went into the hallway and heard, 'Come through,' as they
went into a bright double-length room, which acted as both
bedroom and sitting room. Natalie Curran was sitting on a
two-seater armchair, which she filled entirely. An oxygen tank
and mask stood next to the chair, on the arm of which lay her
activity centre. Remote controls, crossword magazine, bottle
of Coca Cola. She was morbidly obese and clearly not getting
enough help.

'You're welcome to help yourself to tea or coffee. It's all in
the kitchen,' she said, gesturing vaguely into the back, but they
declined. Swift came straight to the point.

'Natalie, we know you were fired from Toxteth Pharmacy for
falsifying prescriptions. Jason Hardman is now dead. Why was
he taking dexamethasone?'

Her face turned white with fear. 'I don't know,' she said. 'I
don't know Jason Hardman himself. I only saw him when he
came to collect his prescriptions. It's Andrew Shepherd that I
know; he was the one who asked me to do it.'

'How do you know Andrew Shepherd, Natalie?'

'He used to come in to the pharmacy and he was so nice to me, then he started helping me to get home, helping me in and out of the wheelchair, and he sort of became my boyfriend, really.'

'Did he tell you why he needed these prescriptions?'

'No, and I didn't ask. I thought it was better not to know, I suppose. He felt bad when I got fired. He kept coming round for a while, doing bits of shopping for me, but he's stopped now. As you can see, I'm in a bit of a mess.'

She almost didn't have the energy to cry, and looked beyond shame in her abandonment.

'When was the last time he visited you, Natalie?' Quinn asked.

'About a month ago. He said he'd be back the following week, but I haven't heard from him since, and I never had his phone number. I know he was just using me for the prescriptions. But still…'

'Do you have any home help, Natalie?' Swift asked kindly.

'I'm on disability, but no help, no.'

'Perhaps we can have a word with social services, see what they can do,' he said as they got up to leave.

But then Natalie said, 'Was the Dexa a cause of Jason's death?'

'No, Natalie, it doesn't look like it, but we don't know yet.'

'And what about the other bloke? Is he OK?'

Swift and Quinn both sat down again quickly. 'What other bloke?'

'I was falsifying prescriptions for two different names. Exactly the same drug for both. One was Jason Hardman; the other was… er… Stuart Killy, yeah that's right, Stuart Killy.'

* * *

As they left, Quinn remarked, 'So sad that someone could let themselves get like that.'

'I know. So many lonely people behind closed doors.' Darren was racked with doubt at his own abilities. He was cursing himself for not asking such an obvious question - was Jason

Hardman the only prescription recipient? *Shit, you almost missed it. You are not up to this.*

And now the name Killy. Everyone in Liverpool knew that name. The biggest crime family in the north-west, with a drug-dealing network that spread across the world.

'Is there any crime in this city that doesn't involve that family?'

'I know what you mean,' said Colette. 'There are loads of Killys, though.'

'But where d'you think the big boss man lives?'

'Meathead? I don't know. Where?'

'Take a guess. Where's posh?'

'Blundellsands?'

'Formby. Just around the corner from those nuns.'

'Shit.'

They stood in the street while Darren took out his phone to call for an address on Stuart Killy, when Colette said, 'Actually I think I know Stuart. Yes, that was one of my first cases on the force when I was stationed at central. There can't be more than one Stuart Killy, right? Armed robbery, and I remember because there was something a bit sad about it. Stuart was one of the Killy nephews and had a low IQ. He was the driver, I think. And I remember thinking it was a shame that he went down for the same time as the rest of them.'

Swift got on the phone, and by the time they had walked back to the car, Stuart Killy's identity had been verified.

'You're right, Colette, he went down four years ago, but listen to this - he was released six months ago on electronic tag, and guess where he lives? Kenilworth House.'

* * *

Back to Kenilworth House, and this time they were on the ground floor, knocking on the door while a group of children on bikes and skateboards looked on from behind, muttering about how they hated 'the bizzies' and playing at being intimidating. There was no answer, and eventually Swift shouted through the letter box. 'Mr Killy, we know you're there. We're coming in now.' But before he had even finished the sentence, he winced at a foul smell emanating from the letter box. According to the probation service, Killy's electronic tag, and therefore his person, was in the apartment, but something was very wrong.

This time Swift had no hesitation in breaking and entering, and he called in a team who arrived within minutes.

As they entered, the smell of rot was immediately overpowering - rancid bins and rotten food. But there was something else as well, something much worse. The uniformed policeman who had knocked down the front door was first to the living room, and he collapsed back slightly against the door frame, put one hand to his mouth and pointed with the other, which was still holding the battering tool. Swift and Quinn moved into the room and saw Killy's heavy round electronic ankle tag, dutifully plugged into the wall and beeping intermittently to signify, somewhat plaintively, that it was fully charged. The tag was lying in a pool of dried blood on the rug. And attached to the tag was a foot, neatly removed at the ankle, and beginning to rot. Swift put his hands to his face and rubbed his fingers over his mouth.

'What the hell is going on?'

* * *

Back at the station, Swift flicked through the updated Policy Book and Action Book, pleased with the way things were going. He called a meeting to update what they had found about Andrew Shepherd, feeling confident; two days in, and good policing had identified their man. Surely an arrest was imminent.

'Right, our prime suspect is Andrew Shepherd.' He pinned up a photo, obtained from Tomlinson's personnel file. 'He's dangerous, he's missing, and he's potentially responsible for two other missing persons, so let's do this update quickly, then get to work. Quinn, let's have a quick bio.'

'Andrew Shepherd, aged forty-five, registered as living at Kenilworth house in Toxteth for the past fifteen years. Very strange employment history. PhD in Genetics from Cambridge University, worked on the Human Genome Project at the Wellcome Institute there from 1995 to 2001. All seems very prestigious. But after he left Cambridge, it all goes blank. He has claimed benefits at various times, and at other times disappeared off the radar completely. According to his medical records, he was signed off work repeatedly with clinical depression. The only record of employment we have is that he worked at Tomlinson Young Offenders Institute from 2014 to 2015, teaching science with a qualification that was not verified, and we can't find a confirmation of it. He was fired for religious grooming, his grooming target being Jason Hardman. Apparently, he continued to see Jason Hardman after he was fired. No evidence of a romantic relationship between them, but we don't know. We also don't know why he was procuring him steroids, or what the hell he was doing with the mad home laboratory.' As she spoke, Swift was pinning up photos of the various rooms in Shepherd's apartment, with their bizarre and dark incongruities. 'But the religious junk in his flat has been confirmed by an expert as being directly linked to the quotation at the crime scene, so we almost certainly have the killer identified.'

'Who's the expert?' someone asked.

Darren stepped forward to take over from Quinn. 'Erm. An expert witness from… the church,' he said unconvincingly, turning to his incident board while Colette raised an imperceptible eyebrow at him.

'Andrew Shepherd had no car, no social media, no siblings, the only family being elderly parents living near Cambridge. He hasn't been in touch with them or used his bank account in the last three weeks. He doesn't seem to have had a mobile phone contract either, and there's no landline in this apartment. A very strangely off-grid life.'

'Right, lads, so firstly,' he pulled down the little finger of one hand as a "bullet-point," gesture. 'Where is Shepherd? Check local CCTV, check door-to-door on all the other storeys of Kenilworth House, check local churches since he was so religious. Second, who was he living with? There was someone else living in the flat, reported by neighbours to be a young woman who was rarely seen entering or leaving. Start with Missing Persons. Third, Stuart Killy.'

At this, he pinned up the photo of the severed foot. Even though everyone already knew, the image raised audible gasps. 'This one is an absolute mind-fuck. One minute this case was all wrapped up as a lone religious nutter, the next we're descending into druglord Hell. Let's see what the Killys have to say about this; one of their lot missing points to gang warfare, but there doesn't seem to be anything going down at the moment. No doubt Titan are going to be all over it in no time, so let's see how far we can get on our own.

'Right, Quinn and I are heading over to Manchester. We looked up Shepherd's two ex-colleagues from Cambridge; this photo,' - he tapped the university photo on the board - 'is clearly important to him. One moved to France years ago, but the other is still working as a geneticist in Manchester. Name of Matthew Clancy. Since Shepherd lived such an off-radar life, we're having to delve quite far back for contacts. Plus, he's obviously still been working informally as a geneticist, God knows why, but he must have got that expensive lab equipment from somewhere.

'OK, good work people, let's close in on this guy.'

Chapter Seven

Northern Genome Limited took up the top floor of a glassy high-rise in central Manchester, one of the many new architectural features that made up the pride of north-western urban regeneration. As they waited in the reception area, Quinn fingered the promotional brochure. '*Northern Genome Ltd. is pioneering the molecular medicine revolution. Our impressive range of services for synthetic biology includes DNA design, synthesis, and custom cloning; antibody and viral engineering, bioproduction and genetically engineered cell lines. Our diagnostics department allows smarter healthcare decisions through high-quality genetic analysis, through our trademark sequencing tools. We work with hospitals and universities worldwide, and we are proud of our reputation at the forefront of the growing genomic medicine market.*'

'Do you know what any of that means, you with your A level Biology?' asked Swift.

'I only got a C, you know. Look, there he is.'

She turned over the leaflet, and on the back page was a face they only barely recognised from Shepherd's photo. His former colleague Matthew Clancy now looked older, but also tanned and confident. Quinn read out loud.

'Professor Matthew Clancy is founder, clinical director and CEO of Northern Genome Ltd. He gained his PhD from Cambridge University in molecular biology before joining the revolutionary Human Genome Project. Following that, he became a lecturer in Genetics at Manchester University, and in 2009, set up Northern Genome with the aim of being at the forefront of the genetic medicine revolution. Professor Clancy enjoys rowing and rugby, having been a Cambridge blue in both sports.'

'He's a bit of alright, isn't he?' She elbowed Swift.

'That's for you to say. He looks totally up his own arse.'

'Ah, hello detectives, sorry to keep you waiting.' At that moment, Professor Matthew Clancy appeared around the corner with benign surprise. 'I wasn't expecting visitors today. Come into my office and we can talk.' He was strikingly tall and broad, with a rich deep voice and kind eyes that looked earnestly into your own. He had a broad face with chiselled features and dark, slightly floppy hair in a style that harked back to the Nineties. He wore an expensive-looking blue shirt, open at the neck, suit trousers and immaculately shined shoes. They went into his office, another glass box from which they could see white-coated figures moving slowly and silently around a lab. The smell was of disinfectant and new carpet, and Clancy's cologne wafted past them as he went to sit on the other side of his desk.

'So. What can I do for you, detectives?' He bounced down into his office chair and placed his hands on the desk.

'We're trying to locate a former colleague of yours, Andrew Shepherd,' said Swift, adjusting himself into his chair.

'Andrew?' Clancy looked genuinely thrown. 'Ah, well, I haven't seen Andrew in a long time, I'm afraid. Is he in some sort of trouble?'

'When was the last time you were in contact with him?'

'Not for years. He was in poor shape - emotionally, I mean - when we parted company. I have felt bad about not keeping in touch, really. What's happened?'

Swift and Quinn declined to answer and tried to look inscrutable.

'Could you tell us about your history with him?' asked Quinn. 'We're just trying to build up a picture at this point. You were on his team at the Human Genome Project in Cambridge in the Nineties.'

'That's right.' Clancy nodded. 'The Sanger Institute at Cambridge was one of the five international sites. But the project was already well-established by the time we joined. We were young mavericks - I suppose we were the glittering genetics juniors at Cambridge, and the university wanted us involved, plus they had extra funding to use up. So, they allowed us to set up a sort of skunkworks team-'

Swift interrupted. 'And that was yourself, Andrew Shepherd, and one other…'

'Laurent Baptiste, yes.'

'And what did you do, exactly?'

'Well, I don't know how much you know about the Human Genome Project?'

'Only the basic idea. To sequence human DNA, right?'

'Almost. The project's mandate was to map all the functional genes. The genes that code for proteins. But that's only one to two per cent of the genome - the rest is what's known as junk DNA. And our rather futuristic project was to look into this junk DNA, this biological dark matter.'

'Dark matter?'

'It's an informal term for junk DNA - biological dark matter is the genetic material or microorganisms that are unclassified or poorly understood. At the time, most of the human genome was a complete mystery, but the potential of this unchartered territory was, and is, huge. It was our team's job to do some preliminary studies on this - to ascertain what could be done in the future, once the Human Genome Project was over. Of course, things have moved on spectacularly since then; other projects have discovered far more about the potential of this so-called junk DNA. Some of which we are working on here, for example. But back then, it was extremely frustrating. We weren't finding anything, and it was like looking for a needle in a haystack. Plus, we didn't even know what we were looking *for*. The data collection and analysis was daunting; fifteen trillion bytes of raw data. With the technology we had, it would have taken three hundred years of computer time to analyse it all. We felt we had been fobbed off, I suppose. Excluded from the actual work.'

'So how well did you know Andrew Shepherd? What was he like?'

'We had been students together, and he was brilliant; prizes, scholarships. I initially felt very lucky to be assigned to his team. And he was the team leader, but unfortunately, he had… well, I suppose some mental health issues, rather serious mental health issues. It was very slow going, and it got to him, I'm afraid. He stopped focusing on the task at hand and his behaviour at work became increasingly erratic, paranoid. In the end Laurent and I felt we had to report him, because he was damaging our reputations. He simply couldn't cope with not finding anything, and so he began imagining things that weren't there, coming up with bizarre theories that would have discredited the whole Human Genome Project.'

'And why did you leave the project?'

'When Shepherd was dismissed our team was disbanded, and there was simply no longer a job for me anymore.'

'And you didn't keep in touch with Shepherd?'

'No, no, there was some unpleasant feeling, I suppose. On both sides. Like I said, I felt bad about that. Tell me, what's happened to Andrew? Is he in trouble?'

Swift ignored the question, looking around the room and through the glass at the lab.

'What is it you do here exactly, Professor Clancy?'

'All the things it says in the brochure you're holding.' He smiled.

'So you decided to leave academia then? Sort of sell out and go private?'

Clancy was unruffled by the provocation. 'Well, I suppose

you could put it that way, yes.' he smiled. 'But you know, this really is the best way to be at the forefront of research. This is the future of medicine; we are at a frontier, but that means we are heavily restricted in what we can and can't do at the moment. There are huge ethical implications in gene therapy.'

'You mean like curing people of things that… aren't everyone's definition of a problem?'

'Exactly, Detective. There's a fine line between what is considered a "disease", and a "trait", and the implications of altering traits perceived as undesirable are large. Trait enhancement could negatively affect what society considers as normal and could promote discrimination towards those with undesirable traits. A slippery slope effect.'

'And what's your take on it?' asked Quinn. This was getting off-topic, but neither she nor Swift could help being interested.

'Well, surprisingly, for a geneticist, I'm rather conservative. I advocate a cautious approach to the moral and legal aspects. And I think it's important for some of us scientists to put on the brakes, hold the floodgates, as it were. There's a lot to be said for "God made us this way".'

'Are you religious, Dr Clancy?' asked Swift nonchalantly, without looking up from his notes.

'Ah no, not at all,' laughed Clancy. 'I didn't mean to give you that impression. Just a figure of speech. But… we all have to believe in something. And I believe in science.' He smiled again.

'Was Shepherd religious?' asked Swift.

'Yes, he was indeed. And that was part of the problem. He had some, shall we say, creationist ideas that were completely untenable for a scientist. Discrediting us, as I said.'

'Did you know that Shepherd had moved up north?'

Clancy paused. 'No, no, I didn't.'

'Bit of a coincidence, isn't it?'

'Not really; to be honest, it's possible he could have followed me up here. He was a rather lonely character. There never seemed to be a girlfriend on the scene when we were at Cambridge, and he didn't have much family. But there wasn't… there wouldn't have been a job for him up here. I certainly couldn't have recommended him.'

'Did you know he was a teacher? In a young offenders' institution?'

Clancy paused again. 'No, obviously I didn't, no. How surprising.'

'And what about the other team member, Laurent Baptiste? Do you know what happened to him?'

'Well, I'm sure you've looked him up. He's rather well known, isn't he? Laurent returned to France and made a lot of money in casinos. If you want to talk about selling out, detective. He was a brilliant statistician, brilliant. I suppose he found a profitable use for it.'

They were about to leave when Swift said, 'So, just out of interest, Professor Clancy. When you do this gene therapy, how do you do it?'

'As I say, it's still really only being done at the very experimental level. But in theory, you create a mutated gene in the lab, then introduce it into the body via a virus, a retrovirus. Initially, the main obstacle is getting the body's immune system to accept the virus.'

'So, you would need to lower the body's immune system. With, say, a steroid?'

'Well, yes, exactly.'

Swift and Quinn headed back to the car, both checking their messages. 'Go on then, say it,' said Swift, without looking up.

'OK then - you were really harsh with your questioning. You're really going for this bad cop thing, right?'

'Just trying to push his buttons, you know. I'm not here to make friends.'

'Is it because I fancy him, boss?'

'Fuck off. Listen, that machine in Shepherd's flat, the Revelon

Sequencer. We can't trace it because he removed the serial number. So where did he get it? They cost over £100,000. I saw three of them in Clancy's lab. Let's get a warrant to check Northern Genome's phone and visitor records. But don't raise any eyebrows here by requesting Northern Genome itself - request the entire building's records.'

* * *

Helen had finished cleaning the stone floor and dusting the pews, and finally rounded off her Tuesday morning rota by laying out the Bibles and psalm books on freshly wiped shelving along the rows. She then took a few minutes to sit in contemplation, trying as ever to speak to God. She had struggled to focus during Terce this morning, and there was another hour before Sext in which she might clear her head and ask for God's help. The Order's daily programme was intense, with six compulsory prayer sessions beginning at six in the morning and ending at eight in the evening, and not including the public services administered by the Deaconess. In between all that there was the rota of cleaning, cooking and other duties, a full schedule of manual tasks that seemed almost designed to prevent any time for self-questioning. Helen usually had to do her University work in the evenings, staying up late under lamplight. When she found time to herself, she used it to pound the dunes and forest paths, trailing wet sand on her skirts and fancying herself as a female warrior in the Wars of Religion, or perhaps a misunderstood Jane Austen heroine.

But today she needed to be in church. She felt His weight upon her, as she had all those years ago, and yet she felt somehow that this time she may be closer to a truth. God was testing her in some way, or was about to test her, and she prayed for the guidance that was rarely forthcoming.

St. Michael's Church had been originally built as an Anglican chapel in the Gothic Revival style, all pointed arches, lattice-work and grotesques. But when it was endowed to the Sisters of Grace, along with the house in the Twenties, the church underwent its own mini-Reformation; a stripping of the altars designed to remove any suggestion of joy. Now, with its austere white walls, plain wooden pews and stone pillars, the only concession to beauty in this church was the large stained-glass window behind the altar, depicting the Crucifixion in glorious, gaudy colours. Other than this aesthetic indulgence, there was to be no distraction from communion with God.

But Helen was currently distracted by the conflating images described by Mikko and Shepherd's drawing, and in particular the details - the cockerel, the wrought-iron railings, the hooded figure, the precisely depicted colours of the sky. Of course, images of the figure of Death and the gate to Heaven were ubiquitous in human cultures, so there was nothing strange in them both having the same dream or vision. But such details - could that really be a coincidence?

She was disturbed by the sound of the heavy door creaking open at the back of the church and the sounds of echoing footsteps, whispers, and a cleared throat. Helen looked behind her. And there they were again, with a certain inevitability. Those detectives. They walked down the central aisle towards her, Swift's voice resonating off the stone pillars.

'What kind of music do you like, Dr Hope?'

Neither of them seemed as gentle, or as on her side, as last time. They were brusque, almost hostile.

'I don't...'

'D'you like heavy metal?'

As they reached Helen, Quinn took an iPad out of her bag, swiped her finger across the screen to bring it to life, and handed it to her. Helen took a few moments to realise what she was looking at. It was a post from Facebook, from a fan page for Total Depravity, with a photo captioned 'Does Mikko have a new girlfriend? No!' It was a slightly grainy photo, taken from far away on someone's phone, but unmistakable nonetheless; it was him and her, sitting on top of that picnic bench at the side of the motorway. They were side by side and the amateur photographer had captured the moment when she had put her arm around him to comfort him. Helen looked in the mirror so little these days that she hardly recognised herself, and she was taken aback at this long-haired female figure in secular clothes, sitting with a man on an adventure that she could hardly believe really happened. And she couldn't help but feel a guilty thrill of excitement that she had been spotted with a sort-of celebrity. *My one claim to fame*, she thought. But Swift snapped her back into the present.

'A coincidence, that double-headed axe. The body. The band. And there you were, in both places.' He paused for effect.

'Where were you on the night of the seventh of October?'

It took Helen a few moments to realise the significance of the question.

'I was at… I was here. Where I always am. Here.'

'You're not always here, though, are you?'

'I was that night. You can ask anyone… I mean, this is absurd.' she was panicking slightly and wasn't sure why.

'OK then, don't worry, we can check that. So why were you with a heavy metal band on the M6 last week?'

'Oh yes, my goodness, that must look so strange to you. I was looking on the internet the evening before - the day the body was found and you came to see me - and I just wished I could help more. I couldn't stop thinking about it. And I found this band with the same symbol as the body, and their lyrics from the same passage in the Bible as the… Oh, I don't really know, I've been idiotic, haven't I?' She was struck with a sudden horror and inexplicable sadness.

'They didn't do it, did they? The band?'

'You're not the detective here, Sister Hope. I'd appreciate it if you stuck to lecturing and… praying. We're perfectly capable of doing Google searches ourselves. And lo-and-behold, when we do, what do we find? You.'

'Well, I didn't think-'

'This isn't Miss Marple or, who is it, Father Brown? Next time you feel like playing detective… come to us. Can you do that?' Quinn winced at Swift's harshness as he continued.

'And next time you fancy a night out, how about a nice girls' dinner and a white wine spritzer at Pizza Express? Instead of satanic metal gigs.'

Swift turned and left, Quinn offering a vaguely placating shrug to Helen as she followed him. Helen stood looking at the church door as it closed behind them, her heart racing from anxiety and, perhaps, a certain defiance.

'Go on then. Say it. I was too much,' Swift said to Quinn as they walked towards the car.

'No, I wasn't going to. She should have come to us with that axe picture, silly woman. Except that - you can't deny she has been on the same lines as us, and she found the band connection before we did. That Kristensen guy was in the north-west at the time. He has a string of convictions - drugs, minor assault, even a church vandalism - and the symbol, the lyrics - it's a coincidence, don't you think? And there are no coincidences?'

'It is weird. I'll grant you that. But it's more likely that Shepherd is using him as a convenient smokescreen. Kristensen has a watertight alibi for every minute of his life - the fella is never alone. None of us have ever heard of him, but apparently, he's some sort of god in the world of heavy metal. We could certainly do him for crimes against music though, and offences against personal grooming.'

They got into the car. 'You know,' said Quinn, 'I read about these Norwegian death metal bands who went around burning churches down. It was a big scandal all over Norway in the

Nineties. These bands claimed to be genuine Satanists, you know, not like Black Sabbath and Alice Cooper, but proper devil-worshippers. There were a couple of murders as well. And OK, this band Total Depravity are too young to have been involved in those particular incidents, but they were obviously heavily influenced by it growing up.'

'You're right,' said Swift. 'There are no coincidences. That singer is a scrawny little thing, but he has a team of huge blokes. I suppose they could all be in it together. It's a bit much to murder someone as a publicity stunt, though.'

'Unless they are real Satanists.'

'My God.'

'You mean, my Satan?' Colette smiled.

Swift frowned. 'This case is properly messing with me head. We'll pay this Total Depravity a visit. Don't make me listen to the music, though.'

He answered his mobile on speaker as they drove off.

'Swift speaking.'

'Boss. It's Dave. The Super wants to speak to you in person - says can you go to Canning Place now?'

'Shit. Yeah, on me way.'

* * *

At Merseyside Police Headquarters on Canning Place, Swift took a deep breath and knocked on the Superintendent's office door. He had only been in here a few weeks ago, formally receiving the promotion, which he wasn't sure he quite deserved. A 'meteoric rise', they had called it in the Liverpool Echo; local lad powers through the ranks and triumphs in the Vice Unit, secondment to the Met, before returning to join the Murder Squad as their youngest DI. But Swift felt he had just been supremely lucky, swept along like the sand snakes on Crosby Beach.

Superintendent Liz Canter sat behind her desk looking formidable and motioned him to sit. Liz Canter was the steely figurehead of Merseyside Police, and could hardly have been from anywhere other than the city of Liverpool. With chiselled cheekbones, skin leathery from decades of hard police work, tanning and smoking, blonde hair and dark eyebrows perfectly manicured, she wore her typically hard expression as a badge of office. She put her elbows on the desk and leaned forward, sighing.

'Tell me I didn't make a mistake with you, Darren. I heard from the forensic team at Kenilworth House - there were some raised eyebrows, I can tell you. What the bloody hell were you thinking, taking some nun to a crime scene?'

'She was there as an expert witness...' he ventured.

'Expert, my arse. She's a potential suspect, and that was a fresh crime scene. It's so against protocol it's not even in the rule book!'

'What about if we appointed her a Specialist Lay Adviser?'

'Darren, come on. There are criminal profilers for that. Specialist Lay Advisers are doctors, social workers, engineers; they're not nuns! The police don't have spiritual advisers. You're going to make us a laughing stock.'

'So what? Are you taking me off the case?'

'No, not at the moment. It's not completely unheard of to have murders around Crosby, but this is high profile. Crucifixion on Crosby Beach? Jesus, it's a field day for the press. To be honest, if I'd known this was going to be your first case, I would have kept you back here for a bit longer. But the hassle of taking you off would be a pain in the arse, so this is your last chance.'

Swift nodded, only half-relieved.

'In any case, it wasn't totally stupid, what you did - asking the nun's advice. Definitely thinking outside the box, getting inside the mind of a killer, all those clichés. That's the stuff that will make you a great detective one day. And I know you will be. That's why I've always championed you, Darren. You're intuitive, and you care. It's just - you know, stick to the Crime Scene Protocols for now, yeah?'

Telling off over, she softened. She was, after all, his unofficial mentor.

'How's it going then, being back in Crosby? Is it hard not being one of the lads anymore?'

'It is weird, yeah. But it's OK. They're good lads. And girls. Leading a team's dead stressful though, isn't it? And with such high stakes. I don't know… how to behave with them, how to be. I feel stupid. Just across the road from the station is the Kwik Save, where I used to work on Saturdays when I was at school, and sometimes I wish I was still there, doing a nine to five.'

'Imposter syndrome is normal, and it shows you care. Your detective personality will come, and in the meantime, people look up to you, Darren. Everyone in this city is a smartarse with a big mouth, and you hold something back. You've got a certain mystery about you, and that commands respect. The girls love you, the lads all want to be you, and you know this city. You live and breathe it, you know what makes people tick. I'm glad it didn't work out in London. Because you belong here.'

Canter smiled sympathetically and leaned back in her chair. Swift hated himself for opening up; he wished she would stop looking at him and felt absurdly close to tears.

'Have you told them yet?' she asked. 'About Matt?'

'Not yet, no. It hasn't come up to be honest with you.'

'I think you underestimate them, you know. It won't even be a thing. You've been burned several times, I know. You were unlucky in London. But this is Liverpool.'

'I know, yeah, it's not a thing. It's just, I've made it a thing. I'll get meself sorted.'

Chapter Eight

Helen was driving around the north of England again and rather enjoying the liberation and mild rebellion of it. Whoever had designed the itinerary for this band's tour had a somewhat flawed sense of geography, because it didn't make any logistical sense. Dipping south from Liverpool to Birmingham, then back up to Newcastle, and now Leeds? She wondered if it was that enormously fat man who had been selling t-shirts and lurking on the bus. As she approached Newcastle, she realised she was quite looking forward to this concert. Despite the bizarre suitability of her robes last time, she had dressed appropriately tonight, in the Total Depravity t-shirt and Mikko's jeans, which she had hidden in her room at Argarmeols Hall and smuggled out with her. Mikko was so thin that the jeans were only slightly too big for her, and they still had that inexplicable chain hanging from them. She would also have a chance to return his leather jacket, which she imagined must be expensive. Yes, she was looking forward to this. She knew what to expect now, and somehow felt a part of the ritual of it all, with her suitable attire and her knowledge of the music. She smiled at how ridiculous she was, and had a strange certainty that God would smile on her, too.

This was a smaller venue than the last one, a side-street basement rock bar called 'Judas', and there was such a long queue that she worried she wouldn't get in. But she finally passed through the door just in time for the beginning of Total Depravity's performance. A sound system was playing ominous introductory noises, and there was the now-familiar sheeting wafting at the back of the stage depicting the double-headed axe.

She beamed involuntarily when he came onstage, and even found herself clapping and cheering, although she was far from joining in with the rituals of the rest of the crowd, and refrained from raising her hands in that devil horns gesture - that would be a step too far. In that way, the brain gradually accepts the unfamiliar. She processed the sounds she was hearing in a different way, and it was becoming clearer. The resultant tones from the amplifiers were emitted in waves like church organ pipes. The doom-laded guitar chords were interspersed with passages of frantic chromaticism that had an almost carnivalesque absurdity to them, alternating soul-crushing melancholy with an almost joyful chaos. The cinematic key changes manipulated her emotions into exhilaration, and the Phrygian structure of the scales and chords evoked mysticism, medievalism, religion, and fear as he growled about the beauty of ephemerality, the horror of nihilism. It all looked remarkably difficult to play, and she marvelled at the technical prowess of the musicians, their ensemble precision, and their camaraderie. Singing about death, horror, and Satan all looked rather fun.

While she stood in silent contemplation, all around her, people shook their heads rhythmically, ran in circles, climbed onto the stage, and jumped off, making her wince. But the jumpers were caught by the crowd each time and were carried aloft back to their positions. She recognised the ritual of it now, every song ending with roars and cheers accompanied by those 'horn' hand signals as a sort of Amen.

Tonight, Mikko had elected not to wear a t-shirt, and his thin naked torso with its almost concave chest, his straggling hair and beard, gave him the look of a demonic Jesus. This was enhanced by the red stage lights that lit up his eyes. His malevolent expression would occasionally break into a grin at his bandmates and he would launch into contorted dance moves. However, tonight he didn't seem as present as the last time, and Helen had the sense that he was somewhere else in his mind, and 'dialling in' his performance.

The concert ended, and the crowds dispersed, but Helen did not see the fat man this time, and when she tried to go through the door at the side of the stage, a man wearing a security bib just folded his arms and shook his head. 'I'm a friend of Mikko,' she attempted weakly. 'Aren't you all?' he said with contempt. She left the bar disappointed, but then she spotted the black bus parked on a side street at the back of the theatre. There didn't seem to be anyone stopping her, so she walked towards it. And there was Mikko, exiting the theatre and hopping onto the steps of the bus. She waved and called out his name too loudly, causing the stragglers outside the club to turn their heads. He was just about to go on the bus when he saw her.

'Motherfuck.' He was struggling with himself, turning and turning again several times and wringing his hands through his long hair, wanting to ignore her but unable to ignore her. In the end, he decided to come down and approach her, and she was confused to see that he was furious.

'What the fuck did you do? I had the police on me! You lied to me. You didn't tell me about that body. You are bad news, dude. Motherfuck. What are you even doing back here?'

Oh goodness, of course. 'I'm sorry, I'm so sorry. I wanted to. I wasn't keeping it from you. There was just no time. Your bus was leaving, and I wasn't thinking straight… But now I really needed to tell you something else.' She blurted. 'The police, they took me to the apartment of the man who they think did this; and I saw what you saw.' He was shaking his head, and she felt she was still losing him. 'He had drawings, many drawings, all the same thing - the gate, the hooded figure, the double-headed axe, the light and the dark. It was exactly as you described. He saw the same thing!'

Mikko had stopped shaking his head, but he was looking

some way behind hers, considering his demons.

'They would have found you anyway,' she continued. 'I mean they did - the axe symbol on the body. That's how they found you, just like I did. We are both connected to this, whether we like it or not.' She sighed. 'I don't know what I was thinking. I'm sorry. I just wanted to tell you about the picture. Here, I can't very well give you the jeans, but here's the jacket.' She began to take it off and make moves to leave, but he stopped her and put it back on her shoulders.

'It's freezing. What are you doing? Keep it on. Motherfuck. I was so freaked out by those police. It's not good for my anxiety, dude. I couldn't even understand what they were saying with that fucked up accent they had. And they were even questioning me about the Norwegian church burnings. That was back in the Nineties. Fuck.'

'Well, that would be crazy, wouldn't it?' said Helen. 'Because not only were you a child in the Nineties, but those Norwegian church arsonists were quite clearly black metal bands. And you, as everyone knows, play melodic death metal. The two are completely different musical subgenres.'

Mikko smirked at that. *Thank goodness*, thought Helen.

'You're becoming a metalhead then, are you, Sister Helen?' He looked at her for a long time, then lit a cigarette, shivering in the cold. 'OK. Fuck it. So, what are you suggesting? That we try to find this guy, this murderer? You really think we can find him before the police?'

'Well, I have some ideas. Some leads we could follow. And even if we don't, we might find some answers about your dream.'

'OK fine, let's fucking do it. Tomorrow we have a day off before we head to Scotland. Tell me where to go.'

* * *

The next morning was impossibly bright and crisp, and a diminutive figure stood outside Manchester Deansgate train station in a cloud of cigarette smoke, rocking back and forth and hugging himself against the cold. He wore a long oversize grey coat with the lapels turned up, a trilby hat with the rim pulled down, and huge sunglasses which contrasted with his alabaster skin. Only a set of fangs could have made him look more vampirish. Helen pulled up in the Beetle, and he laughed at her comedic old-fashioned car, and she laughed at his wraith-like appearance. They drove off into the last of the morning rush hour traffic, and she felt that the awkwardness in the car was not wholly unpleasant. 'Do you mind if I smoke?' he asked. 'No, I don't,' she said, and she realised she didn't. The nicotine incense was foreign to her and yet somehow nostalgic at the same time. They drove in silence for a while, then she ventured something that had struck her.

'Your music. There's something very classical about it, isn't there?'

'I like my scales and arpeggios, yeah. Old-school solos rule. I grew up idolising the great neo-classical guitarists - Van Halen, Malmsteen, Rhoads.'

'I've never heard of any of those people. But it's more than scales and arpeggios though, isn't it? Your songs are structured around the circle of fifths. They have a... yes, a sonata form. And you use a lot of Baroque techniques as well - that ostinato bass, it somehow invokes a Bach toccata. And there's a folk element too. It's incredibly technical, isn't it? Sorry, I'm talking too much, aren't I?'

'Not at all. Talk away, Sister Helen. Look, they're just guitar tricks, you know. Like quotations'. He shrugged.

'No, no, I don't believe you. It's more than that. You have an innate classical sensibility.'

'OK, well, thanks, dude. I guess.'

She continued. 'Did you study classical music?'

'I did indeed. Thank you for noticing. Oslo Conservatoire. But I keep that on the down low, to be honest with you.'

'Conservatoire? Wow, that's very impressive.'

'Yeah, well, I was not a good student at regular school - they said I had ADHD, hyperactivity, whatever. But it was actually that I have this photographic memory. I remember everything, and so there's just too much going on in my brain. Music was the only way to channel it. I don't even need to try with music - I just see it.'

'That sounds like a form of synaesthesia.'

'Whatever. And you're obviously pretty fucking musical yourself, then?'

'I was. A long time ago. I took singing lessons when I was young. I was in a choir and so on. I loved singing, actually.'

'But you stopped?'

'Yes.'

He draped himself over the side of the passenger seat provocatively and looked at her over the rims of his sunglasses. 'There's a story here, then.'

She explained to him that Calvinists don't believe in music other than psalms sung without accompanying instruments. That only the Divine revelation should be put to music, and that using musical instruments is exhibitionist. That this was the Reformation principle of the sola scriptura.

'Calvin thought music was dangerous. It had the ability to lead people to either godliness or to lascivious conduct. He said that music exacerbates the power of words, whether good or bad.'

'Well, I guess I could agree with him there.' Mikko thought for a moment. 'But that is all total bullshit. What about all the incredible religious music? What about Bach - he wrote his music precisely in order to glorify God? I mean, some of the most beautiful shit in the world has been inspired by religion.'

'And yet you hate religion.'

They both clammed up and sat in silence for a while. A tension had been introduced and neither of them was sure why. Then Mikko saw something that he hoped might lighten the atmosphere - a pile of CDs stuffed into the open glove compartment on the passenger side.

'Oh, so you don't like music, huh? Then what is this? Hildegarde von Bingen, twelfth century canticles. OK, that's pretty nunny. But what about this? Abba Gold?'

Helen reddened, embarrassed, and protested, 'That's Sister Mary's. She's the only other person who drives this car, and she allows herself a few musical indulgences.'

'Let's whack this baby on, then. I fuckin' hate silence. It freaks me out.' He put the CD into the player and soon the cheerful, tinny chugging of Abba's 'Waterloo' filled the car. 'Oh my god, I remember the fucking words to this. That memory of mine.' He tapped at his temple. He turned it up and launched into growls and shrieks in a death metal version of the Abba vocals.

Helen laughed out loud, and it felt good. She couldn't remember the last time she had really laughed.

* * *

An hour later, Professor Clancy arrived at Northern Genome Ltd. to see a nun and a man with a tattooed neck in the waiting area. He went to the reception and leaned over the desk to speak to his secretary in a low voice. 'Tanya, who are those people?'

'Oh, they arrived half an hour ago wanting to see you. You've got a window until eleven, so I made them an appointment.'

'What do they want?'

'Actually, I'm not sure. Maybe a couple wanting genetic testing for fertility?'

'A nun, Tanya, planning on getting pregnant? Interesting theory. Give me five minutes, then send them in to my office.'

'Well, this is the strangest week I've had in a long time,' he said, getting up to shake their hands as they came into the room. 'First, I am visited by detectives, and now by a nun and a...'

'Musician.' Mikko finished the sentence for him as they shook hands.

'You were visited by detectives?' asked Helen, as she sat down across the desk. 'Was it about Andrew Shepherd?'

Professor Clancy paused briefly before confirming.

'Yes, it was, actually. So, what can I do for you?'

Helen did the talking. She explained the strange story as best she could; how the police had brought her to Andrew Shepherd's apartment, how she had seen the drawing, and how they wanted to know what it meant. She wasn't really sure where she was going with it herself, and now they were here it sounded ridiculous. 'You see, Mr Kristensen had the same dream that was depicted in the drawing, and so... I saw that Dr Shepherd still had lots of genetic testing equipment in his apartment, so I thought maybe he was still working with you.'

'I'm afraid I don't think I can help you at all, really. I haven't seen Andrew Shepherd for many years, and when we parted company he was... well, he was a troubled soul. That drawing could mean anything.'

'Was he religious himself? Because his apartment was filled with religious books and papers.'

'Yes, he became very religious, and that was the main problem, I think. There are some fundamental contradictions between genetics and religion, as you can imagine, which he struggled to resolve.'

'What was his main concern? Was it to do with creationism?

I suppose a geneticist of certain faiths would have a very hard time resolving their science with their beliefs.'

'Not exactly. Look, it's rather complicated. Let's say that Shepherd struggled with the notion of playing God. Which is what modern science does, I suppose.'

'Was it to do with the biological dark matter?' asked Helen.

Professor Clancy raised his eyebrows. 'Ah, so you have done some research on our project then, Sister?'

Mikko shifted himself more upright in his chair and spoke up. 'Biological dark matter? That is some cool shit for a song, right there. That sort of blows my mind. So, what exactly did he find? In this dark matter?'

Clancy looked at them for a long time, sighing, conceding. 'We, or Shepherd, I should say, discovered a new gene, which he called OS1. It was on a chromosome which is specific to humans, no other animals, and appeared to be dormant, not expressed. And he found a marking on this gene's DNA that he couldn't explain. He became convinced that he had found what he called the soteriological marker. The marker for Heaven or Hell.'

'So, he thought he had found the gene for sin?' asked Mikko. 'Don't tell me, it's the 666. Like in The Omen, right?'

Clancy ignored this comment and looked at Mikko as if he were a mildly irritating child. 'No, no, sin is innate. Everybody has the gene for sin. According to Christianity, of course. No, he found a marker, which he thought was the marker for predestination.'

Helen was now lost in a personal realm of terror, but Mikko was fascinated.

'But if the genome is so vast, how did he even get to that?'

'Well, that is an excellent question.' Clancy looked surprised at this. 'It was thanks to our other team member, Laurent Baptiste. The data we were using came from a maximum-security prison, you know, really the worst criminals one can find. Simply because there was a large group of people from whom cheek swabs could be easily provided. And Andrew spotted a centromere with an unusual shape, which he couldn't explain. It was on the OS gene, so it was definitely specific to humans, and not everybody had it. In fact, only a very few of our data set possessed this mutation. So, he wondered if there were sociological factors at play. Laurent, to humour him more than anything else, ran statistical studies on different populations, and Andrew was convinced that the numbers added up. Bad people, but not all, tended to lack this genetic marker. It didn't seem to correlate to any other factors, stochastically; cognitive ability, disease, sex, sexuality, income. The only correlation, and even that was inconclusive, was with criminal activity. There were also indications that it was perhaps not completely dormant, and was somehow linked to activity in the prefrontal cortex of the brain. The part of the brain that controls our moral behaviour.

'Andrew became convinced. There was no talking to him. He gradually became impossible to work with. He was off on his own agenda, and it wasn't something to which we could subscribe. I mean, it was insane. Very sad, really.'

'Did anyone else know about it?' asked Helen. 'I don't remember anything coming out in the press.'

'Oh no, we kept it to ourselves. I'm comfortable telling you now, because you can see how ridiculous it is, but we would have been completely discredited. And our position within the Human Genome Project was already tenuous at best. The whole thing smacked of creationism, eugenics, and would have done proper genetics a terrible disservice. But Andrew was threatening to reveal his so-called findings. Announce it to the world. Can you imagine what would happen? If people knew their fate?'

'You mean, if they *thought* they knew their fate?' said Mikko. 'Because it's bullshit.'

'Yes, exactly, if they believed, of course. I mean, the world would collapse. It would be unthinkable.'

'Fuck,' offered Mikko. 'This is a mind-fuck. I kind of wanna write that down. That is a sick concept album right there.'

'Quite.' Professor Clancy had no response to this, but Mikko's return to inanity seemed to comfort him. Next to Mikko, Helen was silent. She was teetering on the edge of a precipice. She felt God was with her and that he was leading her somewhere, and that it may be terrifying, yet she must keep going.

'OS1. So - that stands for Original Sin, I presume. What does it look like, this… gene?' she asked.

'It looks very much like all the other genes. You know, they are very difficult to describe. But the mutated version, that is, the supposed,' - he made inverted commas with his fingers here - "marker for Heaven" is a single base change in the OS1 - a guanine replaced with adenine at position 32. Not 666,' he said, looking at Mikko in jokey accusation. 'It's almost imperceptible. A miracle, in fact, that he found it. Well, it would be a miracle if it were anything. The human genome is absolutely packed with this so-called junk.'

Clancy raised his eyebrows suddenly; he had a suggestion. 'I can test you, if you want. Just for fun. For your… concept album.'

'What would that involve?' asked Mikko. 'I don't like needles, man.'

'With all those tattoos? Hard to believe. But don't worry - it's just a simple cheek swab each. And I can call you in a couple of days with the results.'

Mikko slapped his hands onto the chair, arms in agreement, relieved to lighten the atmosphere. 'I'm down. If I'm going to Hell, that is way cooler than Heaven.'

'Hotter.' Helen reminded him, smiling sidelong. It was important to stay on the light-hearted surface of this, because the depths of horror below too unfathomable to contemplate. There were a few moments of expectant silence then, and Helen realised that Clancy's offer was serious.

'I don't know,' she said uncertainly. 'It feels somehow... blasphemous.'

'It totally is. Fuck.' said Mikko. 'But I won't tell God if you don't.'

'God sees everything. And I tell him everything.'

Clancy watched them banter back and forth as they almost forgot he was there.

Something was happening. *Is this flirting?* thought Helen. *Using God's name for flirting. My goodness, what am I doing? If that isn't blasphemy, I don't know what is.*

A few minutes later, as she allowed her mouth to be swabbed by Clancy's gloved hand, while Mikko looked on, awaiting his turn, she wondered if perhaps this was the test - and she was failing.

Chapter Nine

Abandoned churches litter the land; giant tombstones marking the old days of belief. Liverpool is scattered with these austere red-brick corpses, Catholic and Protestant - the Victorian gothic towers and spires darkened by pollution, like dried blood never to be cleaned. Some of these carcasses of Christianity have suffered the indignity of renovation, and are reborn as emblems of modernity; climbing walls, nurseries, office space. Others stand resolute and mournful, with crumbling turrets that sprout weeds, smashed windows boarded with thick metal grilles. Some boast fluorescent posters advertising events long past; although surprisingly few are scarred with graffiti, some innate reverence holding people back from defacement.

St. Wilfrid's stands high and lonely on its mound at the edge of the Rimrose Valley, a couple of miles outside Crosby. This church, with its distinctive castle-like tower on which perches one miniature spire, was abandoned in the Nineties, the Church of England unable to justify supplying a vicar to such a puny and dwindling congregation. Its slightly out-of-the-way location meant that it slipped through the net of community regeneration projects, and so now it stands melancholy and somehow dignified, despite its partially collapsed roof and smashed window. The tallest structure in this part of town it is a beacon calling out to the other desolate formed places of worship across the north of England.

Tonight, the beacon is lit; at the bottom of the church steps a group of teenagers have started a fire around which they sit trading jocular insults, vodka and marijuana. Although Halloween is over, they are dressed in varying degrees of costume. Sparkling red devil horns, a *Scream* mask, a furry werewolf suit. Too old for kids' parties and trick-or-treat, too young to access the night-time delights of the city centre, they make their own fun, playing spin the bottle, daring each other to fumbled encounters. They shiver in the night air, an opportunity for a boy to get close to a girl, a moment to begin. Their faces are half lit by the flames, half-dark, half-golden; their eyes demonic with bravado and fear.

Arran has taken something stronger than alcohol or weed. Unable to sit still, he jumps up suddenly and yells, 'Oh my god, I've got an idea!' He runs up the steps and tries the church door, which creaks ajar. 'Oh, my fuckin' god, it's open!'

'I dare you to go in!' they shout. But he bounds back to his position in the circle and takes hold of the official spinning bottle.

'Right, whoever it points to next has to suck me off, in the church, on the altar!'

The girls giggle nervously, and one boy shouts, 'What if it's one of the lads, then?'

'Ah no, I meant to say girls only,' he protests, but is drowned out by roars of laughter. They push each other and collapse into mini-heaps. 'I'm gonna wet meself,' cries one girl clutching her chest. Amidst hilarity, the bottle is clumsily spun. It careers a little but spins to a halt, pointing, through the flames, to the quietest girl, Hayley. She is pleased because she likes Arran; terrified because she has never done this before. Fear flashes through her, but she brushes it aside; there's no need for anyone to know it's her first time. Best to get this out of the way while she's drunk enough to make herself do it. She clambers to her feet, and he puts his arm around her shoulders, nervous too, now that the moment is real. They go up the steps together to the chants of 'Suck It, Suck It,' and at the top they both turn and each raise a middle finger to the circle as they push back the creaking door and go in.

The church has no roof; it is almost a ruin and the faint lights from the city add a pink tinge to the darkness above them, giving enough light for them to make their way gingerly to the altar, dodging rubble, fallen rafters, rubbish bags full of empty beer cans. He sits on the top of the three long steps, which were covered with ancient carpet. He undoes his flies and leans back on his hands, saying, 'Go 'ed then.'

She does what she thinks she is supposed to do, kneeling in front of him, not really knowing whether to use her hands as well. He does what he thinks he is supposed to do, placing his hands on her head. She smells unwashed skin, a faint taste of urine, and is revolted by the saliva and the slurping sound she is making. She is appalled by the remarkable indignity of it all, and is worried that she will vomit when the moment comes, or even before.

But he smells something unpleasant too and hopes it isn't him. Where he is sitting, it is sticky, and there are soft things on the floor, damp and cold. His hands move from her head to the floor at his sides, and it is wet and viscous, so he pads his hands along, and he touches something freezing and yet familiar. He feels around it and there is bone under skin, and the unmistakable stubble of a recently shaved leg. He looks behind him and what he makes out in the darkness causes him to scream. Hayley's teeth catch his taut foreskin as he jolts her from his crotch and their screams echo through the loose columns, through the rafters, and into the night air.

* * *

As dawn broke, the spotlights could be turned off and the crime scene took on its own natural, grey light. The police photographer continued to snap from every angle, each image more terrible than the last. Quinn had done her crying now, had retched up her stomach to acid, and now she stood numb, unable to look, but unable to stop looking. She had been a police officer for five years, and had seen a few things in her time, but she couldn't imagine that in an entire career she would ever see anything more horrible than this.

The woman's body - or perhaps girl's, as she looked little more than a child, particularly in the vulnerability of death - was slumped against the baptismal font in a seated position, legs splayed, like a rag doll, with her head lolling to one side. Her lifeless eyes looked over to the north window, which still had some remnants and shards of coloured glass. Almost inevitably, on the girl's forehead, was the shape of an inverted axe, neatly carved in blood. The marking itself was fresh and black, but the blood had run down the girl's face, staining it almost completely red. Her abdomen was splayed open, and entrails flopped down the stone steps, their bulbous masses dwarfing the size of her body. The steps were draped in a sheet of blood, which had been smeared in all directions by Arran and Hayley. Behind the body was an incongruous whiteboard, perhaps left over from Sunday schools many years ago. On it had been written, not in blood but in a mocking red marker pen.

As the proverb of the ancients says,
'Out of the wicked comes wickedness.'

A healthy tree cannot bear bad fruit, nor can
a diseased tree bear good fruit.

Who can make the clean out of
the unclean? No-one!

'You OK?' Swift placed an arm around Quinn and gently rubbed her shoulder.

'Nope. This is the worst thing I've ever seen in my life.'

'This is potentially a serial killer situation now. We need to widen missing persons to UK-wide ASAP and run it against women who might have a connection to Shepherd. I'm gonna give Tomlinson a call and see if there were any girls that Shepherd was bothering back then. Maybe it wasn't just Jason. This could be the girl who was living in his apartment, but who knows if there are more?'

They stood in silence for a few moments, since springing into action would cement the reality of this horrible situation. Eventually he said: 'You know what I'm worried about. I can hardly bear to say it.'

Without taking her eyes off the body, she wrapped her coat tighter around herself. 'Go on.'

'Why did they cut open her abdomen? What else was in there?'

'Oh my god.'

* * *

There was a knock on the library door. Helen jumped in her chair and quickly closed down her web browser, even though the screen was facing away from the door. The Deaconess popped her head in.

'Helen? Ah, there you are. There was a phone call for you. Someone called Mikko Kristensen? He says he is on his way to see you, and he'll be here soon. And he gave me the following message for you. She stepped into the library, and read from a post-it note.

Get yourself a… I'm afraid he said the f-word here… mobile phone.' She sighed. 'Are you sure you know what you're doing, Helen? Shall I meet him with you?'

'No, no, it's quite alright, Margaret. He's… a student of mine. He's having a difficult time with the course, and I'm giving him some spiritual help. You know, as we do here from time to time.' She smiled, but Margaret did not smile back. She moved further into the room.

'Be very careful, Helen. I believe this person has been sent here to tempt you. And this is a good thing, my dear. Remember Article 11: "But God, the Father of all comfort, does not let them be tempted beyond what they can bear, but with the temptation he also provides a way out - it's Corinthians 10.13 of course - and by the Holy Spirit revives in them the assurance of their perseverance".' There it was again, that kindness tinged with threat. Helen was finding it unbearable.

'I'll be careful, Margaret. I promise.'

As soon as the Deaconess left, Helen rushed up to her room and waited at the window, a strange buzzing in her head, an increase of her heartbeat, an irritating sweating that she couldn't stop. As soon as she heard the crunch of gravel and saw a taxi turn into the driveway, she grabbed her coat and ran down to the doorway to greet him outside. This was not a visitor that could be deemed in any way appropriate to come into the building, and as he emerged from the taxi, immediately lighting up a pre-rolled cigarette, she saw with dismay that although, the ridiculous slogan t-shirt he was no doubt wearing was covered by a winter coat, he was also wearing a beanie hat embroidered with the word 'SATAN' in capital letters. The inverted cross tattoo on his neck was clearly visible. With unfortunate timing, Sister Mary pulled into the driveway just after his taxi and emerged from the Beetle with two enormous shopping bags filled with groceries. 'What's up, Sister?' he nodded at her. 'Can I help you with those?'

He moved to take the bags from Sister Mary, but she snatched them away and looked at him with grim disapproval as she marched up the steps, glowering at Helen too as she puffed past her into the house.

'Hey, Sister Helen.' Mikko stood at the bottom of the steps, rocking on his heels with his hands in his pockets. He gestured behind Helen to where Sister Mary had gone inside. 'What's her problem?'

'I imagine she objects to your hat.'

'Oh, yeah. Fuck.'

'Come on. You wore that on purpose.'

'I didn't! OK, maybe subconsciously. Anyway, so Professor Clancy has our results, apparently. I'm ready for the big reveal, if you are.'

Helen wasn't really sure how to behave. Should she thank him for coming all this way? People seemed to lightly make fun of each other, with a touch of sarcasm. Perhaps she would try that.

'So, you dressed for the occasion, then? You know I can't bring you in to the building looking like that. I'm pretty tolerant as Calvinists go, but the other Sisters? Not so much.'

'OK, Sister Helen. Let's go for a walk then. Show me your hood. I want to check out this spooky-ass forest. It is awesome around here.'

As they walked away, side by side, a face appeared in one of the upstairs windows of Argarmeols Hall. The Deaconess watched from a room that might have been hers, or might have been Helen's. Then two more faces appeared, Sisters Frida and Mary, in the kitchen window. And another, and another. A leader and eleven of her twelve apostles, watching over their own, the apostate being drawn into the wilderness. Helen did not dare look back, but she could almost feel their gazes upon her. *And lead us not into temptation, but deliver us from evil.*

They headed into the pine forest, walking mostly in silence. This was her territory, and she felt somehow proud to be showing it to him. She knew every twist and turn of the path, every undulation of the hills, every tree trunk. It had rained all that morning, and the pine trees hung heavy with damp and the heady scent of wet leaves, autumnal decay. At one point, a red squirrel darted across their path and Mikko started in fright. 'Fuck! What the fuck is that?' which made her laugh and lightened the atmosphere. Their boots became stained with wet sand and clotted with leaves. Sometimes the path was clearly constructed with pine logs, wooden handrails, and at other times they had to clamber, putting out their hands for balance on mossy rock outcrops, stepping over roots and branches, avoiding prickly gorse. Once in a while Mikko, with his nervous energy, would pick up a pine cone and throw it, skim it like a child, into the forest against a tree trunk. Eventually the foliage thinned and they could hear the sea, smell the sea, and they came out upon the sand dunes of Formby Point. The tide was out and waves crashed far away, perhaps half a mile out across the sands. It was always windy here, and they both automatically stopped and took deep breaths into the wind.

'This is actually pretty beautiful,' he said. 'It's a lot like where I grew up, looking out over the North Sea. When I'm not touring, I honestly can't imagine not living on the coast somewhere. And definitely in the North. I enjoy living on the edge of something, you know, on a frontier. It makes you feel existential, even at the best of times. You know Norway has over twenty-five thousand kilometres of coastline, stretching right up to the Arctic. And it is brutal as fuck up there.' He was talking a lot, and Helen sensed he was nervous.

'So, we have all these legends about the sea,' he continued. 'I mean, not just the Vikings and shit. There are these monsters called draugs, which are supposed to be the spirits of sailors drowned at sea. So if you drown, and you don't have a proper Christian burial, you can't get into Heaven, and so you come back as one of these evil draugs, with no head, like just seaweed instead of a head.'

'A draug...'

'Yeah. It means *living dead person* in Old Norse.'

'I must look that up, thank you. Actually, I don't know much about Scandinavian mythology, and of course it would be so suitable for my course.'

'I'll come and give a guest lecture.'

'Not unless you cut back on the swearing, I'm afraid.'

'Anyway, it's just another version of a zombie. When I die,' - he looked out towards the horizon, where an enormous empty oil tanker was slinking into Liverpool Bay - 'I'm gonna have one of those Viking burials. Just launch me out to sea on a blazing longship, surrounded by my guitars, and let the wind carry my soul to Valhalla.'

'Ah, so you believe in Valhalla then, the great hall of the gods?'

'No, man. No more than I believe in your Heaven and Hell. They're all just stories we needed to tell ourselves in the past, dude. Otherwise, life was just too hard to explain. And now, now that we can explain everything, somehow, we still need stories. Different stories. I don't know.'

He drew deeply on his cigarette and motioned vaguely with his hand to indicate a boat romantically floating out to sea. The river Alt drains into the Mersey at Formby Point, and on the beach, it splits into hundreds of tiny channels that trickled towards the sea like dark blue blood vessels. Down there somewhere, in the intertidal lagoons, the Neolithic footprints of animals, birds and people have been preserved for seven thousand years. Baked by the sun and sealed into the muddy shoreline by repeated layers of sand and silt from the tide, coastal erosion was now revealing these ghosts from Liverpool's ancient hunter-gatherer past.

The vastness of the sandscape here was perhaps an illusion, since it wasn't more than a few miles to Southport, but the horizontal nature of the view made it look as if it went on forever. It always compelled Helen to want to set out and just keep on walking. But eventually, she would always have to turn back. She was tied to this landscape now, this windblown land constantly in motion. Like Mikko, she was always drawn to the coast and enjoyed living on the edge of something. The sense of scale was disorienting, and she thrived on the altered perspectives; she would watch huge container ships lumber into view, obscuring the landscape, before suddenly disappearing into port as if they had speeded up. She would watch them come and go, wondering what was in those containers and what it must be like to work on board those lonely giants. And she would watch the marsh birds prepare for their journey to warmer climates whilst the squirrels hoarded for winter.

There were constant reminders of danger here, not least from the ominous and seemingly permanent firing of bullets at Altcar Rifle Range. There was a Victorian shipwreck three-quarters' buried in the sand, now serving as a jagged fence; while the war rubble that formed the tidal barrier on Blitz Beach between Crosby and Hightown provided another reminder of old conflicts. The frontal dunes were constantly in peril from the elements, as violent storms coupled with high tides could see vast swathes of sand sheared off them, leaving vertiginous cliff faces scarred with marram roots.

Everything that was new here became quickly stained with salt and sand; new brick-built housing estates in Formby village, new cars, new shoes, faces. Helen sometimes felt that her whole body and soul was preserved as if in salt. *A living dead person.* As if he had been reading her mind, Mikko said: 'So, this is like your purgatory, huh? Living here. Total Depravity has a song called "Purgatory" on our second album. It kind of sucks, to be honest with you.'

'Well, the concept of purgatory is Catholic, not Protestant,' she said. 'But I suppose this is… yes, I felt…' she trailed off, because she had no answer to give. They sat on some dry-ish sand on the top of a dune, and looked out at the vastness below, faces braced against the wind, picking pieces of marram grass.

'Why did you come all this way to tell me?' she asked him. 'You could have just telephoned…'

'Erm, excuse me, you don't have a phone, remember?'

'You know what I mean, you could have, you know, left a message…'

'Er, hello, this is a message for Sister Helen, just to let her know God says she is definitely going to Heaven. Thanks, bye.'

She gave him a withering look.

'I don't know, man,' he said. 'I just wanted to see the place. Being close to someone who believes in something makes me happy. Spirituality doesn't just appear, you know. It needs someone with a brain capable of imagining a world they can't see. And that's powerful to be around. Everyone needs to believe in something, right?'

'Yes, I think that's right. Well, I suppose you believe in music.'

'Yeah, I guess. And I mean, I also came here because you're pretty fucking hot for a nun. What can I tell you?'

Helen stared at the ground.

'Sorry,' he said. 'Too much. The truth is... I sort of didn't want to find out by myself. I don't know why, but I wanted to be with you. For spiritual guidance, right? That must be it. So - you ready for this?' He took out his phone.

* * *

Swift and Quinn stood in the cold mortuary room at the Aintree Pathology Department, shivering but not from the cold, relieved that this particularly horrible post-mortem was almost over. The girl's body lay shrouded in front of them, with pathologist Dr Colvin moving around her, completing the required tasks in his usual business-like manner. Perhaps his brusqueness was the only way to cope with such a job. This was by no means the first time Swift had been in a mortuary, but it was the first time as a Detective Inspector in charge of a case, and he hoped to God he would ask the right questions. Fortunately, Dr Colvin was an old hand and would most likely take him through everything. Colvin, however, didn't seem his usual jovial self; something was bothering him, and Swift expected it was simply the grisly severity of the crime.

'So.' Colvin read from his clipboard, adjusting his glasses

with his other hand. 'Let's review. Twenty-something female, cause of death: bleeding. Time of death was estimated between midnight and six a.m. yesterday morning. Bled to death from two deep knife wounds to the abdomen. A very precise disembowelling in one movement. A professional job, if you can call it that. With a very sharp instrument.'

'One disembowelling movement. But you said there were two knife wounds,' pressed Swift. Despite his subdued manner, Colvin was still playing his usual game, making this into a pathology lesson.

'Yes. I did.'

Colvin sighed, shook his head, and placed his gloved hands on the surgical table facing the officers. The sheet remained covering the body. 'You don't need to see underneath it again, do you?' Swift and Quinn both shook their heads; Quinn felt that the image of this girl's body would be imprinted on her memory for a lifetime. Colvin continued.

'The second wound was the disembowelling. The first wound was a rudimentary caesarean. Well, I say rudimentary, but it was conducted by someone who knew their way around the body. I'd be very impressed if... sorry, impressed is the wrong word... *surprised*, if they didn't have medical training.'

'Caesarean? Do you mean she was pregnant? How pregnant?'

'Judging from the large size of the uterus and placenta, certainly third trimester. Just... horrible.' Swift and Quinn looked at each other and shuddered.

'Is there any chance the baby could have survived?' she asked.

'Well. You hear about these things, of course. Usually on those American true crime TV programmes, though. The umbilical cord appears to have been cut carefully, which implies the intention was indeed for the baby to survive.'

'So, the girl was alive when it happened...'

'No illicit substances in the blood, and no blow to the head, so it appears that she may have been awake for the whole thing.'

'Jesus.'

'Now obviously we're still waiting on results from fingernails, stomach contents, so hopefully forensics will have a lot more to work with soon.'

'OK. OK. We'll get back and see where we are with an ID. There doesn't seem to be any match with Missing Persons,' said Swift, nodding uncertainly. 'But when I called Tomlinson back, they mentioned another inmate who had been close to Shepherd, name of Chelsea McAllister. We're heading to her address next.'

There didn't seem to be any way to end this session with dignity for the victim. They stood in front of her body for a few moments, hands clasped in front of them funereally, then they stepped away with as much reverence as they could. But Colvin hadn't finished.

'There's something else, detectives.' Colvin didn't look up from his clipboard now. 'I'm still struggling to fathom it myself, but I've checked several times and I rarely make mistakes with these things.'

'Go on.'

'She… was a virgin.'

He was still staring intently at his clipboard, and Swift and Quinn looked at each other in confusion.

'What do you mean?'

'Precisely that. Hymen intact. That foetus was not the product of sexual intercourse.'

'Artificial insemination?'

'Well, given that we are still, I estimate, several hundreds of years away from inventing parthenogenesis in humans, and I gather we're not Herod's men looking for the Second Coming here, then yes, artificial insemination would seem to be the only explanation. It is conceivable - pardon the pun - that an insemination needle could have been inserted vaginally without breaking the hymen, and since it was almost nine months ago, a small puncture could have closed over. Insemination via a needle in the abdomen is also theoretically possible, although with the skin damage, I haven't been able to find any evidence yet.'

'Why would someone artificially inseminate such a young girl? Unmarried, no reason for infertility...'

'I'm at a loss, detectives. I suppose that is for you to find out.'

Chapter Ten

'OK, let's do this.' Mikko called a number and balanced his phone on his knee between them.

'Hello, Professor Matthew Clancy here?'

'Hello, Professor, this is Mikko and Helen. We've got you on speaker, and we are on standby for our all-important results.' Mikko smirked at Helen, but he couldn't hide his underlying nervousness. They were both glad to be outside with the distractions of the wind and the scenery.

'Ah yes. So, first things first.' said Clancy. 'Are you sure you want to know? Not that it means anything, of course, but I don't want to give you nightmares. It's a bit like an Ouija board, you know.'

'Sure, we're totally down for this. Hit us.'

'OK. Well - scientific bit here - I sequenced the OS1 gene from both of your cheek swabs, and on Helen's we see a guanine replaced with adenine at position 32, which has the effect of replacing a cysteine with a tyrosine in the amino acid sequence.'

'So, what does that mean, then? I mean, who's going where?' Mikko was still smiling at Helen while he said it.

'Well, if you were to believe Andrew Shepherd's theory, it would mean that Helen has the soterion mutation, and therefore is one of the elect. She is going to Heaven. While you are... not.'

* * *

It was late afternoon, and the sky was descending. The tide was coming in, and black clouds loomed low on the horizon over the sea.

'Well, there we are. I guess I'm gonna be with my brother.'

Mikko was trying to keep it light, but she knew he was looking at her for reassurance.

'I don't believe it, you know,' she offered.

'Yes, you do. That's the whole point of Calvinism!'

'No, I mean, I don't believe this genes thing. I don't understand… I'm more confused than ever.'

'What's not to understand? You're a nun and you're going to Heaven; I'm a fuckin' asshole who killed my brother, and I'm going to Hell. And it's all bullshit, anyway. Those genetics guys are as crazy as you nuns.'

They sat in silence for a while. Then Helen took a deep breath. 'The reason it doesn't make sense that it's wrong, is that I know I'm not going to Heaven. I need to tell you what I did. The reason I'm a nun.'

He shook his head. 'You don't have to.'

'I do. I do. When I was twelve, I got a phone for my birthday. This was before smartphones you know, but it had texting and a camera and games, and my friends all had them too, so we got into these texting marathons.'

And Helen was speaking, but she was no longer on the dune, looking out towards the spinning wind turbines that provided a form of hypnosis. She was back in that house, texting her friends, smiling about boys, girls, who liked whom. The TV was on, blaring a Saturday night show that she wasn't really watching, and she was lying on the carpet, propped on her elbows. This was the first time she had been left to babysit her brother while her parents went out, and since she was too young to be anywhere else on a Saturday night, the liberation of the house to herself was exciting.

She had put Alfie to bed an hour ago, impatient to be alone, but he hadn't been asleep yet. Something made her check on him. Perhaps she'd heard a bump through the ceiling, or had a strange feeling. She crept into his dark room and felt for him in his little toddler bed, but she was patting empty crumpled sheets. In a panicked whisper, she patted the floor next to the bed, under the bed. *Oh God, was the window open?* She ran back to the bedroom door to turn on the light switch and when she looked back at the window she saw legs, little legs dangling, and a face with the same expression she would later see on Jason Hardman's body on the beach. She tried to untangle him, to lift him down, but she couldn't undo the ties that had cut so far into his neck she could no longer see them through the folds of skin. Her hands were shaking uncontrollably, and he was so cold, so limp, and in the end, she just had to leave him there, alone, while she called for an ambulance.

'It was the blinds. I don't know what he was doing by the window, but he got caught in the strings of the blinds and was strangled. It happened to a few children before they made new regulations…'

'I'm so sorry.'

She nodded, and they both stared at the ground, both picking at pieces of marram grass more urgently than before.

'It wasn't your fault,' he said, shaking his head. 'It wasn't your fault. For sure, you know that.'

'Yes, yes, it was.'

'It was an accident. You were too young to be in charge. If it was anyone's fault, it was your parents. What happened after?'

Her voice was breaking, but she felt a steely horror, an acceptance of her fate, her responsibility. She could hardly bear to think about the immediate aftermath, never mind to express it in words.

'My parents' marriage didn't survive, and my Dad left. I haven't seen him in fifteen years. My mother and I just carried on, but it was so unbearably sad. I tried to take care of her, but she couldn't even look at me. We were Methodists, we always had been, but she became increasingly religious. And so did I. Anything to be closer to Alfie, to God, to be closer to understanding, to get some sort of comfort. Anyway, I felt that her seeing me was too painful, so I left as soon as I could; scholarship to sixth form college, then to Liverpool University. I found the Sisters of Grace during my first year, and Deaconess Margaret helped me a lot.'

'But did you really have a… a calling for that? A vocation, or whatever?'

'Yes, yes, I did. I couldn't possibly lead a normal life. The rest of my life must be a penitence. No, that makes me sound like a martyr. The rest of my life must be devoted to trying to understand.'

'And you chose the cruellest religion you could find.'

'No, no, it's not like that.' And she tried to explain to him, to herself, the attraction of Calvinism. That she wanted something cruel, harsh, and unforgiving, because she deserved nothing better. That the last thing she wanted was forgiveness, only punishment. But if she were truly honest with herself, there was another attraction of a religion which left her utterly dependent on God's grace, absolved of all personal responsibility. Perhaps then, her brother's death could be God's fault, not hers. That deism in itself is therapeutic, and belief in an all-powerful, all-seeing God absolves us of any will, allowing us to be broken. That there is a perverse comfort, a sort of pride, in knowing that you are depraved, helpless. She enjoyed the challenge of rationalising a set of principles. That she chose Calvinism when she was spiritually immature, naïve, and that if she was totally honest with herself, there was now a certain amount of regret. That this anachronistic little community she had chosen, on the edge of the world, was not so much a life of penance as a life of escape. She wondered if Calvinism was actually Christianity in its most misconceived form, and if she might have made a terrible mistake with her life. But it was too late now.

Both shivered a little from the cold and from other unnamed fears. Now the black clouds were rolling in at speed and the sky hung oppressively low. They hurried back, mostly in silence, each lost in private thoughts. A line had been crossed now, an invisible threshold, and they were perhaps in a liminal space that was impossible to define. They were no longer two unlikely acquaintances; they were something else. Helen tried a little small talk, asked him about his next concerts, his plans for after the tour, but he gave only brief answers. The first heavy drops spattered on Mikko's leather jacket and Helen's anorak as they reached the wet gravel of Argarmeols. It was dusk.

'So,' he said, scuffing his sandy boots against the Beetle's tyres. 'It was nice finding out the destiny of my immortal soul with you. Actually, it was fucking weird.'

'Come on,' she smiled weakly. 'I'll give you a lift to the train station.'

As they drove, Mikko squirmed and muttered to himself, and eventually blurted out,

'You know, I'm pissed. I'm fucking pissed off. I don't believe you. If you had really wanted to cloister yourself, you wouldn't be here, near a big city, teaching at a university. You would be in some hermit place somewhere, with a vow of silence. But you chose to live on the edge of somewhere - on the edge - so you can watch what goes on when people really live. And what's more, you don't want to be forgiven. You want to go to Hell, but you don't have a choice. What's it called? Irresistible Grace. You're going to Heaven whether you like it or not.'

Helen was driving through tears; she loathed herself and everything about this moment. Mikko, close to tears himself, swivelled round in his seat so he could look at her.

'You have to forgive yourself. It was an accident. Guilt is not a way to live - it is crippling you. You were just a kid, and you weren't responsible. It's terrible, what they did to you, how they made you feel. You shouldn't be here. Punishing yourself all your life for something you didn't do. You're going to get old here, and you're going to be bitter. It makes me angry as fuck. This God, he's not your God. I know you - you're kind and forgiving. You're not like these people. If you're gonna believe in God, choose a different church. For fuck's sake. Fuck it, let's go to this church right here. Pull over.'

They were almost at the train station now, and on their left was a large church with a castle tower. It was open and lit up and there were people going inside - an evening service was about to begin. The sign said 'Church of England Angel of Liverpool, All Are Welcome In The House Of Our Lord.' The church was in its own garden that was filled with gravestones. Feeling broken and needing to be directed, Helen allowed herself to obey him and manoeuvred the car into a space next to the pavement. She was wishing desperately that none of this had ever happened, that she had just left it alone.

'Come on,' he said. 'Let's go in.'

'Alright.' She looked at him, wiped away her tears. 'Take off that ridiculous hat then...'

'Oh yeah, right. Fuck.'

The church was almost full, with lots of families; children ran up and down the aisles. As they entered, a jovial man handed them a leaflet and inquired, 'Are you here for the community choir practice?'

Helen opened her mouth to speak, but Mikko spoke first. 'Yeah, we're just trying it out if that's OK.'

'Wonderful. Welcome. Here's the order of service then, and you'll find everything else in the hymn books on your pews.' He spoke as if he were giving them both a hug.

They edged into a space on one of the back pews. This church,

Angel of Liverpool, was much bigger than St. Michael's, centrally heated, and the atmosphere was completely different. There were families, students, young people, old people, and the smiling vicar appeared utterly delighted as he surveyed his congregation. Helen couldn't help notice the contrast with the Deaconess, who looked with genuinely grim dismay at each individual who entered her establishment. At the front of the nave was a choir who wore a uniform, but it was of robes in clashing, garish colours. Behind them on the back wall were the huge organ pipes, and Helen was suddenly thrilled at the thought of hearing music in a church. The organ at St Michael's had been removed decades earlier, no longer needed for the Order's brand of strict Calvinist services, and Helen had always felt a touch of sadness when she saw the faint marks on the white walls where the pipes had been ripped out.

'See, I told you - nice Christians!' Mikko whispered in her ear, looking at the sheet of paper he had been given. 'Nice fucking set list too,' he nodded approvingly as he surveyed the hymn titles. They took a hymn book each from the shelf in front of them, and she studied hers intently, embarrassed, wishing she could be here alone to try something so personal, and at the same time glad she was not alone. As worshippers continued to file in, the organ began to play an introductory piece, its resultant tones reaching her very core in the same way that the distorted guitars of Total Depravity had done through their amplifiers. The organist was decidedly amateurish, she couldn't help noticing, and she had an urge to play again herself. She was sure she could remember how. But despite the odd wrong note, those organ pipes evoked an innate warmth and spirituality.

The vicar announced, 'Let us sing our first hymn of the evening, one that you all know, 'He Who Would Valiant Be.'

'Oh man,' whispered Mikko. 'He Who Would Valiant Be, that is like super-Calvinist. Not only do I know this hymn, I literally stole the words for one of our tracks.'

Reprobation

Helen looked down at the hymn book out of shyness, but she knew the words too - they had been ingrained in her since childhood - those lyrics adapted from Bunyan's *The Pilgrim's Progress* and set to the folk melody by Vaughn Williams. The organ launched into the hymn's dignified, righteous cadences, and Helen sang tentatively, her voice cracking, relieved that she could barely hear herself over the other singers. Mikko began to sing too, in a delicate baritone. Both of them were rediscovering voices they hadn't used in a long time.

He who would valiant be 'gainst all disaster,
Let him in constancy follow the Master.
There's no discouragement shall make him once relent
His first avowed intent to be a pilgrim.

As the first verse drew to a close, Mikko put an arm around Helen, and she welled up with tears again, so he rallied her with a gentle shake and she blinked them back as they launched into the second verse.

Who so beset him round with dismal stories
Do but themselves confound - his strength the more is.
No foes shall stay his might; though he with giants fight,
He will make good his right to be a pilgrim.

At the end of the second verse they looked at each other and smiled, and Helen wondered if she was about to find some answers in this church, and Mikko wanted to do something, maybe to hold her hand, but he didn't and they carried on singing. With the final verse, the organist pulled out the stops in that familiar, irresistible sonic manipulation that filled the church with bass notes and pathos.

Since, Lord, Thou dost defend us with Thy Spirit,
We know we at the end, shall life inherit.
Then fancies flee away! I'll fear not what men say,
I'll labor night and day to be a pilgrim.

When the service was over, the vicar entreated the congregation to offer each other greetings, and people moved around the church, shaking hands, giving and receiving hugs. Helen stifled a laugh more than once as people give Mikko a wide berth or a second look. As they left the church, she felt not the bleak catharsis that she experienced after St Michael's rituals, but a different sort, a comforting sort. Instead of spiritual exhaustion, she felt a spiritual awakening. Perhaps it wasn't always necessary to punish yourself. Perhaps sometimes you could be kind to yourself.

They stood outside the car, shivering in the cold, Mikko scuffing the ground with his boots. 'So. Where to now, Sister Helen?'

'I don't know. I mean, I'll go back to the Order now. But I feel sort of… AWOL. And I feel better. Thank you. A catharsis. Like one of your concerts.'

'You see, you got spiritual counselling from a renowned Satanist.'

'The irony is not lost on me. So where are you going now, then?'

'Fucking… Bristol? We just have two more UK dates, then I have a few days off. Look, I need a fucking holiday, some sun or something. Do you want to maybe come with me? We could go to the south of France, find this other geneticist guy you've been looking into or whatever. Investigate, like fucking… Scooby Doo or whatever.'

'Thank you. But you know I can't do that.'

'Yes, you can. You can do anything you want.' Then he said, 'I read in the paper they found another body. A girl.'

'I know. The police didn't contact me this time. I think… it sounds crazy, but I think… I'm a suspect. I don't know, but I feel like I'm a suspect.'

'Join the fucking club. Did you never suspect me?' He looked down, suddenly worried. 'I mean, I could have done it, you know. That was my band's marking on the body, right there. I was in Liverpool at the time. I hate God. And I have a bus full of huge guys who do whatever I tell them.'

Helen thought for a moment. There had been a trepidation at the very beginning, when she had first found the Total Depravity website. But if she was honest with herself, it was less about fear and more about excitement, the thrill of being on the chase, of being perhaps one step ahead of the police. From the moment she met Mikko, she hadn't given it a second thought. The discovery of that body on the beach, however horrific, had ignited a process in her she couldn't quite explain but which had energised her.

'I didn't suspect you, no,' she said finally. 'Never. Strangely.'

'Strangely. Ha. So come on then, let's carry on the journey, or whatever they say on reality TV. Let's see what this other genetics dude has to say. Whether you believe or not, I mean it's still huge, right? People are dead. And whether I believe or not, I believe they believe, and that's where we have an advantage over the police. Use your skills… come with me.'

'I can't, Mikko. I'm sorry.'

Chapter Eleven

Autumn was creeping exponentially into winter, and as the temperature plummeted a semi-permanent mist descended over the city, swathing its highest points - the Radio City tower, the cathedrals, the cranes - in a fine grey veil that would often hang there all day. At high tide, the bronze men were the only figures on the beach, facing the sea unyielding as martyrs while the colourless surf crashed over them. The angriest waves would surge over the promenade and wash away flowers and tributes that had been tied to the barrier in memory of Jason Hardman. Teddy bears and handwritten cards would be tossed in the swell and would wash up on the beach the next morning as a second offering to the dead.

Despite Darren's attempts to keep the grislier details of the murders out of the local press, a macabre anxiety was taking hold of Liverpool. A city bonded in tragedy, as it had been before, as it would be again, was looking for answers to questions almost too profound to contemplate. The churches that had been full before were now overflowing; the congregations that had been tiny were now expanding as newcomers crept uncertainly into pews. St. Wilfrid's, the location of Chelsea McAllister's unimaginable end, was no longer abandoned on its lonely mound. The yellow police cordons surrounding it were gilded with flowers and offerings, while candlelit vigils took place there every evening as the community huddled together in grief.

Only a mile or so away, the Jeremiah Chapel stood a few doors down from Crosby police station. Another piece of Victorian gothic, its deep red brick sporting intricate tracery windows and a beautiful ogival arched doorway. Its small size and busy location allowed the Jeremiah to lend itself to all sorts of spiritual and non-spiritual activities, and it was thriving. The notice board in the church's front garden, which had once listed times of worship, was now pasted with a fluorescent poster that cheerfully invited locals to an incongruous mixture of free activities, including bridge, ballroom dancing, Zumba, 'messy church.'

Quinn nudged the heavy door open with her shoulder. She admired the understated beauty of Crosby's low-key churches, and loved that they always seemed to be open, even nowadays, the possibility of sanctuary always available. It was testament to the residual respect for religion, she thought, that more were not vandalised. She saw Swift sitting in one of the middle pews.

'I thought I might find you here. Everyone's still there in the office, but it's late. We should do the meeting and wrap things up for the day, yeah?'

'Yeah, sorry. Just needed a few minutes to… I don't know.' He looked up at the church's focal point, a giant crucifix that hung above the altar, from which the forlorn figure of Christ stared at him with pleading eyes. He continued to stare at it as he spoke.

'This case was looking clear-cut until the Killys came up. Why are they involved? I'm trying to find a link between the drugs and the religion here, but other than those steroids, it's all hearsay. How are you doing on that sequencer machine in Shepherd's flat? What's it called? The Revelon?'

'Slow going. Almost a hundred of this model were sold last year alone, so it's a case of tracing the serial numbers to their owners one by one. We need more manpower.'

'I know. But that could be the Killy link. A missing serial number implies it's stolen. Maybe the Killys stole it for Shepherd, maybe he borrowed money from them to buy it, maybe he was procuring drugs from them, maybe he became indebted… I'm clutching at straws.'

He finally prised his gaze away from the crucifix and smiled grimly at Quinn. 'You can follow the training manuals all you like, tick all the boxes, but it goes out the window when it comes to getting inside people's heads.' He leaned forward so that he was almost in a prayer position and rubbed his face with his hands. 'This case is doing me head in.'

Colette tentatively put a hand on his back. 'It's getting to all of us, boss. It's getting to the whole of Liverpool. Apparently, churches are packed to the rafters all over the city. Mad, isn't it?'

'It shouldn't even be about the religion. It should be about all the vulnerable people just passing through the case, the people who can just disappear unnoticed. Chelsea McAllister wasn't even registered missing - can you imagine her parents were so wasted they weren't even bothered that she'd been gone for weeks? And I keep dreaming about that baby. But it's the whole Bible thing that's freaking everybody out. Stupid, isn't it? I mean, we're in the realms of fantasy land.'

'Yes, but what's fantasy land to us is real to someone. You can't discount the power of other people's beliefs.'

'But who do you know who actually believes in God?'

'I do,' said Colette.

'You what?'

'I do! Loads of people I know do.'

'But when you think about, really think about what that means; the logical conclusions of that it just doesn't make sense to me.'

'It doesn't have to make sense. And you don't have to go to church to believe. Everyone has to believe in something.'

'But it just isn't possible that people can do things, kill each other, based on belief.'

'Think about what you just said, and think about the world.' said Colette. 'That's exactly what people do, all the time, throughout history.'

'Yeah. Sorry. The truth is....' He paused and took a deep breath. 'The truth is, I did used to go to church. For years, growing up. Me parents were - are - members of Mainstreet.'

At this, he looked at Colette to see if that meant anything to her.

'Mainstreet. Aren't they those happy-clappy nutters who do exorcisms, try to convert gay people and that?'

'Nutters, yeah.' he nodded. 'That's about the size of it. The church was the biggest thing in our lives. So I did used to believe, because I didn't think there was an alternative. But once I hit me teens, I couldn't wait to get out of there.'

'My God. That's mad. Even in a place like Liverpool, you can get these pockets of intolerance. I dread to think what Mainstreet are saying about this case in their sermons. No wonder you've got a thing about nuns. Listen, you're doing great, Boss. Everyone is impressed. And everyone is behind you.'

'Sometimes I feel like I'm just arsing about with paper clips and marker pens, making it up as I go along.'

He leaned forward again, rubbed his hands on his face, and she shuffled closer along the pew to put a hand on his shoulder. It was awkward, but it was a moment, she thought.

'Let me tell you a secret. Nobody knows what they're doing.'

'What, you're telling me Dr Colvin doesn't know what he's doing?'

'Fine. Some doctors know what they're doing. But the rest of us are just arsing about with paper clips and marker pens, making it up as we go along, joining the dots, hoping something will stick. You're heading a murder investigation by yourself, aged thirty. And you're teaching everyone else how to do it as well. Believe in yourself, since you don't believe in God.'

'Nice one, Colette. What would I do without you as my right-hand woman?'

'You'd have Dave, mate.'

'Fucking hell. That lad. If he stopped joking around for five minutes, he could become a great police officer. And if I grew a pair, I could become a great police officer, too. Come on.'

They edged out of the pew and walked back down the aisle.

'Tell me the truth, Colette. Do they all think I shagged Canter to get this job?'

'No! Jesus, that hadn't even crossed my mind! Come on, grow a pair like you said, and let's get back and sort that lot out.'

'What do we do now, then?' he asked as they reached the church door and turned around to look back at the crucifix. 'Is it the sign of the cross? Oh, you religious expert. Is there anything you're not an expert on?' he nudged Colette.

'Yeah, it's spectacles, testicles, wallet, and watch.' She did the movements solemnly.

'You what?'

'Oh no, that's Catholic, isn't it? What are we in now, Church of England?'

They doubled over with giggles, which they hushed to a whisper, then realised the pointlessness of whispering, which made them laugh even more.

* * *

A few minutes later, Swift and Quinn restored their solemnity for the incident room.

'Attention please, everyone, the victim's name is Chelsea McAllister.' Swift spoke while Quinn placed on the incident board a blown-up selfie of the dead girl, obtained from her Facebook profile. 'The only reason we know that, is we went back to Tomlinson asking if Shepherd had any other so-called favourites when he was working there, and they mentioned Chelsea. To be honest, I'm kicking myself for not checking that out sooner. She was nineteen years old, from Litherland, hadn't been seen by her family for six weeks, although they didn't report her missing.'

'Why not?' someone asked.

'The parents are drug addicts, and barely even noticed she'd gone. She had also taken drugs in the past, and had learning difficulties, suspected foetal alcohol syndrome. Her drug dealing, which was what sent her to Tomlinson, was instigated by her parents. She'd been in and out of care but returned to her parents' home after her time at Tomlinson, and that's how she dropped off the radar. A very vulnerable young person who slipped through the net.'

'So boss, was she the one living in Shepherd's apartment?' asked Dave.

'I think we can assume so, yes, particularly since there was that baby and pregnancy catalogue in her bedroom. But we can verify that with forensics. Speaking of forensics, the crime scene hasn't yielded anything yet in terms of footprints or fingerprints. Again, tracks have been covered carefully.'

'Any CCTV nearby?'

'Not within a workable radius. It's probably the most remote church in the Crosby area, and presumably that's why it was chosen. The only thing we have to go on is that whiteboard. He tapped at the photo on the incident board. Let's get a handwriting expert to compare that with the scrawlings on Shepherd's bedroom wall.'

'How d'you do that, boss?'

'To be honest, I don't know. But I'll find out. Lads, this is all as new to me as it is to you. Quinn, do you want to carry on?'

Quinn stepped forward.

'So that's two victims from the young offenders' institution. We need to find anyone else who Shepherd was in touch with, especially young people. Try the neighbours again. Try the CCTV in the vicinity of that church on the night. DI Swift and I are going to contact other former inmates of Tomlinson, those who had been there at the same time as Shepherd but not swayed by him. Maybe get some explanation from them of what he was trying to do? Some sort of weird experiment gone wrong? Difficult though, as there's unlikely to be anyone left who was there three years ago.'

Swift took over again.

'We need to up the urgency now, lads. This is approaching serial killer territory, and Stuart Killy is still missing. Who knows how many others are missing? There are nearly two hundred people on the Missing Persons list on Merseyside, and any of them could be connected. Dave, Baz, have you got anything for me?'

'Erm, we went back last night to talk to more of Jason Hardman's mates, but none of them had seen him in a while. It was absolutely chock-a-block. Heaving, wasn't it?' Dave looked at Baz, who nodded solemnly to confirm that it had, indeed, been heaving.

'Never mind nightclubs. What about the timber yards and vans?'

'Erm, no. No vans were spotted on CCTV from Hall Road Station that night by the beach. Whoever it was must have driven the other way. No sightings of Shepherd from the CCTV cameras across the road from Kenilworth House. Not so far anyway, but we need to go back further - it's just finding the time. On the timber - checked a few timber yards locally, nothing. Checked a couple of cars, hire firms for van rentals, nothing.'

'A couple? Check them all! Dave, you know what?' sighed Swift. 'You are a proper joker. Give me something to show me you deserve to be here.' There was stifled laughter around the room, but Dave looked hurt, and Darren instantly regretted his severity. In the absence of manpower, they had been piling every ad hoc task on to the poor lad.

Quinn had a question. 'Boss, how are we doing on motive? What are we saying was the motive at the moment?'

Swift opened his arms in a hopeless shrug. 'He's an arch manipulator, preying on vulnerable people, but what was he trying to achieve? Was he testing them for this so-called sin and them bumping them off if they were sinners? Was he trying to change them in some way? The baby is an absolute mind-fuck. I know we're supposed to get inside the mind of the killer, but priorities are forensics, police work, finding this bloke.

'There has to be a drug connection. Jason Hardman and Chelsea McAllister, both with convictions for drug dealing, and then the Killys get involved. Titan haven't taken this off us yet, so let's work on Shepherd.'

Chastened, Dave put up his hand.

'Boss. How do you look for a baby that might not exist?'

'Call the local hospitals, put out something to all the doctors' surgeries in the Sefton area. Other than that, I haven't got a fucking clue.'

He looked out of the window, at a loss. Outside the police station it was pitch dark, the tarmac glowing orange in the street lamps as the last of the evening rush hour traffic was easing its way into Crosby, crawling through the multiple sets of traffic lights in this busy community. Swift looked around the office at the exhausted faces.

'Right, who's coming down the Angel for a quick bev? We need a morale booster.'

But he stopped, because Tracey, on the phone in the corner, had raised her hand and was flapping it about to show the significance of the call she was on. A hush fell over the room and everyone waited in silence as the call wound down with, 'Right, thank you very much, Father. That's brilliant, and we'll be back in touch shortly.' She put the phone down and stood up to a sea of expectant faces.

'So - that was a response to the Most Wanted appeal we put out on Shepherd. It was a Father Anthony,' she read from her notepad, 'who runs St. Cuthbert's Hospice in Croxteth. Apparently, Shepherd has been going there recently as a volunteer, visiting sick people, you know. He was last there three weeks ago, and apparently he was acting strangely.'

'Three weeks ago - so that's the most recent sighting of him, and that's after the death of Jason Hardman. Nice one. Right, Quinn, let's get down there.'

'Oh, sorry, boss,' Tracey stopped him in his tracks as he was grabbing his coat, 'the Father also said he's happy for us to go over there, but would we mind not coming tonight - visiting hours only, you know, for the sake of the patients.'

Swift paused for a moment, turning.

'Oh, right, yeah. But fuck that, this is the best lead we've had. Let's go, Quinn.' He clapped his hands together, feeling buoyed. 'The rest of you. Bevvies.' *Where are you, Shepherd?*

* * *

Deaconess Margaret Mills was in full flow, reading from the Gospel of Matthew, holding her Bible up to the rafters and waving her other hand flamboyantly.

'And as he sat upon the Mount of Olives, the disciples came unto him privately, saying, tell us, when shall these things be? And what shall be the sign of thy coming, and of the end of the world? In the Gospel of Matthew, Jesus tells us the parable of the ten virgins. Then the Kingdom of Heaven will be like ten virgins who took their lamps and went out to meet the bridegroom. Five of them were foolish, and five were wise. Those who were foolish, when they took their lamps, took no oil with them, but the wise took oil in their vessels with their lamps. Now, while the bridegroom delayed, they all slumbered and slept. But at midnight there was a cry, "Behold! The bridegroom is coming! Come out to meet him!" Then all those virgins arose and trimmed their lamps. The foolish said to the wise, "Give us some of your oil, for our lamps are going out." But the wise answered, saying, "What if there isn't enough for us and you? You go rather to those who sell and buy for yourselves." While they went away to buy, the bridegroom came, and those who were ready went in with him to the marriage feast, and the door was shut. Afterward the other virgins also came, saying, "Lord, Lord, open to us." But he answered, "Most certainly I tell you, I don't know you." Watch therefore, for you don't know the day nor the hour in which the Son of Man is coming.'

She paused and looked at her congregation for a long time, lingering on each pair of eyes until they were forced to look down in wretchedness.

'Are you watchful? Are you truly watchful, like the five wise virgins? Are you ready for the Second Coming of Christ? For the Bible tells us that we must be ready at all times; that the time of the Lord will come like a thief in the night. So, there is the good news; Christ is coming. But why must we be ready? Because here is the bad news. The Bible also tells us that the end times will not come in peace and safety, but with plague and terror!

'Thessalonians!' She pulled down the finger of one hand to begin her bulleted list. 'While people are saying "Peace and Safety", destruction will come upon them suddenly, as labour pains for a pregnant woman, and they will not escape.

'James!' She screeched this second bullet point so suddenly that several people jumped in shock as she reeled off more passages of the Bible by heart. 'The Judge is standing at the door! Thessalonians again!' Third. 'The lawless one will be revealed, whom the Lord Jesus will overthrow with the breath of his mouth and destroy by the splendour of his coming.

'The lawless one. Satan. Satan is here already, I tell you! Daniel tells us that "He shall speak pompous words against the Most High, shall persecute the saints of the Most High, and shall intend to change times and law". The Revelation tells us to beware the beast with seven heads and ten horns; that this beast was mortally wounded but *survived*.'

The Deaconess said this last word as a terrifying whisper, the volume of her rage subsiding suddenly at the very moment when Helen sneaked in at the back of the church, trying to close the heavy door as quietly as possible, and failing. Margaret stared at her for the entire length of her theatrical pause. Attendance at Margaret Mills' commanding weekly sermons was effectively compulsory for the Sisters of Grace residents, as well as being relatively well attended by locals and guests. Helen had noticed their leader's firebrand quality becoming more and more pronounced in recent months. The regular themes of humility, faith and hard work were gradually morphing into themes of readiness, watchfulness, a new era approaching. The Sisters joked amongst themselves that she had been watching too much *Game of Thrones*, known to be her weekly televisual indulgence. Helen's adoration for Margaret had dissipated in recent months, and was building into a negative feeling that she didn't like and was fighting against.

'Let's talk about the Revelation,' continued the Deaconess, with a sardonic tone. 'Is it as crazy as you might think? Is it? Because the Revelation tells us about plagues, famines, earthquakes... yes, these things are here already! The prophets warn that the earth will experience great turmoil, wickedness, war, suffering! The prophet Daniel said that the time before the Second Coming would be a time of trouble such as the earth has never known. Sound familiar?'

She nodded, looking out at each terrified, gulping face of her congregation.

'And most important of all, the Bible tells us to beware of false prophets. False prophets!'

Helen had a fleeting thought that her fiery eyes reminded her of Mikko when he was performing.

'False prophets! They are mentioned all over the Bible! And perhaps they are all over our world! Mark: "For false Christs and false prophets shall rise, and shall show signs and wonders, to seduce, if it were possible, even the elect."

'Matthew: "At that time many will turn away from the faith and will betray and hate each other, and many false prophets will appear and deceive many people. Because of the increase of wickedness, the love of most will grow cold, but he who stands firm to the end will be saved... For false Christs and false prophets will appear and perform great signs and miracles to deceive even the Elect- if that were possible. See, I have told you ahead of time."

'You see, we have even been warned. So be watchful. Be as the wise virgins. And remember Revelation 22: "Behold, I am coming soon! Do not seal up the words of the prophecy of this book, because the time is near. Let him who does wrong continue to do wrong; let him who does right continue to do right; and let him who is holy continue to be holy."

'These things *cannot be changed.*' She emphasised these words with her theatrical whisper again. 'It is the word of the Lord.'

As always, her caustic tone softened at the end. Helen sighed inwardly. These tricks and manipulations no longer worked on her.

After the congregation had shuffled out into the cold and into their own private nightmares, the nuns made their way to the dining room, which they nostalgically called the Refectory. They took it in turns to cook, and nobody was particularly looking forward to tonight's effort, a beef stew by Sister Frida. But they sat together in amicable quiet, the twelve of them, the twelve apostles of Margaret Mills, murmuring appreciation at the food steaming in front of them, and waiting for the Deaconess to take her place at the head of the table. At the other end was Sister Mary, the Deaconess' official deputy, rubbing her hands together in gleeful anticipation of dinner. Now approaching the age of fifty, she had entered the convent fifteen years ago, having received a calling to the monastic vocation shortly before the end of her medical studies. Thanks to Mary's energy and expertise, the Order was able to care adequately for the elderly nuns, plus the odd pregnant or drug-addicted waifs and strays that landed on their doorstep. She was a gossip and a glutton, but everyone appreciated her burly, jovial presence in such severe surroundings. Next to her were Sisters Josephine and Anke, who had arrived at Argarmeols seven years ago on secondment from a Calvinist

Order near Antwerp and had never left. They barely spoke, other than to each other. Sister Alice had taken the veil after being widowed, and Sister Frida had also apparently been married, but was now so pious that she rarely left the chapel other than to cook. Other than Helen, only Mary had taken the veil as a young woman. As for the Deaconess, her journey to Sisterhood remained something of a mystery to all of them; she spoke a lot, but rarely about herself.

Helen was usually seated next to the Deaconess; as a university lecturer and a bringer of revenue to the Order, she was accorded a special veneration. Furthermore, the Deaconess far preferred her company to anyone else's. Opposite Helen were Sisters Elizabeth and Elsie, the two most elderly nuns. The Order effectively operated as a retirement home; with only Helen, Margaret, and Mary of working age. Helen looked at the women who had become her family. They didn't wear their veils indoors when they were together, and apart from Margaret and Helen, every head was white or grey. The scent of carbolic soap, old lady, and unwashed wool. They were supposed to be an evangelical Order, to spread the word, to convert people, but nobody from the outside had taken the veil, or even come close to considering it, since Helen ten years ago. Apart from a relatively tiny but loyal local congregation, the only genuine interest in the place nowadays came from desperate people seeking short-term refuge, or chancers pretending they were desperate, or people with obvious mental instability, or journalists seeking a story. A TV crew had once pitched up and requested making Argarmeols Hall part of a reality documentary on the modern cloistered life. Margaret had sent them packing with a spectacular brutality that had become legendary amongst the Sisters. But without interest or support from the public, without any true relevance in the world, they all wondered how long this place, this little anachronism, could continue.

The ladies straightened in their seats and bowed their heads as Margaret swept in and began to say grace. 'Dear Lord, we thank you for this food we are about to enjoy. We thank you for each other, for our community, for your love. We pray for the poor victims murdered within our community; we pray for their families, and we pray God helps them to understand why they had to die in such a way. Amen.'

The Sisters began to eat, murmuring approvals and assents.

'Terrible business with the bodies on the beach and now the church,' ventured Sister Hazel from the other end of the table. 'Do you think they are connected, Deaconess?'

Margaret opened her mouth to speak, but was interrupted by a loud 'Pardon?' from Sister Elizabeth, who was very deaf. Margaret placed a hand on Elizabeth's arm and leaned in.

'The bodies, dear. On the beach and in the church, the murders.'

'Pardon?' said Sister Elsie benignly.

Sister Mary came to her aid, changing the subject through a mouthful of roast potatoes. 'That was quite a sermon today, Margaret. Really got them going!'

'It was nothing to do with getting them going, Mary. I meant every word, as always. These are portentous times. I think we all feel it. A change is coming, perhaps even the Great Tribulation. I feel as if, unlikely as it seems, our Order is needed more than ever in the world.'

'Oh, Margaret, that's a bit dramatic, isn't it?' chuckled Mary.

'Pardon?' contributed Sister Elizabeth.

Margaret visibly rolled her eyes and turned to Helen, signalling that group discussion was over and that they should talk amongst themselves. In a hushed voice, she said,

'What is happening to you at the moment, Helen? Yesterday, Sister Mary needed to use the car to deliver some boxes for the Salvation Army clothing drive, and it wasn't there. Did you know she has been having to hire a van? In the past, you always told us where you were going. You haven't really been going to see your mother, have you?'

Helen looked at her plate, feeling a childish insolence. Margaret continued, looking out at the other nuns with a hushed voice.

'I know you haven't, because I telephoned her. She and I had such plans for you here. I mean, we *have* such plans for you here. You are to be the future of this place, my dear. After everything that happened to you… they say that the best Sisters are those that bring with them to the cloister some grievous sin to expiate. And with your sin, you are going to be the most wonderful nun. You *are* the most wonderful nun.'

Helen continued to look down and eat in silence. She had, of course, chosen this life in order to be constantly reminded of her grievous sin, and yet it still irritated her to be constantly reminded of it. *It is only what you deserve*, she told herself again.

'There has been talk, you know,' continued the Deaconess. 'Some here feel that you are no longer fully participating in the community. That you might question your faith. Tell me, how is your faith, Sister?'

Helen felt she needed to offer something, at least.

'I am working through some issues. It's true, Margaret. Sometimes I feel that my faith is stronger than ever, at other times I feel I am losing it completely.'

'Then talk to me. It doesn't have to be like last time, in the retreat. Although having said that, I would like to go there soon, and check on the renovations. I'm hoping we can start painting soon. I'd also like to discuss the finances of this place with you, Helen. You're the only one who can help me. I mean, look at this lot.'

'They're wonderful,' said Helen, looking at them, and noting with bitter amusement how the Deaconess could flit effortlessly from questions of mortal sin to interior decoration. Helen meant what she said, too, because these quiet ladies had become her family.

'Yes, yes, wonderful and all that, but if we don't get new

blood, we are finished here. There's only you and I who are even of working age and bringing in salaries. I have a lot on my mind too, you know. It's by no means clear that our grant from English Heritage is going to continue. And if we don't find some new recruits - and I had hoped you might bring one or two in via your position at the university, as I brought you in. Our grant from the United Reformed is truly hanging in the balance. It's supposed to be conditional on conversions.'

Helen pulled and twisted and stroked at her wooden cross as Margaret continued, wishing she would stop.

'You are being tempted, you know. And that's no bad thing - Jesus was tempted. Can't you see, Helen? The signs - how much clearer do they need to be? An actual Satanist came here! I know who he is, you see, I looked him up. A Satanist, within our grounds, and you went for a walk with him, for goodness' sake! You're on the brink, Helen, I'm telling you. Turn back to God.'

Then she softened. 'This is a huge moment for you. This could be the test you've been waiting for your whole life.' Now Margaret was gripping her arm on the table and staring at her, and Helen felt she had no choice but to look back.

'Thank you, Deaconess. I will bear it all in mind. And I will pray.'

But tears were welling in her eyes and she could sit there no longer. She abruptly pushed back her chair and stood up to leave too quickly so that everyone stopped to look. She gasped in shock as the cross on which she had been pulling suddenly broke free from its necklace of wooden beads. The cross fell on to her plate and became soaked in beef stew, while the tiny beads scattered, rolling across the room in all directions. The Deaconess stood up too, pushed back her chair in anger, saying, 'Well, I... I never did!' before plucking the cross from Helen's plate and drying it urgently on her napkin. She looked at Helen incredulously, almost with disgust, and made a point of not handing the cross back. The other Sisters sat motionless in wary silence. Helen wavered, looking around, wondering whether to pick up the beads, unable to bear it any longer. 'I'm sorry, I'm so sorry, excuse me,' she said, and left the room at almost a run, heading straight for the phone in the living room. *Don't think about it, don't think about it, just do it.*

She sat on the armchair in the living room, took from her pocket the scrap of flyer on which Mikko had scrawled his mobile number, and in one movement took the old-fashioned phone and dialled the number. A voice answered, over the top of a lot of background noise, and she could hear the thud of drums and guitars and loud voices in the background. 'Yo. Mikko.'

'Mikko. It's Helen. OK, I'll come with you. To the south of France. When you've finished your tour.'

'Yes! I knew it. I will arrange everything, Sister Helen, and I will see you at the airport. But do me one favour - lose the habit, just for a couple of days. I'm not saying you have to wear a bikini, although you can be my guest, you know, by all means.' Suddenly he shouted to someone in the background, *'Hey fuckheads, be careful with those fucking guitars… sorry, we're just* loading out. Those guitars are my babies, you know - but… just to get some fucking vitamin D, you know?'

Later, there was a knock on Helen's door. It was Sisters Josephine and Anke, in their dressing gowns, smiling kindly and holding Helen's repaired cross and necklace. 'Here you are, my love,' said Josephine. 'We collected up most of them and re-strung it for you.' Helen's eyes filled with tears as she took the cross and clutched it to her chest. 'Never mind the Deaconess, my dear,' said Anke. 'She loves you. We all love you. We want you to be happy here. It's alright to waver, you know. We all do. God understands.'

Helen was overwhelmed by their small kindness, and she longed for one or both of them to come forward and hug her, to have some human touch other than the Deaconess's threatening hand on her forearm, or Sister Mary's sweaty and exuberant shakes of her shoulders. But she knew that neither of them would. It just wasn't done here.

That night in bed, she knew she would again dream of falling. The Bible was filled with stories of falling; the house built on sand that falls with a crash; the seed that falls on rocky ground; the Great Falling Away. And all these allegories meant the same - spiritual descent, apostasy, an abandonment of God. As she waited for the sleep that refused to come, she tossed and turned and writhed and her hands slipped down towards her thighs and this time she allowed herself not to stop.

Chapter Twelve

St. Cuthbert's Hospice comprised a large red-brick Edwardian manor house, flanked by single-storey modern wings, all standing in a large leafy garden on the edge of Croxteth Country Park. Run since the 1960s by Franciscan friars, it functioned in odd harmony with the National Health Service in a similarly effective anachronism to the Roman Catholic schools' arrangement with the Department for Education. In some ways, it was comparable to the Sisters of Grace; a minor stately home donated to the church, a place where the spectre of death was constant and questions of destiny were foremost in people's minds. Whereas at Argarmeols Hall, death meant fear and judgment, here there was care and compassion.

Swift shuddered as he and Quinn pulled into the car park.

'I hate these places,' he said, too flippantly.

But Quinn said, 'Actually this place is really lovely. My uncle was here, so I've been before. They do a great job.'

'Oh, sorry. I just mean, it's terrifying, isn't it? Can't really get me head around it.'

'Yeah.'

They walked towards the entrance, passing a little shrine to St. Cuthbert in white marble, around which several bunches of fresh flowers had been recently placed. 'So this place is run by Franciscan friars? What is it with nuns and monks in this town?'

'I told you,' said Quinn, smiling, 'Liverpool is full of believers. Anyway, this is a proper hospital. Apparently, it's the state-of-the-art palliative care centre in the North West. You see, boss, religion can put itself to good use.'

They went to the Reception desk, and Swift immediately felt a lump in his throat at the meaning of the place, but was surprised at how kindly the atmosphere felt. Father Anthony came around the corner with hand already outstretched to greet them, and when he took Swift's elbow with his other hand and looked into his eyes, Swift had a sudden urge to burst into tears. The Sisters of Grace made a statement with their overly traditional monastic uniform, and Father Anthony also made a statement, but in the opposite direction. Instead of a habit, he wore jeans, trainers and a grey zip-up hoodie, under which he displayed a Liverpool football shirt onto which he had somehow fashioned a dog collar. He took them down a wide corridor to his office, past a brightly decorated living area where a few visitors were seated in family groups. There were children amongst the patients and the visitors, and some of them looked desperately sick. Swift could hardly bear to look, and he marvelled at the strength of people, the terrible things with which they could cope, the crosses they had to bear.

Swift and Quinn sat down in Father Anthony's office, and he bounced down onto his chair on the other side of the desk. He had a kind yet jovial Irish accent tinged with Liverpudlian after decades spent at St Cuthbert's. 'So, detectives, I'm only sorry it took me so long to contact you about this. I didn't spot it myself. It was one of our families who saw his picture in the paper and sent it to me. Unfortunately, one family had found this man a bit of a nuisance, this Andrew Shepherd, and that's why they remembered him.'

'A nuisance?'

'Well. I'll start at the beginning, shall I? I just feel horrible about this. We would never have guessed. I mean, do you really think it was him? Anyway.' He put out his hands, gathered his thoughts. 'Andrew Shepherd started coming here six months ago. We have a volunteer programme. We have about fifty regular volunteers in fact. There are all sorts of things people can get involved with - cooking, entertaining, massage, beauty treatment, fundraising, and so on. It's a very important part of our set-up. Anyway, Andrew Shepherd applied to be on the befriending scheme. His CV said he had done it many times before, said that he had a counselling qualification, and so on; and he provided references. But since his Criminal Records check was clear, and we needed befrienders quite urgently, I have to admit that we didn't check those references. He seemed such a lovely man, it didn't seem to matter.

'His role was to come in for three hours a week during visiting time, to chat to patients that didn't have visitors. And he was very reliable. But... he turned out to be a little strange, unfortunately.'

'You said he was a nuisance?' asked Swift.

'Yes, that's right. For starters, he was very picky, which is not really in the spirit of things here. He seemed only interested in talking to certain patients. Now, obviously, there are situations that are too traumatic for some people to cope with, I understand that, but this was something else. He wanted to be with those who were closest to death, and in particular those who had almost died, you know, had near-death experiences. He was bothering people when they were with their families, questioning them, making them upset. I began to think he had some sort of death fetish. Then the final straw came in the visitors' lounge one day when he started harassing this poor child who was terribly ill and who we'd almost lost the week before. He was urging the girl to draw what she'd seen when she was... when she almost died. Thrusting paper and crayons at her. He became very forceful about it, and we had to drag him away. I believe he took the drawing with him as well. That was the family that spotted him in the newspaper. How could you forget his face after such an upsetting incident?'

'So why did you allow him to continue coming?' asked Swift.

'We talked to him immediately, of course, about his behaviour, and he was terribly apologetic. But you know, these places are very difficult. Some people take a while to learn how to cope. So we gave him a chance. And then - and this is the main reason we allowed him to stay - he had become very close to one particular patient, Lily Taylor. She doesn't have any visitors at all. It's quite sad really, and she became very attached to him - she needed him, in fact. We allowed him to continue coming on condition that he only spoke to her. And that was easy to enforce, because she can't leave her room, so he just went in there. As I say, I feel terrible, and I suppose with hindsight maybe I should have spotted that he... well, he had some sort of agenda of his own.'

'This patient, this Lily Taylor, is still alive?'

'Yes, she's just clinging on. It's a miracle, really. We almost lost her several times over the past few months. Obviously, we haven't told her he's a murder suspect. But she doesn't seem to miss him, hasn't been asking about him, which is also strange. As if she knew he wasn't coming back.'

'Father Anthony, would it be possible for us to speak to her?'

He thought for a moment, breathing deeply and gazing into the space above their heads.

'To be honest with you, I don't see why not if she's awake. She's not going to have any other visitors this week, sadly. But she's very weak and on a lot of morphine. I'm not sure whether you'll get anything.'

As Father Anthony took them upstairs, he explained that Lily Taylor was eighty-two, had terminal lung cancer, and had been placed here four months ago by her family, but then effectively abandoned. 'Very strange because they seemed like a nice family - her son and daughter and so on - but apparently, she wasn't well-liked, even by them. An *evil person*, those were their words - can you imagine? I know not all old people are angels, but still, you'd think...'

He trailed off as they had reached a small hospital room where the door was ajar, and Swift and Quinn could see a desperately frail elderly woman lying in a hospital bed. Her skeletal body was almost consumed by the pillows on which she was propped, and a plastic oxygen mask hung around her neck, ready to be used. Her breathing was audible and laboured, and her half-closed eyes vaguely watched the television screen in the top corner of the room, which was showing some soap opera with the sound turned off. A nurse was in the room taking a reading from the monitors, and she smiled and leaned forward to Lily, almost shouting. 'You've got some visitors, Lily.'

In a moment that made Swift well up again. The old lady's eyes widened slightly, and she opened her mouth and turned to them, perhaps expecting to see someone in particular and then realising it wasn't them. Swift leaned forward vaguely.

'Hello, Mrs Taylor. We want to ask you a few questions about Andrew Shepherd.'

There was no response from Lily, and the nurse said, 'She can't hear you, detective. You need to speak up.' Swift squirmed with embarrassment. He remembered how much he had hated having to visit old folks' homes for his school community service - struggling for things to say, the stale smell - and how he had envied those to whom it came naturally. Quinn took over, sitting next to Lily and taking her hand. 'Andrew Shepherd!' she shouted. 'Is he your friend?'

The old lady's eyes brightened, and she looked straight ahead of her, lost in memories.

'Andrew. My saviour. A wonderful man.' Her voice was a croak, pitchless and breathy, barely there at all. She turned to Quinn and patted her wrist with her shaking hand. 'He saved me. It's true. I am saved.'

'What did Shepherd say to you when he last visited? Can you remember?'

'He said he can't come back. But it's alright, he gave me the last dose. And it's our secret. They don't know about me, you see. All I have to do is wait now.'

Suddenly she gasped, closing her eyes, frozen in silence. Swift and Quinn looked at the nurse in panic, but she said, 'It's OK. She just needs a bit of oxygen. And some rest.' Father Anthony had been standing behind the detectives and put a hand on each of their shoulders to signify that the visit was over.

'As you can see, she's a little delirious. You won't get anything more out of her today.'

The detectives got up, smiling their thanks at the nurse and leaving Lily Taylor to her own personal purgatory. Outside the room, Swift asked Father Anthony, in a whisper, without really knowing why: 'Is it possible that Shepherd could have tampered with her medication? Given her something?'

'I mean, to tamper with the drip - very unlikely, but not impossible, I suppose. To have slipped her something? Well, we don't search for people when they come in. But her condition hasn't altered. I mean, if anything, she's living longer than we would have expected. So he hasn't harmed her.' They walked back down the corridor. 'What sort of thing do you mean? You mean he wanted to watch her die? Is he one of those playing god types?'

Swift and Quinn looked at each other with raised eyebrows.

As they got back into the car, Quinn said, 'What a lovely man, that Father Cuthbert. I feel bad that he feels bad. Don't tell me, you didn't like him.'

'No, no, he was sound. But why was he so apologetic? He was helping us, not the other way round.'

'Well, I suppose he's pretty shocked that he let loose a murder suspect in his hospital. I mean, imagine the damage he could have caused in there?'

'Yeah. Not good for their reputation, I suppose. But it appears no harm done in there, at least. Did we actually learn anything?'

'Other than some minor tracing of Shepherd's movements three weeks ago, and more confirmation that he's our prime suspect, not really. Pieces of the puzzle, I suppose.'

Chapter Thirteen

Helen and Mikko were sitting on an aeroplane waiting to take off, Helen in a parallel universe, where she wore a floral dress with a man's coat over the top and went on a plane with that same man. She had told Margaret that she was going to stay with her mother, knowing that Margaret would check and discover she was lying, and somehow not caring. And she told herself that with this trip to find the third geneticist, she was researching something eschatological; perhaps even an academic paper might result. In the seat next to her, Mikko looked exhausted. His eyes were sunken and had deep shadows under them, and without his usual black eye make-up, he looked older and more fragile. She wondered when he had last been home, been taken care of by family, and thought that his life was perhaps no less constrained than hers - living on a bus, never left alone, constantly being judged. It was late on a Friday afternoon, and the flight from Manchester to Nice seemed to be filled with hen and stag parties who were already at varying stages of merriment. Mikko looked around him at the revellers. There was a raucous group of women all wearing sparkly halo headbands and matching white polo shirts emblazoned with 'Gemma's Angels'. Some of them were kneeling up in their seats to chat across the aisles, ignoring the hostess's pleas to put on their seatbelts ready for take-off. And no doubt by design, there was a group of young men wearing devil horns and matching red football shirts proclaiming them to be 'Ste's Sexy Beasts.'

'This is a proper flying piece of reprobation right here,' said Mikko. 'What does the nun make of this, then?'

Helen smiled. 'This is my first time on a plane, actually.'

'Oh my God, seriously? You've never flown?'

'Never! I took a vow of poverty, remember? I can't afford plane tickets. And also, a vow of obedience. So no holidays. I went to Amsterdam once, to an academic conference funded by the University. I gave a paper on Satanism there, in fact. But that was on the Eurostar, and let me tell you, it was so difficult to persuade the Deaconess to give me permission that I haven't tried since.'

'Amsterdam… nice. I have also been known to get up to some satanic activity in Amsterdam. Man. So you're an aeroplane virgin? I mean, you're an everything virgin. Sorry.'

'Indeed. That's the other vow. Chastity.' she said, looking straight ahead and feigning as much interest as she could in the laminated safety instruction sheet.

He went quiet and looked out of the window, smacking his lips repeatedly in some personal drumbeat. A sudden roar of mutual laughter from the Angels and the Sexy Beasts further down the plane provided a welcome distraction, as the stags and hens shook the seats and threw crisps at each other. Helen and Mikko both looked back and smiled at each other.

'Is it always like this?' asked Helen.

'Only on EasyJet. And never take the flight to Prague on a Friday night - oh my god, those guys put Total Depravity to shame.'

The sky was turning a deep red as they took off, and in that moment of universal human disbelief, that leap of faith as an aeroplane leaves the ground, Helen automatically gripped both arms of the seat. But his hand was there too on the central arm, and as they accidentally touched and looked at each other and then looked down in embarrassment, she wondered whether this whole thing hadn't been a terrible mistake. She quickly took her hands away, took out the wooden cross which was hanging on a necklace underneath her dress, and began fingering that instead.

Relaxing into the sensation of flying, and eager to distract herself, Helen took out of her rucksack a red folder - the dossier she had collected. She began sifting through the papers, mainly sheets she had surreptitiously printed out from the university and convent computers. Biological dark matter, Calvinism and genetics, the labrys... academic papers written by Clancy, Shepherd, and Baptiste. But the largest section of the file, simply because he constituted the easiest aspect to research, was that on Laurent Baptiste, and his fabulous and infamous life since leaving genetic research. Mikko peered over Helen's shoulder.

'Oh, is that your research? This is super-exciting. Is it a holiday, or are we on the trail of a murderer?' With this, he made a faux-fearful movie trailer voice. 'I am so pumped for this. So, tell me all about this Baptiste.'

'Well, research is what I do. And I have a lot of time on my hands, I suppose.' Helen wasn't sure whether he was making fun of her. 'Baptiste was a statistician, so it figures, I suppose, that he could make a lot of money in casinos. He now owns a chain of them across the world, plus two hotels in Monaco, one of which we are staying in, I believe.'

'Yes. I booked us into the Paradise. Separate rooms, of course.' He leaned in knowingly, wagging his finger. 'Fun fact - his other hotel in Monaco is called the Underworld.'

'No, really?'

'No, not really. It's called the Monaco Grand. But that would be cool, though, right?'

'Anyway. There's lots of information about Baptiste because he lives a sort of celebrity party lifestyle. Used to date a supermodel, apparently.'

'Me too.'

Helen looked at him with faux exasperation.

'I did! And I bet you knew that because I bet you googled me the way you googled this guy. Come on, admit it. She actually turned out to be a fucking bitch, to be honest with you.'

'I can neither confirm nor deny having googled you. Anyway, what's most interesting, I think, is this: when you type the three names into the search engine together - Shepherd, Clancy, Baptiste - you get their research papers, the Wellcome Institute, et cetera et cetera... and then you get... some anomalies... But scroll down a few pages, and eventually you get to this.' She turned the page. 'Grantchester United Reformed Church. It's just outside Cambridge. Or was - it doesn't appear to exist anymore. But look, on the Grantchester village website, there's this report from their annual AGM, July 1999. And here's the photo of their central committee - I printed it out.' She rummaged around until she found the paper and showed him a slightly pixelated colour photo of a group of around twenty people squinting into the sun. Standing together on the back row were Shepherd, Clancy, and Baptiste.

'At one time, at least, they were all Christian. Practising Christians. Reformed Christians.'

Mikko studied the photo. 'Actually, I don't think that Genome guy Clancy said whether he was religious or not.'

It was almost dark when their taxi arrived in Monaco. November in the south of France offered a balmy twenty-one degrees Celsius, and both Helen and Mikko enjoyed the sensation of relative warmth on their skins after the bitterness of the northern European winter. The Paradise Hotel perched on one of the craggy corner clifftops of Monaco, a pink alabaster monolith with a neon red sign that began flashing as soon as the sun began to set, and continued flashing until dawn. The red flashing was accompanied by a slight electrical buzz that would irritate anyone trying to sleep in the rooms nearby. However, it was expected that guests at the Paradiso would sleep mainly during the daytime, the night-time being reserved for the restaurant, the rooftop club, then the casino. As they moved through the revolving doors to enter the hotel lobby, Helen was mesmerised by the fleet of luxury cars on display outside - Lamborghinis in fluorescent colours, Hummer jeeps in ghostly matt paint - and she accidentally swung round in the doors a second time. Mikko laughed 'What, you've never seen a Lamborghini before? I have like two of those at home.'

'Do you really?' she asked.

'No. I do not. Metal musicians do not make any money at all. Unless they're in Metallica.'

'I don't know what that means,' said Helen vaguely, looking around wide-eyed and child-like at the ostentation surrounding her. From the reception desk, they could see the entrance to the casino; there was no door, just a wide entrance like a gaping mouth that led into a red carpeted windowless space so vast she couldn't see the end of it, so that she imagined it must be cut into the very mountainside itself.

Mikko had booked two single rooms on the same floor, and they parted to deposit their things and prepare for the evening. Helen threw her bag on the bed and sat down next to it, marvelling at the thought of a real duvet instead of a rough blanket, of using hotel toiletries that weren't carbolic soap, of not having to wake up at five-thirty the next morning for Lauds. *But I am here for research*, she told herself. *I am an eschatologist on the trail of a theological mystery, possibly on the trail of a murderer, and I am completely in control of this situation.*

A few minutes later Mikko knocked on her door and they headed up to the rooftop bar where, she had read on gossip websites, Laurent Baptiste was wont to permanently hang out. The rooftop was filling up with beautiful bodies. A DJ was playing house music, and lights flashed. Despite the warm weather, flaming torches had been lit at intervals, bathing people's faces in half-light. They were high up here and could survey the realm of Monaco laid out before them; an entire country clinging to a tiny hillside, a retreating army of high-rises forced onto the coast with nowhere further to go. Chased across the mountains and teetering at the water's edge. Peach and silver skyscrapers crammed on top of each other like one enormous piece of quartz, shards erupting towards the sky. The principality was like a hydra, continually sprouting concrete and glass. Mikko watched an impossibly beautiful woman walk past.

'This definitely feels like Paradise,' he said.

Helen felt more uncomfortable than she had ever been, far more so than at the heavy metal concerts. She supposed the atmosphere here was what you might call sleazy, and at least, she supposed, nobody would leer at her. And yet she still wished she was wearing make-up like the other girls, had her hair highlighted, wasn't wearing these awful leather sandals and a charity shop dress. She had lingered in the duty-free shop in the airport, considering whether to buy some product or other to improve herself, but not having any idea what that would be, or any money to buy it. They perched at the bar, and Mikko ordered himself a whisky and her a glass of champagne.

'Are you sure that's a good idea, Mikko? I don't seem to tolerate alcohol very well.'

'It is definitely a good idea. Cheers.'

They looked around but there was no-one who fit the description of Laurent Baptiste, so they sat for a while, contentedly people-watching. And how enthralling it was; she wondered where on earth in the world all these people had come from, and how they had so much money. After a while, two young women tottered over and stood at the bar next to them. They wore tiny shorts that appeared to Helen to be made of plastic. The heels of their shoes must have been over six inches tall, she thought, while those breasts could not possibly be real. They were fascinating, and she found it hard not to stare, but Mikko had already turned to them and asked one of them a question.

'Excuse me, miss. Do you know where we can find Monsieur Laurent Baptiste?'

The woman spoke in stilted English with a heavy Russian accent, so Mikko switched into fluent-sounding Russian and began an animated conversation with the two women that seemed to Helen to last several minutes. She noticed and pondered the bizarre streak of jealousy that she felt. Mikko finally turned back to Helen.

'So, she said, amongst other things,' he smiled teasingly, 'that when Baptiste is not here, he's usually on his boat. It's down there in the marina, and she said there's usually a party going on so we can't miss it. Called the S… something beginning with S… Soterion, that's it.'

'Of course,' said Helen. 'What else? *Soterion* means salvation in Greek.'

'Let's fucking go then.'

* * *

They walked down the winding roads and stone staircases that took the city state down to the yacht marina, which was overlooked by the royal palace. Here, the most expensive yachts in the world had been herded in, like prize specimens in an enclosure. They bobbed almost imperceptibly in the dark; giant wedding cakes on an unstable tray. They were ungainly and bovine, with decks piled upon decks, some with helicopters absurdly balanced on top, almost tied on. One even had a jeep precariously balanced on one side of the deck, causing it to lean unsteadily. This was a competition in which size mattered more than anything. Most of the boats were quiet and dark, locked up for the winter, but further down the jetty, in pride of place outside the Monaco Yacht Club, they could see lights and hear voices, laughter, music. When they got closer, they saw the gold lettering of the 'M/Y Soterion' lit up, a red carpet on the dockside, flanked by a uniformed sailor and a security guard who was visibly armed.

Mikko went up to them. 'Good evening, sir. We are looking for Laurent Baptiste. Is he in?'

Both men automatically stepped forward to block the entrance to the gangway.

'Mr Baptiste is not available right now, sorry. You will have to leave.'

Mikko put up his hands to show that no hostility was intended. 'OK, OK, we'll leave. But do me a favour. Just tell him it's about the OS1. Go on, humour me.'

The sailor and the security guard whispered to each other, and the sailor went inside. A couple of minutes later, he came back out on to the deck and called, 'Please, come aboard.'

Mikko and Helen stepped gingerly along the narrow wooden gangplank onto the boat, where they were asked to remove their shoes, and a door was slid open into the yacht's main living area. It took them a few moments to get their bearings in this unfamiliar place, which had a dizzying amount of gold and chrome, including a floor-to-ceiling pole, and odd, disorienting soft lighting. The sofas were coated in red velvet and, it appeared, so were the walls, while the thick, plush carpeting was black. There were several seating areas, occupied by groups of impossibly glamorous people, and in one corner a DJ was playing dance music incongruously, quietly. It was immediately obvious who Laurent Baptiste was. He was sitting on a long sofa at the back of the room, flanked by two very young and very tall women with expressionless faces. He looked as bored as they did, and was clearly drunk. On the low table in front of him was a bucket of champagne and a scattering of glasses, vodka and whisky bottles, ashtrays. He didn't get up, but called and beckoned to Mikko and Helen. 'Welcome, friends. Please, sit down.' He spoke perfect English but with a strong, almost affected French accent. He had lustrous, thick, dark hair, and a slightly unkempt beard and moustache. His body was that of someone who had probably been very muscular in the past but who had softened to flab and paunch. 'What can I do for you? You who know about OS1? Let me guess, you are looking for the serial killer, Andrew Shepherd. But you are not from the police, I see. Unless they have vastly improved their undercover disguises.'

Mikko began the introductions, and while he did, Helen realised they didn't really have a decent story about why they were there at all. She tried starting in the same way as they had in Manchester, asking Baptiste about the drawing she had seen in Shepherd's flat, and how it matched with Mikko's vision.

'Ah, the gates of Heaven and Hell,' Baptiste said with grandeur laced with sarcasm. 'You saw them too, did you?' He looked at Mikko but seemed only mildly interested in something that, to Helen, was an astonishing phenomenon.

'Vous savez, Andrew was obsessed with near-death experiences. He collected them. Searched out stories on the internet. Visited hospitals, dying people, made a terrible nuisance of himself. He often talked to me about those gates.'

Helen nodded. 'He wanted confirmation that everyone was seeing the same thing. And were they?'

'According to him, yes. Everybody saw the gate, the path that forks, the mysterious figure, the two skies. But my friends, that can all be explained by neuropsychology. And it cannot be the only reason you came here.'

One of the women flanking Baptiste on the sofa took out a silver case, opened it, and prepared a line of cocaine. Baptiste admonished her in French, nudging her too roughly to get up and leave, so that some of the white powder spilled onto the table, and she licked it up with her finger as she slunk off grumpily. 'Sorry about that.' he smiled. 'Filthy habit.'

'Oh please, don't mind me,' said Mikko. 'You won't find any judgement from this guy.'

'Then would you like some, my friend?' Baptiste took something out of his pocket, and Mikko looked keen to partake, but Helen glared at him disapprovingly.

'OK, no thanks, dude. Another time.'

Helen asked, 'When was the last time you were in touch with Andrew Shepherd?'

Baptiste looked at her for a long time; but since he wasn't answering, she continued: 'Did you know he had a laboratory inside his apartment?'

'Ah, so you know about that as well. Alright, yes, Shepherd last contacted me three years ago. He wanted me to buy him a Revelon Sequencer. They cost over a hundred thousand dollars, you know. And you can't just buy one from a shop. He said that I owed him. And I did, I suppose.'

'Why did you owe him?' asked Mikko. 'If it was his fault that your team was disbanded, and you lost your job?'

'Let's say I owed him in other ways. He took care of me on a… spiritual level. And anyway, look around you! Everything that happened has led to this. I am a very wealthy man, a very fortunate man, with not a care in this world.' He said this with an odd bitterness. 'One hundred thousand dollars is nothing to me, so why not?'

'Do you know what he was doing in that home laboratory?' asked Helen. Again, Baptiste did not answer, but focused intently on lighting his cigar, so she continued,

'We spoke to Professor Clancy, and he told us about the marker for the Elect. Was Shepherd testing people to see if they were going to Heaven or Hell? Do you think he killed those people because he thought they were sinners? To stop them from sinning in the future?'

'You're not quite on the right lines, shall we say? Shepherd tested himself, that's for sure. And he didn't have the marker. He was a Reprobate, destined for Hell.'

'So, he decided to just go crazy, start murdering people, because it didn't matter?'

'No. Not that.' Baptiste was enjoying this. He put down his cigar, poured himself a large whisky, and drank most of it in one go. Helen was very glad he was drunk, since this might help him reveal more of what he knew. He leaned back and slid his arms along the back of the sofa and around the girls, the second of whom had slipped back into the room sheepishly, sniffing through one nostril, then the other.

'What's the next step after genetic testing?' he asked rhetorically. 'Gene *therapy*. Andrew wanted to mutate the gene, to add the marker to his own body, and then to the bodies of others. To play God. And I mean, that's what we do. We're geneticists, and genes can be modified. But who on earth was going to sanction that? Who was even going to believe him? We had to stop him, and that's why the team was disbanded. I mean, the idea of fixing the gene we could dismiss. But telling people - it would discredit all of us.'

'OK, so perhaps he was trying to add the marker to these people. But then, why would he kill them?'

'Perhaps it didn't work. Gene therapy is still a very new and experimental technique. We don't really know if it works, or what the side effects are. It could be very dangerous.'

Mikko leaned back and put his arm around Helen in a gesture that unconsciously mimicked Baptiste, but she looked at him with the same disapproval as before and so he shied away, asking quickly, 'So if you were Shepherd, how would you do it? How would you change someone?'

'Well. There are two types of gene therapy. The first is called somatic cell gene therapy. This involves obtaining blood cells from a person with a genetic disease, or in this case without the x marker, and then introducing a good gene, i.e. with the marker, into the so-called defective cell. It's normally done virally, by injecting a retrovirus into the body and hoping it will spread. And it would have to be done several times over the course of a person's life, as the effects don't last very long. The retrovirus inserts its genetic code directly into the chromosomes of the host cell. But the problem is you need to weaken the patient's immune system first so the virus can take hold. There are other ways, but the viral method is the most effective.'

At this point, Mikko had lost track, but Helen was concentrating intently, trying to understand. 'And would this… cure… then be passed on to the next generation?'

'Non non, pas du tout.' Baptiste wagged his finger as he downed another large slug of whisky. 'This type of gene therapy is not passed on from generation to generation. And in any case, the marker - the soterion mutation we, sorry, he called it - is not inherited. It occurs spontaneously on the OS1 at the moment of conception. Like a genetic disorder. Or the opposite of a genetic disorder, I suppose. Since it is a rather, shall we say, favourable mutation?

'But you raise an interesting point there, Madame, about the other type of gene therapy. The other type is known as germline therapy. Germline therapy takes place in the reproductive cells. It involves the genetic modification of germ cells that will pass the change on to the next generation. This type only has to be done one time to be permanent. You can treat a pre-embryo before it is placed back in the mother by IVF. Or, you can treat both adult sperm and egg cells so the genetic - defect, shall we say - is not passed on to children?'

Helen tried to process this. 'Do you think Shepherd wanted to remove the gene for sin? Remove original sin… forever?'

'Perhaps. But for that, he would need a pregnancy. I suppose he could try to get a job in an IVF lab and do it covertly. Or find someone willing to be his Sainte Vierge.' Baptiste poured another large whisky. Helen wondered if his drinking was something to do with having had to cope with the enormity of these ideas.

Mikko spoke again. 'So, Monsieur Baptiste, I get the impression you don't believe in Shepherd's theory. But presumably you still tested yourself?'

Baptiste said nothing; he just laughed enigmatically.

'And after all this happened, you decided not to pursue your career as a geneticist?' Helen asked.

'Look around you, I think it was a pretty good decision, no? Look, I'm a statistician, and I got treated badly by my research institution. Academia is a brutal and corrupt profession, much more so than any of the business I do now. I gave ten years of my life to pointless stochastic variations. So I decided to use statistics for something else. And look at me. Couldn't be happier.' It was said with that same hint of bitterness that failed to convince them fully.

'Clancy tested us, you know,' Mikko said, eyeing Baptiste from behind his raised whisky glass.

'And?'

'She has the marker, I don't.'

'Then you had better find Shepherd, my friend. So, he can do his God thing and send you to Heaven. If you believe, that is.'

'It's OK, I don't.'

'Ah, in that case, you're fine. Always better to be on the safe side, though, no?' he asked mischievously. 'Atheism is a dangerous game. Even the devils never fell into that vice. For the devils also believe and tremble.'

'Book of James, chapter two, verse nineteen,' said Helen.

'Indeed. I'm a gambling man. I play the odds. And as you can see,' he gestured to the luxury surrounding him, 'it has worked well for me so far, no?' Baptiste poured both himself and Mikko another whisky, and clinked glasses with him, before looking at him provocatively as they drank. 'So, you really don't believe in God, my friend? No Heaven or Hell for you? No paradise filled with beautiful women, no fiery torture, just eternal blackness as your body is slowly decomposed by worms?'

'Look, man,' said Mikko. 'All I know is what I saw. And that was one hooded dude. One dude. Or lady, I guess; sorry, don't mean to be sexist. But it didn't feel like God or Satan; it felt like both. I mean, God and Satan are basically the same, depending on which way you look at it.'

Helen shuddered and hid her face in her drink. She felt she had displayed an extraordinarily high tolerance for blasphemy over the past few weeks, but she was struggling with this drunken and facile way of discussing religious belief.

'Look,' said Mikko, 'even if I believed. It just seems ridiculous - to trick God? Trick your way into Heaven, like He didn't notice what you were doing? Come on, dude.' But at Mikko's words, Baptiste just shrugged theatrically.

Helen spoke up. 'Do you think Andrew Shepherd killed those people, Monsieur Baptiste? I don't profess to know him at all, but I was in his apartment, and he was clearly struggling spiritually. He didn't seem like the type of person who would really want to play God.'

Baptiste thought for a moment. 'Andrew was capable of a lot of things. In many ways, he was the most brilliant man I ever met. I wouldn't put anything past him. But there are other people who might have a lot more to lose from what he was doing. In fact, just about everybody in the world stood to lose out if his theories became public knowledge. Imagine a world where we all knew or thought we knew the future? It would be a nightmare. People would go crazy. People could do whatever they liked!' At this, he gestured around him and laughed. 'And now, my esteemed guests, on that bombshell, as they say, who would like another drink?'

The talk descended, the volume of the music increased, and one of the vacant girls began dancing languidly around the pole, even though nobody was watching. Mikko and Helen soon extricated themselves, since Baptiste was almost paralytic by then. As the walked back along the quay, Mikko said.

'That guy is like the least happy person I've ever met. Anyone who says "Look how happy I am!" is definitely not. Anyway, let's review. First of all, it seems that plenty of other people had the same vision as me, and that freaks the shit out of me. I can't even go there. Let's talk about Shepherd. From what Baptiste says, Shepherd was trying to help these people, to save them. But if he was trying to help them, why would he kill them? Maybe it didn't work? But why make a statement about it?'

But Helen was quiet, racking her brains and trying to remember all the things she had seen in Shepherd's room, wishing she had Mikko's photographic memory. She felt close to Shepherd's struggle and wanted desperately to understand it. But most of all, she wanted to think about the other thing. The other type of genetic modification - to create a human born without sin - those were Baptiste's words. It made her shudder, and she could hardly articulate it. Surely, there could be no greater blasphemy?

But Mikko did not seem to have picked up on the significance of this, and had moved on. 'Here's the big question: this guy has clearly tested himself, and clearly believes it. So which is he? Heaven or Hell?'

Helen sighed. 'That really is the big question - and it centres on whether human nature is fundamentally good or bad.'

'I mean,' continued Mikko, 'I'm not going to suddenly start sinning because I'm going to Hell, anyway. I mean, I wouldn't, if I believed I was... anyway, whatever... And you're not going to start sinning just because you're definitely going to Heaven, and therefore you're safe. Or are you?'

'It's certainly a fascinating question.' she said, and she tried to add some theological exegesis to Mikko's musings; to elaborate on the ideas of antinomianism to which she had alluded in her lecture the previous week, and which now seemed somehow so much more real. But it was late. They had been drinking, and the layers of belief, disbelief, and the grey spaces in between were too overwhelming for either of them to comprehend. Part of her terror lay in the fact that antinomianism, the principle that the Elect had no need to follow moral laws, it could be argued, was effectively the principles of Calvinism, the religion that she had chosen, taken to their logical conclusion. And there were other feelings too; feelings about Mikko that she could neither admit nor deny to herself.

Mikko nudged her, and she smiled back at him. But there were levels of awkwardness in this conversation that were impossible for either to decipher. They walked back to the hotel slowly, dragging their feet, wanting and not wanting this moment to end. It was out of season, so tourists and party-goers were few and far between. The occasional party group trampled past noisily, but it was mainly couples, residents of Monaco, or foreign rose-sellers eking out the last of the year's business. Helen and Mikko walked past a couple passionately kissing, leaning against the promenade, and they automatically shrank away, giving the couple a wider berth.

As they approached the hotel, they both made some awkward efforts at small-talk. And then they fell silent as they entered the elevator up to their rooms. They both made exaggerated fumbling gestures of taking out their room keys and then faced each other in the corridor.

'Well, goodnight,' he said, swaying from foot to foot with his hands in his pockets. 'God bless. I guess.'

'Goodnight, Mikko.'

Helen closed the door quickly but held on to the lock for a moment and pressed her forehead to the door, closing her eyes, trying to breathe, and to lower her heart rate. This state of agitation was unbearable. To pray in this state was unthinkable, to sleep was unthinkable, and she wondered whether to go back out, walk along the promenade, or even go to a bar and obliterate everything. She sat on the bed, because the room was spinning, swirling into different dimensions, scattering into pixels that reformed into images of Mikko, of her brother, of the detectives, of dead bodies, and of the black gates and the hooded figure.

In one movement, she stood up from the bed, lurched out of the doorway and across the corridor, and knocked on his door. He opened immediately, as if he had been standing right behind it. They kissed, and she tasted nicotine and smoke and alcohol, and when she felt his hands on her, she did the same and touched his shoulder blades, his ribs, and his waist. He looked into her eyes and put his hands to her cheeks.

'Are you sure?'

'Yes. Yes.'

As they fell to the bed, the same phrase kept running through her mind, even though she had never been Catholic. She mouthed the words repeatedly, *'Father forgive me for I have sinned, Father forgive me for I have sinned.'* She was teetering on the brink of that abyss now, and she allowed him to take her over the edge, falling, falling, and she didn't want to stop.

Chapter Fourteen

High above the River Mersey, another body is about to fall into darkness. The Runcorn Bridge is another liminal space, a bridge between worlds, or between Liverpool and the outside world. The old bridge is now dwarfed by the Mersey Gateway Project, a symbol of regeneration, the new versus the old. But the old bridge remains, and parallel to it is the Runcorn Railway Bridge, also known as the Ethelfleda. Ethelfleda is the wonderfully evocative name of the Lady of the Mercians, sister of King Edward the Elder, who helped him to build fortifications at Runcorn in the tenth century. Appropriately then, this bridge has a castle-like structure at either end. Now derelict, these mini castles have been poorly locked-up, so that anyone desperate enough to be needing shelter out here would find the doors easy to open. A man opens the door, looks around as if to check the coast is clear, then drags out a black refuse bag from behind the door. The man has matted hair and an unkempt beard, and his face is gaunt although his body shape is disguised by the layers of clothing and filthy shapeless coat he is wearing. He kneels down and takes two items out of the bag, placing them on the ground in front of him. A laptop and a hammer. He takes the hammer and begins smashing at the laptop. For several minutes he smashes, sometimes tentatively, sometimes with a desperate anger, until tiny springs and pieces of circuit board fly at him and the laptop is as nothing. He then puts down the hammer and climbs the ramparts to the very top of the battlements.

The night is still with no wind to displace him, and so he stands on the edge, toes over the edge, unperturbed, and stays like that for what seems like a long time, blinking in the lights and taking in the freezing darkness. He takes some items from inside his jacket and clutches them - three Polaroid pictures and a sheaf of papers. He lights a cigarette lighter so he can look at them. Three Polaroid pictures. One of Jason Hardman, one of Chelsea McAllister, one of Stuart Killy's foot. There is still a chance to save Stuart, perhaps, if he ends things now. He lets the photos fall, one by one, and they flit down to the water below. The tiny flame from the cigarette lighter now reveals the title of his sheaf of papers.

'Spontaneous versus artificial mutation of the OS1 gene. A soteriological approach' by Andrew Shepherd, PhD

He applies the flame to the dog-eared corner of the papers, and watches them burn to nothing, until he is forced to drop the dying embers as they scald his fingers. Behind him, the wrought iron of the bridge proper is black against a yellow sky, and he heads towards his own iron gate. He leans forward until there is no going back and falls. Calmly, his body drops through the night. Limp and heavy, it takes both forever and no time at all on its journey to the freezing black waters below.

* * *

Mikko and Helen lay facing each other in the bed, arms across each other uncertainly. The curtains were open and the infernal red flashing of the neon sign above their room, coupled with the city lights, provided enough for them to see the shapes of each other's features and expressions.

'So,' he said. 'I don't really know what to say now. How was it for you? I guess?'

'It was… I liked it. I'm sorry. I didn't really know what I was doing.'

'You were perfect. Actually, it was my first time, too. With someone I actually like, that is'.

Helen was mortified in so many different ways. For once Mikko was quiet, but she felt that to not talk now would be much worse than to talk. She was so racked by different emotions that she again felt as if she was floating above the situation. She had a sudden urge to tell him something else about herself, perhaps to make herself seem a little more interesting.

'There was another time, you know. But not with a man.'

'What?' He shuffled his body in closer. 'No way. Lesbian nuns? Tell me everything.'

And so she told him. It was another confession with no priest, no box, no curtain. She was looking at him, but she was no longer in the room. She was back in the retreat, almost ten years ago, in that damp bedroom with the motorway traffic rushing by outside. She had passed the novice stage, the aspirant stage, worked her way through the different coloured habits, the different levels of commitment, the different levels of sacrifice. Now she was at the novitiate stage, aged twenty-two years old, and preparing to take her full vows. She was struggling with it, of course, as everybody did, and Deaconess Margaret suggested they go to the retreat for a couple of days, for a change of scenery, to clear her head. Unlike other aspirants, Helen had little family with whom to discuss the huge sacrifice she was planning to make; her mother could only murmur assent. And although the Deaconess was at pains to avoid pointing it out, she was far younger than any other recent aspirants, had lived very little of her life already, which made the sacrifice even greater.

The retreat was in the Pennines, an hour and a half or so by car from Argarmeols. Helen had expected it to be a larger institution, a place for groups from other religious orders, perhaps. But it turned out to be just a house, and it was just the two of them, a sort of extended counselling session. They prayed, and walked, and prayed, and walked, and studied the retreat's library of Calvinist texts. Charles Spurgeon, the Genevan Psalter, the Canons of Dort. It was a hot, sultry July, and they would sit in the garden with their books. The second evening, they even walked to a nearby pub, and the Deaconess allowed them to have a glass of wine each. And later that evening, when it was time to sleep, the Deaconess had suggested that they stay together, so that she could be with Helen through the night during her spiritual crisis.

Margaret had a way of making her do things, of rationalising everything. She said it was God speaking through her, giving Helen her final temptation before the time came. The same temptations seemed to be able to come from either God or Satan, depending on her point of view. And it was such a relief, such a comfort, to finally be held in someone's arms after all those years of loneliness; to touch bare, warm, soft flesh and be touched back. To be wanted, to do things she didn't even know people did, to give herself up to someone and be led to pleasure. She found herself in a place beyond unease, beyond reality, where she could manage events by stepping outside her own body and watching them unfold as if they were happening to someone else.

In the morning she and the Deaconess returned to Argarmeols, and a few days later Helen took her final vows. During those last days of her novitiate, as the countdown to her sacrifice began, a part of her was willing someone, her mother, the Deaconess, anyone, to come forward and try to save her from herself. And she imagined that if they did, she would fight them, insist on the necessity of her martyrdom, her marriage to God. But no-one did, and she tried to brush aside the feeling that it was a sort of conspiracy. The Deaconess needed her to bring new blood into the Order, and of course there were great celebrations, even a press release, a photograph in the *Crosby Herald*. Meanwhile, her mother needed Helen's continued self-blame to validate her own existence. And so, Helen's childish rebellion against the possibility of her own happiness was allowed to take place.

The encounter between Margaret and Helen was never openly spoken of again. From then on, Margaret was almost unwavering in her natural severity towards Helen, and Helen craved her harshness like a drug. Margaret occasionally alluded to that night, skirted around the possibility of it happening again, but Helen never allowed herself to be drawn on the subject. To incur the Deaconess's wrath was part of her continued rebellion against herself.

'You cannot leave me like this. I need more details about this *incident.*'

'Mikko, it's not funny. And I'm not going to give you any more details. Perhaps there was some romance in it at the time - the summer heat, the enormity of my situation - but it was hardly Mills and Boon stuff. I mean, the retreat is just this little white cottage which would be in a beautiful setting, except you can see it from the M6 - there's a constant roar of traffic. You will have driven past it yourself on your way up to Newcastle.'

'I mean, I have to be honest with you. That image of you and that strict Deaconess together is gonna get me through the next tour. Fuck.' He shook his head, smiling, lit a cigarette, and drew deeply. 'But at the same time, it's kind of dark. You were vulnerable, and she manipulated you. In a lot of ways, I hate that she locked you away.'

'I locked myself away. And now I suppose I have let myself out. Like the contents of Pandora's box.' As she said it, she glimpsed at the black snake tattoo that coiled around his upper body. She lay on her back and looked up at the ceiling.

'What have I done, Mikko?'

When she woke in the morning he was still asleep, his back turned, and she traced the images on his back with the gossamer touch of her fingertips. When she got to the double-headed axe on his neck, she drew back. She had broken all three of her vows the previous day, and in the cold light of dawn, she was appalled at herself. *Did I do it because I know I am safe, one of the Elect?* she wondered. *Because if so, then I am a monster.*

* * *

Spirits were low in Swift's incident room at Crosby police station. Six weeks had passed since the discovery of Jason Hardman's body, and since then, there had been only bad news. A murdered girl, a premature baby that was murdered or abducted, a severed foot, at least one missing person, who knew how many more. And not a trace of Andrew Shepherd, their prime suspect, indeed, their only suspect. He had seemingly vanished. His trail, which had had such momentum those first few days of the trace, had ended abruptly at Stuart Killy's flat, and since then no sightings, no credit card usage, no communications - nothing.

The buzz of October and November had gradually subsided to a low hum, as officers worked on vague trails with an increasing despondence, the missing baby having shaken everyone.

Swift studied the incident board he had been so proud of a few weeks ago. His 'persons of interest' now seemed truly pathetic - nuns, guitarists, ex-colleagues from decades before - none of it had got them anywhere.

He turned to face everyone. 'Right, lads, what have we got? Anything yet on the baby - hospitals, GPs?'

'Nothing in the North West.'

'Broaden it to UK-wide then.'

'Boss, are we still not planning to put out an announcement on the missing baby?'

'We're still working on the theory that revealing we know could draw a kidnapper deeper into hiding. But I'm torn, since we're not getting anywhere. Let me talk to Canter.'

He hated that he needed advice from a superior on this.

'Right, moving on to Stuart Killy. Anything?'

Colette said, 'No trace of his phone, nothing on his laptop. There was a Bible and a few other religious books in his apartment, but no-one knows of a relationship with Shepherd. None of his neighbours have heard from him since the beginning of November. It sounds like he's been a real loner since coming out of prison, though. He missed his last appointment with the probation officer, which was two days before we found the foot. Since the tag was still showing in his apartment, it wasn't followed up.'

'CCTV find anything yet?'

'We're still looking, but it's a huge job.'

'As you all know,' Swift said, 'it's a race against time with Killy. He could still be alive. And of course, if that baby is alive, it may need urgent medical attention.'

What they all knew was that there had been a time lag between the disappearances of Jason and Chelsea, and their deaths, which meant that they had been held somewhere alive. So there was still a chance that Stuart Killy was alive, even if his being a suspect or an accomplice of Shepherd was unlikely.

Tracey put up her hand. 'Before we wrap up - I feel awful but... Christmas party. We always do it in the Angel function room, and its two weeks on Friday. Just so you know, boss, since you're part of the team this year. And it's plus ones as well. You know, partners allowed.'

The usual banter ensued. 'Who are you bringing, Dave?'

'He's got a waiting list, haven't you, lad?'

'Fuck off, I'm bringing yer ma.'

'Right,' said Swift, clapping his hands together to signal the meeting was over, 'any of yous fancy coming along while I pay a visit to our old friend Max Killy?'

'Meathead? Rather you than me, boss.'
'Thanks. Come on, Colette.'

* * *

'Look at this - it's all over the British newspapers.' Mikko and Helen were at Nice airport, and he picked up a copy of the *Daily Mirror*, which was running the headline 'Liverpool serial killer. Organised crime link.' Mikko skimmed the article, which ran onto the second page.

'Apparently, there's another missing person, and he's linked to some local mafia family. The Killys? Man, you English people have some weird names. Someone cut off his foot... Jesus. So - what does that mean for our... quest?'

Helen didn't know what it meant, and would need to process the myriad aspects of it, but right now, she was relieved to have a distraction from the tension between her and Mikko. She was racked with guilt and an unbearable, wistful sadness at the immensity of what she had done and the thought that now she must - absolutely must - go back. She was filled with dread at the idea that she was now guilty of this antinomianism she had lectured about.

Mikko's flight to Oslo was now being called.

'It's gonna be fucking freezing back in Norway, oh my God. Are you really going back to the Order, then?' She nodded, almost apologetically. He moved in close to her, to embrace her, but she shrank back. And then he did that stamping thing with his foot, in frustration this time.

'See, this is where God comes in. This is where the guilt comes in. See, this is the part I don't understand. I can't help you with that anymore, Helen. We did what we did, and there was nothing bad about it. Nobody got hurt, nobody...' He trailed off in frustration and turned to walk away but came back.

'So, here's the thing about your God. Your Calvinist God. He's a fucking asshole. Calvinism is basically religion with all the fun bits taken out. No music, no rituals, no confession, no chance of redemption. We had fun this weekend, right? And you still believe in God? So switch to a different religion.'

Helen couldn't help but smile.

'God is an asshole. I'm not sure that attitude is going to help you get to Heaven, Mikko.'

'Well, according to your religion, the asshole has already decided for me. I could spend the rest of my life washing people's feet or whatever, and I'm still headed to the fiery pits. Look, I'm just saying that they haven't destroyed you yet. It's not too late. I saw that spark. I'm in Oslo now until the middle of December, then we're back in London performing at this fucking Satanic Christmas Festival or whatever. I guess you won't be coming to that. But you know, if you do…'

Helen was desperate for him to walk away through that aeroplane gate before she was tempted to change her mind. She would pray, and God would tell her what to do. For once in her life, please let Him tell her the right thing to do.

Chapter Fifteen

Litherland Muscle Gym took up the whole first floor of a six-unit commercial strip in this run-down district behind the docks, not far from Chelsea McAllister's and Jason Hardman's houses. The units had once included a fish-and-chip shop, newsagent, butcher, and solicitor's office, which had together provided a community focal point of sorts. But now these were boarded up with metal shutters daubed in fluorescent graffiti. All that remained open was a tanning salon of dubious legitimacy. The streets around were dotted with odd businesses - scrap metal, car workshops, construction yards, a taxi firm, a laundrette - that may or may not have been connected to the Killy family empire. Despite its insalubrious location, this gym acted as the unofficial headquarters for one of the biggest cocaine and ecstasy networks in Europe.

Swift and Quinn parked their car on the almost-deserted street. The winter mist had descended low upon Liverpool that afternoon, shrouding the container cranes that hung on the skyline like blue and yellow ghosts.

'Boss,' asked Colette as they crossed the street. 'Aren't you supposed to ask Canter before you deal with the Killys? I thought we were supposed to give them a wide berth?'

'Fuck that. She told me to follow the rule book, so that's what I'm doing. Missing person means you interview the relatives. And anyway, there's nothing in the manuals about Canter's cosy relationship with drug barons.'

'How d'you know he's even here?'

They entered the building and headed up the staircase to the gym, from which emanated the echoed smacking and grunting sounds of someone engaged in a heavy work-out.

'He's always here during the day. It's his office. I had a few run-ins with him when I was on the drugs squad. Would you believe this fella doesn't have a conviction to his name? In fact, I don't think he's ever even been questioned at a police station. One day. Here we go.'

They raised their eyebrows at each other before entering the gym, a long, low room that was filled with exercise machines and weight-lifting equipment, completely devoid of clients. In front of them hung a punch bag that was being viciously attacked by a bald-headed, thick-necked, squat man. He wore Liverpool football shorts, boxing boots and gloves, and his orange-tanned muscular torso glistened with sweat. Around his neck hung two gold crosses. Standing next to him was a tall, blonde girl in a sports bra and tiny shorts, holding a clipboard, who appeared to be his personal trainer. The only other people in the room were two bald and burly men, almost identical to Max Killy, who leaned against the wall, arms folded, wearing black polo shirts emblazoned with the gym's logo. Darren knew them to be Killy's bodyguards. Behind a glass wall was a small office, at which a man in a suit sat behind a desk having a heated telephone conversation. This was the Killys' lawyer, another character with whom Swift had had past dealings.

Max Killy eyed Darren briefly but didn't look surprised, and didn't stop his violent exercise routine. He spoke with a Liverpool accent so strong as to be affected, more so since he enunciated every syllable slowly and clearly.

'Detective Inspector Darren Swift. To what do I owe this pleasure? Tell me you've found me nephew.'

'Hello again, Mr Killy. No, not yet. We've come to ask you a f–'

'Sorry, I can't hear yer. Speak up,' Killy shouted over the noise of his punches and kicks. Darren cleared his throat and squirmed internally. He knew the game - Killy was a master at making you feel uncomfortable.

'We've come to ask you a few questions about your nephew, in case there's anything that could help us find him.'

Killy continued to focus on the punch bag, and Darren used the wait as an opportunity to examine the man's tattoos. Amongst the anchors, snakes, roses, and stylised names of his children, there were numerous weapons on display on this contoured body - guns, a dagger, a cartoon bomb - but no visible axe. Killy finally stopped exercising, threw down his gloves, and held out his hands for a water bottle and towel that were handed to him by the girl. He walked over to Darren and stood squarely in front of him, several inches shorter but so intimidatingly close that Darren was forced to inhale the humidity of Killy's sweat. They looked each other in the eyes and then Killy moved sideways to stand eye-to-eye with Colette.

'Who's this, then?'

'Hello, Mr Killy. Detective Constable Colette Quinn.'

'Nice. Very nice.' As he looked her up and down, Quinn remained tight-lipped.

Killy suddenly softened his expression and stepped back jovially, creating a sort of performance space for himself.

'This lad,' he wagged his finger at Darren while addressing his entourage, 'this lad was a pain in my arse when he was in Drugs Squad. Like a dog with a bone, he was. A terrier.' He over-enunciated the word 'terrier' and pushed Darren's shoulder in a faux-friendly gesture, which caused Darren to stumble backwards slightly. Killy suddenly laughed manically and entreated his entourage to do the same. 'I told Canter, I said "This young fella, he'll go far."'

He approached Darren again and said in a stage whisper, 'Sorry to hear what happened to you down in the Met. If anything like that happens up here, you let me know, lad. I'll fuckin' lay waste to the bastards. We don't have that up here.'

He emphasised the word 'waste' with gnashed teeth.

But Darren was tiring of this charade now. 'Mr Killy, do you know Andrew Shepherd?'

'Nope. Never heard of him.'

Darren ignored the answer. 'Was Andrew Shepherd indebted to you for some reason?'

'I told yer. Never heard of him.'

'When was the last time you spoke to Stuart?'

'I sent him a text when he got out of prison. And that's it. Look, Darren. Detective. The Killys have got nothing for you on this. Stuart is me nephew, God love him, but the lad was fuckin' useless. And apparently, he went religious when he was in prison. Half of them do, and they're lost to us after, honest to God. Anyway, d'you really think he'd be working for us while tagged?'

Colette decided to speak. 'Mr Killy, you live in Formby, and we know you do a lot for the community. Do you know the Sisters of Grace, at Argarmeols Hall? Ever help them out with anything?'

Killy didn't even look at her. He approached Darren again, this time so close that his sweat brushed onto Darren's suit lapels. 'Listen carefully. Yous are barking up the wrong tree, coming here. There's nothing going down at the moment. But me sister is off her head with worry, and the talk is he's been kidnapped by the LaLa Mob. So find me nephew, before you make the Killys a laughingstock. Otherwise I'm gonna have to kick off just to save face. D'you know what I mean? And by the way, does Canter know you're here?'

At this point he signalled to the man in the office cubicle, who came out saying with a smile, 'OK officers, I think we're all done for today?'

'Unless you fancy going a few rounds? No? How about you then, queen?' Killy began his punching and kicking routine again and laughed at Darren and Colette until they left with as much dignity as they could muster.

'My God, he scares the shit out of me. He seems almost unhinged,' she said on their way down the stairs.

'I'd like to tell you his bark is worse than his bite. But it wouldn't be true.'

'What happened in London, then? And how does he know?'

'Long story. For another time.'

* * *

In a dim basement under a house, there are no windows and all the lights are off, but the whirring refrigerators and monitors give off enough blue and red light to make out shapes. A baby lies sleeping in a Moses basket. Arms and legs splayed, tiny fists lightly clenched. In a white babygrow and with white blankets, it could be a boy or girl. The baby's breaths shorten and become audible as it emerges from the depths of sleep to a light doze, eyelids fluttering. Its facial muscles begin to twitch, lips smacking, and the little fists go to the mouth, which gnaws from one hand to the other. Leisurely at first, then frantically. The baby is awake and hungry now, and its whimpers crescendo into screams. There is a determined rhythm to it now, as the screams alternate between anger and desperation. Legs kick and head tosses from side to side, and the baby's contortions will not fade until exhaustion hits yet another time, and the screams will subside to whimpers again. This time they have left her too long. A baby without sin can still cry. The baby's cries drown out the whir of the refrigerator, and also the cries from the other side of the room. Here there is another figure contorting, twisting, this time a large man on a hospital bed. He is in agony, his face in a permanent grimace, his clenched fists pounding the mattress. One set of knuckles is tattooed with letters that spell 'LOVE'; the other 'HATE'. Only three of the four shackles are needed for his limbs, and he has twisted himself as far as his body will stretch in order to face the baby.

'I can't help you queen, sorry, they'll be back soon. Please stop crying. For God's sake, please stop crying. I can't stand it.' He wishes they had just locked him in to the room, allowed him to move freely so he could at least feed the baby. Cartons of formula lie tantalisingly close by. His remaining foot points and flexes as fresh waves of pain hit, and then he breaks down into a coughing fit. He is wearing only a hospital gown, his blanket having fallen onto the floor, and the baby has kicked off her blanket too. But the low temperature of the room is the least of their problems.

Above the prisoners, the roar of daytime traffic on the M6 continues.

Chapter Sixteen

It was still dark as Swift ran through Crosby towards the sea, down South Road with its discount stores, still shuttered but ready to do a roaring Christmas trade that day; past St Wilfrid's church where Chelsea McAllister's body had been found, through the deserted marina car park. This was his usual route, and he loved the way it toyed with his sense of scale. As he jogged along the marina path towards the beach, the docks to his left were already at work, lights twinkling atop the giant blue cranes as they swung containers through the air, gantry levers cranking and the occasional shout of a hard-hatted worker. To his right, the marina lapped against its stony shore, and tiny sailing boats tied up for the winter tinkled as their masts knocked against each other in the wind.

Winter had properly arrived now, and it was bitterly cold. Swift wished to God he had put on gloves and a hat. He couldn't seem to do anything right at the moment, and he knew he was missing something. Something to do with religion, genetics, hunches, things that weren't in the Police Investigators' Manual. All he could see in his head was that incident board; that mess of characters, leads, tangents, possibilities. And all he could feel was a profound unease. He really needed this run to clear his head before work, because if he couldn't focus in on anything, how on earth could he lead his team? He was hanging on to this case by a thread, and knew that the moment he asked Canter for help, it would be taken away from him. *Where are you, Shepherd?*

As he approached the beach, a very faint dawn light began

to appear, and Swift prepared for that moment of exhilaration when the vast plain of sand would be ranged out before him. And there it was, space to think. The wind hit him too in a welcome icy blast, flapping his grey tracksuit behind him, freezing his ears. The tide had not long gone out, and each footstep was a slap on the wet sand. It was hard to see in the almost pitch dark, his only guide being the lights from the exploratory oil rig out in Morecambe Bay, and at one point he almost crashed into one of the Iron Men. He cried out in shock and backed away with palms up, as if apologising to the peaceful figure.

He passed the place where Jason Hardman's body had been crucified, and by now it was light enough for him to see the hundreds of bouquets of flowers that had been tied to the promenade barrier above. It was really time to turn back now, get to work, but it was so hard to resist the daily allure of that horizontal plain, as if the whistling wind was a siren imploring him to keep going. Past Hightown, the dune cliffs of Formby were visible now in the dawn light. It was misty, and the wet sand was quickly becoming sprinkled with a layer of frost. Through the mist, Swift thought he could make out a ghostly figure coming towards him. It didn't seem to have a shape but glided along, flapping grey in the wind. As the figure came closer, he laughed at the moment of terror he had felt, because he saw it was a woman wearing a long grey skirt and a shapeless grey coat, the hood of which was pulled over a veil. It was that nun, Dr Hope. He slowed down, and they approached each other warily, both unsure of the etiquette. There had been no contact between them since that day in the convent chapel, when he had been rather harsh with her.

'Hello, Detective,' said Helen, holding her hood on and wincing into the wind.

'Sister Helen,' he nodded, catching his breath. 'Come here often, do you?'

'Oh yes, I walk on the beach all the time. I do my best thinking here. More and more so, recently.'

'Yeah, me too,' said Swift, looking around him, wondering if this was completely against protocol.

'I was so sorry to hear about that poor girl in the church. How terrible. And now that missing man. I suppose there was a part of me that half-hoped you would come and ask for my help again. It was exciting, in its way. But I suppose I made a nuisance of myself last time. Silly.'

'No harm done. It was good of you to help. And we asked you.' He was about to take his leave, but she began to say something else.

'How is the case going? Any closer to finding Andrew Shepherd?' She was wondering if she should tell him about going to visit Clancy and Baptiste. *Of course not, Helen, you're in enough trouble already.*

'I can't talk about the case, sorry. But thank you for the help you gave us. It was... really interesting to meet you.'

'Likewise. Don't discount the religious aspects of the case, Detective. I know you don't believe yourself, but sometimes belief is more important than truth. Because people act based on what they believe.'

'Yeah.' He jumped up and down, blew warm air into his sleeves where his red-raw hands were hidden. 'Well, anyway. No more heavy metal concerts for you, then?'

She smiled and shook her head. 'No, no. That was an... odd interlude in my life. But there might be some changes to come. This murder case - it sparked off a... an unusual chain of events for me. It has tested my faith in ways I never imagined possible. I have to thank you for that.'

'It's testing mine too, to be honest.'

'Really?'

'I don't know what I mean by that. Faith in meself, maybe.' At that moment, the phone in his pocket started ringing, and he was glad of the convenient end point to this uncomfortable exchange. 'Well, have a good Christmas then.'

'Goodbye, Detective, good luck.'

They both turned around.

'Yeah. Swift.'

'Boss, it's Dave.' He sounded anxious.

'You're in early. Go on, what is it?'

'It's Shepherd. They've found his body.'

'You're joking…'

'Sorry. Not his body. Shepherd - he's alive. But he's in a coma. Jumped off the Runcorn Bridge.'

Swift turned around a few times on the beach, as if unsure which direction to go in. Then he set off at a fast jog back towards the marina.

* * *

Superintendent Liz Canter and Swift sat in the intensive care ward waiting room at Halton Hospital, watching a laptop, which was balanced on Canter's knees. The video they were watching, over and over again, showed the relevant CCTV footage from the Runcorn Bridge. It was unequivocally a suicide attempt; as a transport hub, the place was crawling with CCTV cameras and Andrew Shepherd had made no attempt to hide his climb on to the ramparts. A camera positioned halfway along the bridge, capturing traffic heading in and out of the Ethelfleda castle, had caught him in the corner of its screen. The zoomed, slowed-down footage was grainy, and Swift and Canter found it somehow hypnotic to watch a man as he prepared to kill himself. They watched him clamber up with purpose, then stand calmly, eerily, on the edge, light up something and watch it burn. Then he fell forward neatly, as if executing a perfect slow-motion dive. It was clear that he jumped and was not pushed.

He appeared to have been sleeping rough nearby; underneath

the bridge, in fact, inside the castle-like structure on the Liverpool side. Down here he had been out of the reach of security cameras, and Swift and Canter had not seen the moments when he expertly smashed his laptop; only the wreckage had been found, of circuit boards and broken shards of screen, plastic letter keys.

Shepherd had been put in a private room, from which a doctor slipped out into the hospital corridor, nudging the uniformed officer out of the way and making it clear that no-one was to enter. Swift and Superintendent Liz Canter stood up quickly and went towards him, expectant.

'He's in a coma, but stable,' said the doctor. 'Hypothermia, broken leg, pelvis and clavicle.'

'When do you expect him to wake up?' Swift peered past the doctor, trying to see through the blinds into the room.

'Look, detectives, I can't guarantee that he will wake up. It could be weeks, if at all. And if and when he does, he may not be in a fit state to talk to the police.'

Canter said, 'This man is wanted in connection with two murders, particularly horrible murders, and he may know the whereabouts of at least two missing persons. So, I'm sure you can understand our concerns.'

'Of course. I don't suggest you stay, though. It could be a very long time. It's really impossible to say how long. We'll call you, of course, with any changes.'

Swift and Canter sloped to the hospital café for a coffee. The lovingly decorated Christmas tree near the till only served to highlight how depressing this café was, filled with people dealing with their own varying levels of nightmare. Outside it was pouring with rain, which had caused the windows to steam up completely. At the table next to them, against the window, a toddler was gleefully drawing shapes in the condensation with his finger, standing on a chair, while his mother and grandmother spoke in hushed tones. Swift and Canter both turned their cups round and round on the table. Swift felt empty in a way he couldn't define. Canter looked at him. 'Tell me.'

'I suppose we found our man, then.'

'Yep. Looks like it. Look, Darren.' She leaned forward and touched his arm, tried to meet his gaze. 'I know it doesn't feel satisfying. But these things never do, honestly. Even when a case has been properly cracked. The main thing is, we've got him. He's safe here. He did it.'

Swift was tutting, shaking his head and tapping the table with his fingernails. 'There are just so many questions, though. We still don't know how he did it. Where he did it. Where is Stuart Killy? Where's that baby?'

'If and when he wakes up, he can tell us what the bloody Hell he was up to. And in the meantime, we'll keep looking, of course, although, between you and me, it's very likely they are dead. If Shepherd was sleeping rough all that time, it's very unlikely he had a proper lair. The rest will come.'

They were silent for a minute and continued to turn their coffee cups. The toddler who was drawing on the window teetered too far, and the plastic chair tipped over. He banged his head on the table as he fell to the floor, then erupted into screams. The mother dragged him up off the floor, tutting and comforting, berating the boy, berating herself, while the grandmother remained staring at the table, unmoved. Swift and Canter sat watching as this miniature family drama played out, and the boy was eventually bundled into a pushchair and the family made their way to the elevator. The rain was coming down even heavier now, and in no time, the boy's drawings had been re-steamed.

'Look, Darren, you did good police work. You really did. You should be proud of the way you led the team. It's a great start.'

'Come on.'

'It's true, really. Nobody could have handled it any better. But look. To be perfectly honest, this case was always outside of your jurisdiction, and we're going to transfer the next stage to headquarters. There's a huge case to build now.'

Swift protested, but she wouldn't let him, saying kindly, 'So the Crosby team can get back to local policing. You know it must be piling up… it's Christmas, and you've been working on this 24/7 for six weeks. It's time to let go, just a little. When we've finished here, you can go back and tell the team. It's been a great experience for everyone.'

'Just let me keep going on Killy, on the baby. Give me another week. There are still leads we're working on, still things we haven't tried.'

But Canter was firmer now. 'To be honest, Darren, it's not as simple as that. Nobody has championed you more than me, you know that, and it hasn't changed. But you know the Killys - so you know they've been working with Titan since last year. We've made a decent deal; they give us information on rival groups, things going down, all sorts, and then we… well, you don't need to know the details. Anyway, now they're kicking off big time about their nephew Stuart, accusing us of not doing enough, of incompetence, of leaving it to local police on purpose. They're threatening to go vigilante. The last thing we need is them coming down here and causing trouble. And by the way, I know you went to see Meathead.

'Now you and I both know they didn't give a shit about their precious nephew when they stitched him up to do four years for them. This is all just posturing, so they don't look weak. The poor bloke apparently he only had two weeks left with that ankle bracelet.'

Swift shook his head and tapped the empty Styrofoam cup repeatedly on the table. 'I've just got this feeling Stuart Killy is still alive. Jason Hardman was taken somewhere before he died, possibly for several weeks. And Shepherd-'

Canter interrupted. 'Darren. Feelings, hunches, that's all good, I've told you that. But pick your hunches. And pick your battles.

This case is bigger than you now. It needs a full Murder Squad team, and the decision has been made to hand it to DCI McGregor. You'll come back to Canning Place and transfer to another case.' Darren rolled his eyes in frustration, but Canter continued.

'If Stuart Killy is going to be found, McGregor will find him, in no small part thanks to your work. Another big case will come, I promise. The Crosby lot are exhausted and in over their heads; let them get back to local policing.'

'Yeah, there's probably been a couple of bikes vandalised by now. Maybe even a drunk and disorderly down the Bowling Club Christmas do.'

'Come on.' she laughed. 'It's not as boring as that. It's your home turf and you love it.'

'I do love it, it's true.' he nodded. Maybe this was a relief after all.

Chapter Seventeen

It was the final lecture of Helen's course, and the last day of the autumn term before the university Christmas break. She had always found this last lecture, the so-called 'secular one', the hardest to give. Firstly, because she would have to update it based on world events, current affairs. Secondly, because she felt obliged to round off with some of her own personal reflections. Otherwise, what was the added value? And it was scary to talk about herself. Particularly this year, when her personal reflections had changed dramatically.

'Many of you are studying Theology because you have religious beliefs, whatever religion that might be. But some of you do not. Some of you are atheists, agnostics, humanists, sceptics, freethinkers - call it what you will, but you are here for the intellectual challenge. And of course, eschatology is not just about religion. That's why this eighth and final lecture, Secular Eschatologies, is particularly important.

'Because secularism continues to rise exponentially, particularly here in the UK. And secondly, because in 2017 we are hearing a lot of secular eschatologies. These are portentous times, don't you think? The nuclear age and its possibility of total destruction - the unquantifiable nuclear fear - brought with it a secular eschatology that, unlike religious eschatologies, creates nihilism and apathy rather than ultimate meaning. Then we had Y2K, and the millennial fears which it engendered, the fears of the technological unknown. And now we have climate change, pollution, the Anthropocene. A whole new language has grown up around this idea of the Anthropocene, and that this era of mankind's dominance on Earth may be coming to an end. Cultural language has become apocalyptic, with talk of omnicide, of immanentising the eschaton; all of this designed to convey a sense of magnitude, of urgency, of impending doom. Some things happening in the news seem to confirm that sense of impending doom. For example, the extinctions of species; President Trump pulling out of the UN climate accords the refugee crisis; North Korea. And yet, we still seem to be in a sort of collective denial when it comes to doing anything. Are humans destined to be nihilistic? Are we unable to face death?

'The fact is that all eschatologies stem from our fear of death, from our desire for immortality. In 1972, cultural anthropologist Ernest Becker published his seminal work, *The Denial of Death*, in which he claimed that the fear of death, or thanatophobia, is the mainspring of human activity. Most human action is taken either to ignore or to avoid the certain inevitability of death. The terror of absolute annihilation creates such a profound, albeit subconscious, anxiety in people that they spend their lives trying to make sense of it.

'This theory was developed more recently by Greenberg, Pyszczynski and Solomon, who in 2015 published *The Worm At The Core*, reviewing the vast body of research supporting Becker's central claim. They came up with the idea of Terror Management Theory, which proposes that human cultural and societal values are self-preservation mechanisms designed to protect them from awareness of their own mortality. Religions offer literal immortality; the promise of an afterlife that never ends. Whereas secular eschatologies offer symbolic immortality, achieved through accomplishments in life, the bringing up of children, memories left behind.'

Helen had strayed from her lecture notes now, and although

she continued to speak, she was absorbed by one of those mini-revelations that had been striking her recently. Having spent her life so far devoted to the question of literal immortality, she was realising that she cared more about symbolic immortality, about making a difference in this world. She talked to the students about not being afraid, about living the eternal depths of the present moment. It was as if someone else was speaking through her, and it felt good.

'I'd like to leave you with a quotation from the eighteenth-century French philosopher Denis Diderot. He was certainly not a fan of nuns, as you will know if you have read *La Religieuse*. But I believe he might have been a friend of mine.'

She read from her notes.

'"The thought of our destruction is like a light in the middle of the night that spreads its flames on the objects it will soon consume. We must get used to contemplating this light, since it announces nothing that has not been prepared by all that comes before; and since death is as natural as life, why should we be so afraid of it?"

'So, we've come to the end of our semester here. I've thoroughly enjoyed marking your essays, and there's just the final one to hand in now, after the Christmas holidays. The title and reading list are in front of you. Now, does anyone have any questions?'

She looked around expectantly, but today there was nothing, even from Paul.

'Well, I've obviously covered everything perfectly, then,' she said. 'But since it's our last session, perhaps I might ask a question of you. Has this course changed your minds in any way, changed your thinking about what happens after death? Paul, you've been my faithful adversary these last few weeks. How about you?'

Paul shuffled in his seat and cleared his throat, unused to being in the position of being grilled himself.

'I'm an atheist. I don't think there's anything after we die. I don't see how any other point of view can be compatible with proven scientific knowledge. All religions can be explained by the stories we needed to tell ourselves in the past. And they have persisted for so long, even after they've been disproven, because they happen to be convenient for controlling people. So, yes, I'm an atheist. But that doesn't mean I'm a nihilist. Quite the opposite, in fact. It doesn't mean we don't have responsibilities. In order for life to have any meaning at all, we have to do everything we can while we're alive. All we can do is our best.'

'Paul,' she smiled, 'there are aspects of that on which we can definitely agree.'

As Helen gathered up her things, switched off the projector, and prepared to leave, she realised several students were hovering around the lectern. They had come up to thank her, to tell her how much they had enjoyed the course, to wish her a happy Christmas. A couple of them even shyly invited her to the pub. 'Oh thank you, how terribly kind of you, but I'm afraid Calvinist nuns don't go to the pub.' *Although, she thought, I may not be a Calvinist nun for much longer.*

People filtered out so that soon there were only her and Paul left in the theatre. She had been surprised at how nervous he had been to speak about his beliefs, having been so combative with her throughout the course, and so confident in his writing. 'Paul,' she said. 'May I say that your essays have been outstanding this term? Beautifully written, clear analysis. Well done on an excellent term's work. I'm sure you will do very well in the exams.'

'Thank you, Dr Hope.'

'It's unusual for an atheist to take a Theology degree. Not unheard of, and in many ways, it makes sense, but... may I ask if you have a plan for the degree, where you want to take it?'

'Oh, actually I'm not doing Theology, I'm just taking this course as an extra credit. And I suppose it has a certain link to my research. I'm doing a PhD in the Biology department.'

'Oh, really?' Helen thought that she really must get to know her students better in the future, not be so distant. Another change she was going to make.

'What area of biology, may I ask?'

'Genetics,' said Paul. 'My doctorate is going to be on the ethics of gene therapy.'

Of course it is, she thought.

* * *

Christmas is upon the city of Liverpool, heralded by music and lights. Here is the old God; the cathedrals are floodlit and glowing with city pride and ecumenical harmony. And there are the newer gods. The football stadia, also floodlit in a Christmas truce. In three days' time, the Boxing Day derby will resume the red/blue balance of ironic hostilities on which the city thrives. And here are the newest gods of all. Consumerism - shopping centres open late for business. St John Lewis, the shrines of Primark and Debenhams, Liverpool One is the new cathedral. And then, of course, the timeless gods of alcohol, fun, and love. No coats for the pilgrims in vertiginous heels and bare legs, short-sleeved shirts tucked into best trousers. In this city, to wear a coat is a sign of weakness. The worshippers totter and swagger down Matthew Street, cackling with joy, paying their respects at Heebie Jeebie's, Flanagan's Apple, where the bars are altars at which a different sort of eucharist is performed.

Out on the black waters, the Mersey Ferry lights the way from the Albert Dock to New Brighton and back, Slade's Christmas classic blasting from its foghorns into the sky.

* * *

But many different musical forms can equally herald the season. Somewhere in a decrepit, cavernous club on the outskirts of

London, Total Depravity was performing at the Christmas In Hell Festival. Tonight's crowd have added festive elements to their regular metal uniforms; tattooed skin garlanded with tinsel, headbangers lost their elf hats on the sticky floor; angel wings crushed against bodies in the pit; there are even, somewhat incongruously, sparkling devil horn headbands. Mikko had also been persuaded to don a red and white Santa hat, which he wore with an expression of grim acceptance.

Tonight, he has been unable to reach a state of flow, the emotional zone that he always craved where he thought of nothing but the notes, when the sounds would envelop his mind and he was at peace. The crowd would not realise, of course. They saw his lightning fingers, his thrusting tongue, his demonic eyes, and were satisfied with his performance. But behind those eyes tonight, the musical effect would not come. His eyes were mirrored glass. He looked for her in the crowd, hopelessly, knowing she wouldn't be there. As usual, images of the past overwhelmed him, but this time of the recent past. He kept seeing Helen's face, and then he saw that other nun, that fucking horrible fat nun with the scrubbed reddish face and the shopping bags, who had looked at him as if he was the devil incarnate. And then he realised he had seen that face somewhere else. Still scrubbed and plain and with that judgemental expression, but younger and thinner this time.

On a grainy photo, smiling in front of a church, with a group of other young people. In Cambridge. In 1999. On the photo from Helen's folder, that she had shown him on the aeroplane. Now Mikko's eyes were wide. He needed to get to Helen. He continued his performance on autopilot, furiously calculating how he was going to do this, cursing her for not having a phone, cursing himself for being so far away. The crowd had somehow picked up on his intensified expression and were going wild, the many-headed hydra at full range of motion, with stage-divers and crowd surfers spread to all corners of the venue.

When the song came to an end, the hydra erupted into a deep roar, a thousand hands raised in the signal of the horns. As the approbation died down, Mikko grabbed the microphone with one hand, pointed his other across the crowd, and shouted.

'Alright, you Christmas motherfuckers, this is gonna be our Last. Fucking. Song.'

The rest of the band looked at each other uncertainly, since they were scheduled to play several more, but Mikko was the boss. They shrugged and launched into a death metal version of 'O Come All Ye Faithful'.

* * *

Two hundred miles away, Helen was also singing. Ever since Mikko had taken her on that impromptu visit to the Angel of Liverpool church a few weeks ago, she had dreamt of coming back to recapture that feeling again. Tonight, she had plucked up the courage, and despite having broken all her vows - indeed she was breaking the vow of obedience by even being here - she felt God was somehow with her more than ever. The interior of the Angel church glittered with festive decorations, including an enormous Christmas tree, and red and green tinsel hung between the stone columns. A large nativity scene had been constructed in front of the altar, with rag dolls playing the parts of Mary, Joseph, the shepherds, kings and angels, and stuffed toys as the stable animals. The young children of the congregation could play with the nativity, and some of them ran up and down the aisles with the cuddly sheep, squabbling over who got to hold baby Jesus. Helen smiled as she thought to herself of the small plastic tree that Margaret conceded to be erected in the Order's hallway. St Michael's chapel at Argarmeols remained unadorned throughout Christmas save for a small wooden nativity set, and Helen imagined the expression that would form on Margaret's face if a child attempted to touch one of those figures.

She threw out her voice to 'Hark The Herald Angels Sing', holding up the hymn book, but delighted that she remembered almost all the words from her childhood. When they reached the final verse, the church choir performed a harmonised melody over the top, while the organist pulled out the stops to emphasise the bass line. The whole effect was so beautiful that Helen was moved to tears.

She thought of Mikko wistfully. Something was over, something was lost, but something else had begun. A new God was with her now - a kinder and more forgiving God. Soon it would be time to leave the convent, embark upon a new chapter. Faith was not stable; it could change, adapt, and it was not apostasy to see God in a new light. It was not apostasy to break vows that she no longer believed; perhaps had never truly believed. The Angel of Liverpool could be her new church; it was close to the university after all, and perhaps she could find a useful role for herself here, a more practical role in the community. She would join the choir, perhaps even lead the choir, perhaps learn to play the organ. She was going to see her mother for Christmas, and after that, things would change. She was sure of it. There had been no thunderbolts, no flashing lights, no apparitions from Heaven, no revelation at all, really. But something felt different. Perhaps this was as close to revelation as people ever got.

When the service was over, people shook hands, hugged each other, bundled their families out into the freezing evening in a catharsis that was not bleak and exhausting, like one of Margaret's sermons, but energising and warm. She pulled her coat close to her, wrapped her arms around herself and puffed the cold air away, darting across the busy road to where the Beetle was parked. She hopped in and rubbed her hands together, not looking forward to putting them on that cold steering wheel. It was pitch dark in the car, and she fumbled to get the key into the ignition. But suddenly, alongside the familiar car smell of air freshener, carpet, and petrol, she noticed she could also smell another familiar, pungent scent of unwashed wool and carbolic soap. She jumped in fright, her hand to her chest, when she realised there was someone in the passenger seat.

'Oh, my goodness, it's you! You terrified me! What are you doing here in the car?'

'You know, Helen dear,' said a familiar voice, 'you really must stop taking the car without asking. It's becoming a terrible inconvenience for us.'

Too late, Helen felt the presence of yet another person behind her, then a sharp pain as something stabbed into her upper arm. Then everything went dark.

Chapter Eighteen

Darren Swift was in his bathroom shaving carefully, more carefully than usual, trying to prolong the process of getting ready for as long as possible. It was the Crosby police station Christmas party night, and he had to strike that difficult boss's balance between fun and responsibility. Not only that, but he had added an extra complication to the evening, one that had been preying on his mind almost as much as the Shepherd case. The murder investigation was over in time for Christmas. He had survived his first three months in the job, his probationary period, his first big case. But something didn't sit right, and he was uneasy in more ways than one. He heard his phone ringing from where he'd left it on the bed.

'It's some foreign number,' shouted Matt from the bedroom. 'Do you want me to answer it for you?'

'No, it's probably one of those insurance scams. I've been getting loads. I need to put a block on me phone.'

Matt came up alongside him in the bathroom, placing the phone on the porcelain counter. 'Are you alright? I can feel the stress coming off you from in there.'

'Yeah, I'm alright. Just can't really be arsed with tonight.'

'Office parties are a minefield at the best of times. Are you sure you want me to come? I really don't have to, you know. I get it, I promise. You're allowed to have a private life. Especially as a police officer. And especially after what you've been through.'

Matt put a hand on Swift's shoulder, and Swift stopped shaving and put one on top of it.

'No, I want you to come, definitely. I really do.'

His phone buzzed, and a text message appeared from Colette.

Looking forward to seeing you tonight! Not my boss anymore! xx

'Shit. I've been a dickhead about this for too long.'

The Angel pub function room had served as the police station's Christmas party venue for as long as anyone could remember. Why would they go anywhere else other than their local? Finger buffet, free drinks until nine, coloured lights flashing over the makeshift dancefloor. A couple of secretaries were already dancing tentatively, but most staff were still grouped around the bar, taking advantage of their extended happy hour.

Swift turned the corner of South Road with a confident stride and some deep breaths, and he and Matt went into the pub and headed for the back room, where disco lights could be seen flashing through the coloured glass on the wooden doors, and 'Come On Eileen' was thumping through the speakers. He whispered to Matt, 'I can't promise you decent music.' They swung through the wooden doors, and immediately there was that disorienting moment when he saw his colleagues in a different context and had to do a double-take to confirm he was in the right place. But then there was Colette, and she looked beautiful in a sparkly dress and heels, with tinsel around her neck. And there were Baz and Tracey and the others. A few introductions, handshakes, pints bought, and it was done. Perhaps they were surprised, perhaps they would talk about it afterwards, but nobody was the slightest bit bothered one way or the other, it seemed. The inner relief he felt was almost overwhelming. Matt whispered in his ear, 'Bit of an anti-climax, wasn't it? I told you - this is Liverpool. It was never going to be a thing.'

Swift nodded into his pint, the weight of the world off his shoulders. But Colette had turned away to the bar. She blinked back a tear and steeled herself, downing a shot and fixing a smile.

Swift nudged Colette. 'You look gorgeous.'

'So do you. So does he.'

They both looked down and into their drinks.

'I'm really sorry I didn't tell you. It's just… it's complicated. There are good reasons, I swear.'

'It's alright Darren. Story of my life, fancying the wrong lads. I'll be OK. Unless it turns out that bringing a boyfriend is just your roundabout way of trying to prove you didn't shag Canter.'

They were silent for a moment, then she decided to pull herself together, because what else could she do? She motioned over to where Matt was chatting with their colleagues. 'He seems lovely anyway. Matt, did you say his name was? How long have you been together?'

'Nearly a year now.'

'And what does he do?'

'He's a firefighter.'

Colette pursed her lips. 'A policeman and a firefighter.'

'I'm gonna stop you there,' said Darren. 'And if you even think about requesting the Village People from the DJ, you're fired, I swear.'

Colette burst out laughing and put her head on his shoulder. And everything seemed to be OK.

'Is that why you didn't want to go down to Zeus, then?' she asked.

He nodded. 'Yeah, I just… I've been there socially, you know, so I didn't fancy them spotting me as a police officer. I'm sorry I didn't tell you before. There are good reasons, I swear. I haven't had the easiest time in the past.'

'My God, you grew up in the Mainstreet church.'

'Yeah. That's not the half of it.'

When Darren's phone started vibrating in his pocket, he was glad of the welcome distraction. It was the station calling. Over the inevitable sounds of Wham's 'Last Christmas', he mouthed to Matt and Colette, 'I have to take this.' He pointed to the phone at his ear and went out onto South Road, leaving them standing awkwardly together with their drinks.

'Swift?'

'Yeah, boss, it's Dave.'

'Yeah, go on, what is it?'

'I've found something. Can you just come back to the station?'

'Dave, what are you doing at work? I thought you'd be on the dance floor by now.'

'I know, but I wanted to finish chasing up those leads before Christmas.'

'On the Shepherd case? Dave, we're finished with that, you know that…'

'Seriously, Darren, you need to come, honestly.'

'OK fine. If this is a wind-up…'

* * *

Swift went round to the station at a half-jog and found it almost in darkness apart from the duty office. Dave was sitting at his desk under the light of a desk lamp, and Swift immediately noticed that Dave had transferred some of the case files to his desk and had built his own mini-incident board. He stood over him somewhat impatiently.

'Right, what is it, then?'

'Boss. I don't think it was Shepherd. At least, not by himself.'

'You what? Start at the beginning. What have you been doing?'

'So, as you know, I got nowhere on the timber planks or the van or Zeus, so I moved on to these… tang… tang…'

'Tangential.'

'Right, tangential links, you suggested. Anyway, I finally got the visitor records and phone records for Northern Genome through. They were difficult bastards over there; they wouldn't give them up, citing data protection, and the warrant took ages. Anyway - basically, Matthew Clancy lied. Shepherd visited him nine months ago, on three separate occasions.'

Swift rubbed his palm across his mouth, rocked on his heels, looked around at nothing, put both hands to his head. The ground was moving beneath his feet now.

'What shall we do, boss?'

'Wait a minute. Let's see the phone records.'

Dave handed him a pile of papers itemising phone calls to and from Northern Genome, and Darren skimmed through them.

'What are you looking for?'

'Liverpool numbers. Especially over the last few months. Wait, 01704, that's a Formby number, isn't it?'

He ran his finger down the lists, and the same 01704 number kept appearing, phone calls to and from, right until that day.

'Quick, look up this number, Dave.'

Dave typed the telephone number into Google, and there it was, unmistakeably. He looked up at Swift and said.

'Argarmeols Hall. The Sisters of Grace.'

Swift rubbed his hands across his face in frustration and a mild but growing panic.

'Those fucking nuns. Right, let's go. Call this in to Canter. I'm going to grab Colette and get over to Formby. I'll take a squad car.'

Swift ran back to the pub and into the back room, where he yelled through the door, 'Colette, I need you. Grab your coat.'

He looked over to Matt. 'Sorry, something urgent has come up. I'll see you back at home.'

'Don't worry, we'll look after him, boss!' Swift stopped for a moment to notice that Matt appeared to have settled in nicely. Swift drove to Formby above the speed limit but resisting the urge to put on the siren, telling himself to stay calm, that they still didn't know what was really going on.

Quinn sat in the passenger seat trying to pull down her short sparkly dress and pretend to herself that she hadn't had several drinks. They used the fifteen-minute drive to analyse this new information. 'So, let me get this straight,' said Quinn, hoping that her voice wasn't slurring. 'Shepherd, Clancy, and the convent are all in on it?'

'We don't know who exactly is in on it at the convent. Maybe all of them, who knows? But it has to at least involve that lecturer, Helen Hope. There was something weird about her from the start. No coincidences, right? I should have followed my own advice, followed my hunch. Plus, apart from anything else, the rest of them are all ancient.'

'Apart from that Deaconess.'

'True.'

'Also, they may not have been physically involved, but they might have known something. We could bring in the lot of them for obstruction of justice.'

'My god, can you imagine the cells full of old nuns?'

'Dealt with by our drunk rabble after the party.'

Finally, the car pulled onto the gravel at Argarmeols Hall, which was already dark and quiet for the night. The Deaconess opened the door in a dressing gown.

'Officers? What is going on?' she asked incredulously.

'Where is Helen Hope?' asked Swift.

'Goodness me, I've already had that dreadful rock band here looking for her tonight. What on earth is going on?'

'The Norwegians? They were here?'

'Yes, not half an hour ago. I sent them packing, of course. She's not here.'

'So where is she, then?'

'She went to… well, she said that she went to … I'm not sure. She's been very mysterious lately. Sister Mary might be able to tell you, although I'm afraid she is out as well tonight. She went up to the retreat in the van.'

'What van?'

'Well, our van, of course.'

'Do you keep it here? We didn't see a van either time we visited.'

'When it's not here, it's up at the retreat. We had to start renting one a couple of months ago because Sister Helen has been taking off in the car so much.'

Swift and Colette looked at each other. *The retreat*. The Deaconess was shivering in the doorway, so the three of them moved into the hall, where she continued talking. 'To be quite honest, we've had some major problems with recalcitrance from Sister Helen recently, and I'm somewhat at a loss with her-'

But Swift interrupted.

'So why did you rent a van and not a car?'

'We needed the space, Detective. For the renovations at the retreat. Sister Mary found all these cheap building materials.'

'Building materials? Like timber planks?'

'Well, yes, exactly, I suppose. She's very good like that. Sister Mary saved us a lot of money. She's been overseeing the renovations, working with some architect firm in Manchester.'

Swift and Quinn looked at each other again. *Manchester*. As his mind raced, Swift felt a black hole of hubris swallowing him up.

'How well do you know this, Sister Mary, Deaconess?'

'I've known her for fifteen years. But sometimes I wonder how well any of us know each other, really know each other, in this place. Do you think we have both made terrible mistakes, Detective?'

He ignored her and asked, 'Where's the retreat, then?'

The Deaconess wavered for a moment and was about to tell them that the location was a secret. But she realised she had no choice and gave them the address. 'It's around an hour to an hour and a half's drive from here. Just get on to the M6 and keep going.'

As they left, she called out from the doorway,

'Make sure Helen is safe, detectives. I need her.'

Chapter Nineteen

As the crew packed up the coach outside the stage door, Mikko called the convent and tried to call that policeman, Swift, the one that had come questioning him weeks ago. But there was no answer from either number. Music was still thumping from the next band on stage. He told the rest of Total Depravity that they needed to drive up north. It would take a few hours. They would have to trust him. He would make it up to them. And there were few complaints other than from the driver, who had been hoping to join in the after-party himself rather than staying sober. The band and crew packed the coach with as many hangers-on and alcoholic drinks as possible, and by the time they were past Birmingham and approaching the North, most of the passengers in the huge vehicle were very drunk indeed. But as the debauchery developed, for once Mikko was not at the centre of proceedings. He sat in the front seat, just diagonally behind the driver, looking out of the window and fiddling with the GPS on his phone. Surely, he could work out where this place was. She had described it as a stone house set in the hillside and visible from the M6, in the middle of the Pennines. It had to be here somewhere, and he must be watchful not to miss it.

* * *

Here is another nativity scene, of sorts. There are sheep in the fields, those hardy Northern breeds that need only be brought down from the fells for the winter. Instead of the guiding star, a full moon, assisted by the orange lights of the motorway and the Doppler streaks of car headlights. In place of the stable, a stone cottage, where a baby born without sin lies not in a manger but a Moses basket bought from Mothercare. No shepherds or kings to visit this miracle baby, but a large black coach, speeding up the M6, and filled not with gifts of frankincense and myrrh but with vodka, marijuana and groupies.

And where are the angels? Perhaps Swift and Quinn, also speeding up the M6 but a good couple of hours behind, hoping for back-up from Canter and desperately trying to enlist the local police in the nearest big town of Lancaster.

And what of Herod, who massacred the innocents, who sought the Anointed One to kill him and prevent the new kingdom of God on earth? In Judea, King Herod sent his men far and wide to seek and destroy the second coming. But tonight, the threat of Herod is already there, inside the cottage.

* * *

Helen awoke in a place that was familiar and unfamiliar at the same time. She was terribly dozy, almost euphorically so, her body slumped like a dead weight. She could barely move anyway, but had a sensation of being tied by the leg to something. That she couldn't move even if she tried.

'Ah, you're awake. Hello, dear.' Through blurred vision, Helen made out a large grey and white figure, and recognised the voice of Sister Mary, who came over and put her face close so that Helen could confirm it was her. 'You've not been out for too long, dear, just a bit of sodium thiopental, so we could get you here safely without any fusspotting.'

'Sister Mary, what's going on?' Helen's voice sounded far away and detached from her body. Her instinct was that this was a serious situation, and yet she was struggling to break out of the drugged stupor, and Sister Mary seemed so calm, her usual cheerful self.

'Oh, Helen, you have been such a disappointment to us all. Working a secular job, missing prayers, no evangelism whatsoever, taking off in the car, that dreadful heavy metal man… I mean it absolutely beggars belief. And then this… you had no business getting involved with all this, did you, dear?'

She tapped a large folder that lay on a worktop. It was Helen's red research folder, with everything she had found about Shepherd, Clancy, Baptiste, Total Depravity, all her notes and theories, everything. 'You went in my room?'

'Well now, we couldn't have this going around, could we? Because you know, despite her utter charmlessness, stupidity, and despite those homosexual proclivities - oh yes, we all know about those, dear, we all know what used to go on at the retreat - our venerable Deaconess was absolutely right. These have been portentous times, filled with rapturous signs. And the crucifix on the beach served as a wonderful warning, don't you think? A great change is coming. And here it is, my dear.'

Helen realised that Sister Mary's bustling about while she spoke was the bustle of someone preparing a baby's bottle. And she looked around, trying to gauge her position in this long room, as things gradually came into focus. She was sitting on a bare concrete floor at one end of a windowless room, leaning against the wall and handcuffed by the ankle to a thick central heating pipe. A couple of metres in front of her was a Moses basket on a white wooden stand. The basket was traditional wicker with white frilled sheets. It was moving slightly on its rockers, and Helen could make out the tops of tiny hands and feet occasionally waving over the top. Her ears still felt blocked by the anaesthetic, but she was starting to make out little squeals and murmurs.

'Here, make yourself useful. Hold this, will you?' said Mary cheerfully. Mary lifted a baby out of the Moses basket and held it inexpertly in front of Helen, who struggled up on her elbows into a seated position. She had no choice but to hold this tiny child that was offered to her. Helen was no expert, but the baby seemed very small and couldn't be more than a few weeks old. The last time she had held a baby was twenty years before, when she had held her baby brother.

'Now, you're not going to faint again and drop her, are you? I imagine your blood pressure is still low. No? Jolly good. She doesn't look very hungry actually, for once in her life she's not screaming the place down. Noisy little thing, aren't you?' She leaned down and prodded the baby's chest. 'Inclines me to believe she's the one thing rather than the other. You know how tired parents accuse their babies of being little devils? Well. Just saying.'

The baby was crying now, and Helen cradled it awkwardly, trying to find a comfortable position for both of them. Mary handed her a bottle of milk. 'Here, just shove this in her. That will keep her quiet.' The baby took the bottle readily, greedily, while Helen tried to ascertain what was going on in the rest of the room. She recognised the smell now, that damp moorland smell - she must be in the retreat, even though she had never been down to the basement. She could also smell that this baby had not been changed or washed properly, and behind that slightly fetid, sweetly pungent smell, there was the scent of disinfectant. The same hospital disinfectant she had detected in Shepherd's apartment. And she could see similar brushed silver laboratory units to the ones she had seen in Shepherd's living room, and similar machinery and equipment.

Then she realised there was another figure moving around on the other side of the room, no, two figures, one of which was prostrate on a hospital bed. There was a drip and a monitor, and the lying-down figure seemed to be in restraints - not psychiatric restraints with soft velcroed fabric, but leather and metal shackles, as if in a prison hospital.

'His vitals are dropping quickly. I'm struggling to keep him going here. But according to the last sequencing, I believe the virus has taken. So, we're OK.' Helen knew that voice. It was the deep, velvety voice of Matthew Clancy, although now it had lost some of its kindness and possessed an ominous urgency. He was wearing a lab coat and busying himself with his patient, but he turned around and said, 'Oh yes, hello Sister Helen, by the way. How nice to see you again.'

'What's going on here?' she asked, trying not to panic. 'Who is that on the table?'

'Oh, I think you know already, my dear, don't you?' said Sister Mary, and Helen realised she did. 'I thought you had it all figured out? That's Stuart Killy, dear. We just need to make sure he's clear of the soterion before he, you know, *snuffs it*. She said these words with a bizarre comedic emphasis. He's not responding very well at the moment, though.' She went over to hold a piece of equipment for Clancy, who was holding out his hand for an assistant. She peered down into Killy's face. 'Not co-operating, are we?'

'What on earth happened to his foot?' asked Helen. She could see now that his leg was wet and seeping, and tried to suppress her growing horror.

'Oh this? Revolting, isn't it?' Mary poked at Killy's stump, causing him to scream in pain. 'We had to take off that blasted ankle bracelet, and I'm afraid my amputational skills are not what they were. In fact, they were never anything, really. It was the first time I'd done it - a terrible mess, wasn't it?' She nudged Clancy, and he tutted as if she had burnt a cake or reverse parked the car poorly.

'Yes, Helen, I'm afraid it has been a long time since my medical training at Cambridge. And emptying bed pans for those disgusting old nuns does not exactly count as keeping up your medical practice, does it? But if he hadn't been on those steroids Shepherd gave him, it wouldn't have gone gangrenous, so it's hardly my fault.'

Stuart Killy stopped screaming when she moved away from his foot, but his head was moving from side to side in weak desperation, and muffled murmurs of pain were emanating from beneath his oxygen mask. The beep of the monitor was gradually decreasing in speed. Clancy leaned towards Mary. 'We're losing him. I think we'll lose him some time tonight, actually. But the virus has taken.' He emanated the calm seriousness of an emergency room doctor.

'Excellent. You'll be off where you belong then, won't you, dear?' she said to Killy.

Then Mary and Clancy stood silent and still for a few moments at his bedside, and Helen realised they were praying. She tried to manoeuvre herself closer to them.

'Mary. Talk to me. Tell me what's going on. Have you been working with Andrew Shepherd?'

Mary looked at her with theatrical disbelief. 'Goodness me no, quite the opposite! We're simply trying to reverse what he did. Can you imagine - to introduce the deigned reprobate to Heaven? A veritable demon in Heaven? You can't imagine, can you? It's too horrible.'

Helen tried to elucidate what that might mean - for a member of the reprobate to be accidentally introduced to Heaven, to overturn God's natural order of things. Even the Bible didn't say anything about that. Lucifer was cast from Heaven, of course, a fallen angel, but nowhere did the scriptures mention the possibility of him coming back.

'Mary, what have you done?' said Helen.

'Oh, don't be like that, Helen. You've not exactly been an angel yourself recently, have you? And we all know that Shepherd is the so-called bad guy here. There's no greater crime, is there, than to deviate from God's plan. How could we let that happen?'

'The only mistake we made,' said Clancy, who had now left

Killy to suffer alone and was removing his surgical gloves and approaching Helen, 'was overestimating Andrew's faith. We thought he'd accepted his fate of reprobation. And I suppose we did rather underestimate his ability as a geneticist. By the time he came to see me last year, he'd only gone and made it work. When we got hold of his first subject, Jason - and frankly, going into that nightclub to find him was like going to Hell in itself - we tested him here and couldn't quite believe it.'

Mary and Clancy began talking amongst themselves. Mary said, 'It's just as well these retroviruses don't last long. By the time Shepherd comes out of that coma, he'll be back amongst the reprobate for certain. I mean, what was his plan? To vaccinate the entire world? Ridiculous man. To say that the consequences would be untold.'

'Something of an understatement, my dear.'

'The police are going to find you, and you are going to prison,' Helen said.

Mary smiled pityingly. 'We shall be judged by the eternal judge, and I already know what the result will be, my dear. Don't you remember your Romans? Chapter eight verse thirty-three. "Who will bring a charge against God's Elect?" No-one!' She said this last part with the fury of Margaret Mills. 'God is the one who justifies, Helen. God is the one who justifies. And therefore, Matthew and I can do whatever we like.'

'In any case,' added Clancy, 'we're not going to prison. You are. You and that idiotic excuse for a musician. His UK tour provided us with the perfect cover. And I have plenty more hints to throw the police's way. It's all arranged.'

Through the layers of confusion and panic, Helen mused that there were perhaps four people in the world who knew they were of the Elect. Mary and Clancy were psychopaths, Baptiste was a drug-addicted gambler, and she herself - well, she had broken all her vows, committed the sin of fornication... in fact, several of the other deadly sins.

The baby had finished her bottle now and was squirming uncomfortably, so Helen tried inexpertly to hold her upright, which she thought might be the sensible thing to do. She looked into the baby's face. She seemed healthy, but small, and Helen wondered how much of her brief life she had spent screaming for comfort.

'Mary,' she drawled. 'Where did you get the baby?'

'Ah, now that's a whole other story, as I said. Fascinating in its way. Shepherd wasn't content messing about with the soterion. He wanted to remove the entire OS1 gene! Can you imagine? You can't, can you? A human born with sin to pass on to future generations? So, he found this poor young girl, and he impregnated her with a vile, depraved version of an embryo.'

Mary came over and wrenched the baby from Helen's arms, and Helen yielded in order not to hurt the child. 'But that left us with something of a theological conundrum. Because a child born without sin, I mean, medically, biologically, officially born without sin.' She held up the baby. 'Is this the Second Coming, or is it the devil incarnate on earth? We just didn't know, and so we couldn't simply kill that girl. We had to take it out. Very unpleasant, it was, wasn't it?' She looked at Clancy, who nodded and looked at the ground.

'Mary. What are you going to do with the baby?'

'That, my dear, is the question. And we are rather hoping you could help us with that, Sister Helen. What with all your training and knowledge?' She said this with no small amount of bitter sarcasm. 'We have been praying and praying, but God, in his wisdom, wishes us to decide for ourselves. It is the ultimate test of our faith, I believe.'

Helen couldn't help but wonder about this conundrum herself, insane as it may be. *What does it mean to be born without sin*? When Adam and Eve disobeyed God in the Garden of Eden, when they ate the fruit from the Tree of the Knowledge of Good and Evil, they brought sin and death into the world.

And they passed it from generation to generation, so that our very nature as human beings was corrupted in such a way that life without sin was impossible. *To be freed from that innate sin, what would that mean? And do I even believe this anymore?*

* * *

'There, that's fucking it! Take the next exit!'

The shepherds and kings advance, following the moon through torrential rain. The ungainly coach lumbers down country roads, tossing the revellers inside on top of each other, accompanied by much hilarity.

'Dude, where the fuck are we going?'

'It has to be that woman he's into.'

Mikko ignored them all, peering desperately into the gloom at the side of the motorway as orange lights glistened upon raindrops that trickled down the window.

* * *

In the cottage basement, Clancy suddenly stopped still, put a hand out to warn Mary to do the same, and a finger to his lips for silence. 'Listen. There's somebody upstairs. Absolute silence.'

Helen immediately began to scream. 'Help, Help, we're down here!'

'Oh, for goodness' sake, Helen, do be quiet.' Mary put down the baby roughly in the Moses basket and grabbed Helen by the mouth, stuffing a baby grow into it, which she secured with a muslin cloth. Clancy picked up a ready syringe and opened the door silently, tip-toeing up the stone steps. In the living room he saw a dark figure moving uncertainly, facing the stairs to the upper floor, contemplating going up. Clancy came up behind him, overpowering him, and grabbed him from behind as he struggled. 'Easy now.'

'Where's Helen?' Mikko said as he fought against the thick arm around his neck.

'You know, Mr Kristensen, you are a real pain in the arse. And your music is bloody awful.'

Mikko felt a sudden stabbing pain in his neck, and everything went dark.

* * *

Clancy dragged Mikko's body down the stairs feet first. His head and torso bumped onto the hard wooden steps multiple times, and Clancy was so rough with him that Helen dreaded to think what injuries Mikko might have. If he was still alive.

Clancy tossed him into the corner near to Helen, saying,

'Would you believe it's our friend, Mr Kristensen? And it's rather convenient that he is here, since you two are, of course, the prime suspects. Now, we don't have much time, because there will no doubt be others behind him.'

Helen tried to reach Mikko to check if he was breathing, but she couldn't get close enough.

Much time for what? Helen realised with mounting horror that Clancy and Mary were now busying themselves with something else. In the middle of the room, against the wall opposite the doorway, was a wooden table that had been fashioned into a sort of altar. *A sacrificial altar.*

'Mary, what are you going to do?' she tried to scream through her gag.

'Well, we're still not sure to be honest with you, dear.' Mary was less cheerful now, and had taken on some of Clancy's urgency. Helen realised that the room contained a lot of religious books and papers; not strewn chaotically as in Shepherd's apartment, but in an ordered, academic fashion, with a neat bookcase. Clancy and Mary had been studying. And they clearly hadn't found the answer. Mary's stress was mounting now, and she jiggled the baby too roughly as she implored.

'Think, Helen, think. What does this mean? We now *know* that Shepherd was sent from Satan. Look at what happened when he tried to commit suicide? Which, by the way, as you know, is the ultimate blasphemy. He survived! The Revelation tells us about the Beast who came from the sea. "One of the heads of the beast appeared to be fatally wounded. But the mortal wound was healed, and the entire world was astonished and followed the Beast". And so, Shepherd came out of the water alive. Wounded but alive. Satan, get thee hence! Lord, come to my aid!'

Mary's eyes were wild, and Helen realised she would have to think quickly. She was going to have to play-act now; she was going to have to pretend to understand their project.

'Mary, Professor, you're wrong, both of you. You can't possibly believe this genetics of original sin - it defies all logic. Predestination is precisely that - preordained - it doesn't depend on good or bad works. That's one of the fundamental points of our religion. And so to associate a gene with someone's moral behaviour during their lifetime goes against our religious beliefs. It defies all logic.'

'Oh Helen, whoever said God had to be logical?' asked Mary, looking at the baby and seeming genuinely amused.

'OK then, so what if it's the opposite of what Shepherd thought? What if the soterion mutation is the marker for Hell, not Heaven, and you have it all the wrong way round? What if those criminals, those maximum-security prisoners who provided you with the genetic samples, what if they weren't evil and destined for Hell? What if they were the Elect? What if they committed those terrible crimes because they lost their moral inhibitions? They might have been the antinomians!'

There was a flicker in Mary's eyes as she considered this, but Clancy was busy sharpening a knife, laying out a cloth, filling a cup of wine, in a bizarre travesty of a Christian ritual. 'Hurry up, Mary, if we're going to do this.' But Mary was wavering now at the thought of killing a baby, and Helen had to seize her chance.

'Mary, think about false prophets. Margaret told us to beware of false prophets; the Bible tells us there are false prophets everywhere. What if Shepherd wasn't a false prophet? What if the false prophet is Professor Clancy?' Helen struggled on to her knees, trying to implore Mary.

'I believe that Shepherd himself is the prophet. Think of John chapter three verse five. "You know. He appeared in order to take away sins; and in Him there is no sin". Think of John chapter one verse twenty-nine. The next day, John saw Jesus coming towards him and said, "Look, the Lamb of God, who takes away the sin of the world". That's it. Shepherd was trying to take away the sin of the world!'

Now the baby was screaming, and Mary's jiggling became more pronounced as she wrestled with herself. She shouted again. 'Satan, get thee hence! Lord, come to my aid!'

'Mary, listen. John chapter two verse two. "He Himself is the atoning sacrifice for our sins, and not for ours alone, but also for the sins of the entire world". That is Andrew Shepherd, Mary! What if he didn't change himself? What if he didn't give himself the soterion mutation? I saw his apartment, I saw the spiritual struggle he was going through, and I don't believe he changed himself. He was prepared to make this sacrifice. His own eternal damnation in return for the sins of the entire world.

'And you, Mary! You are a prophet as well! All of you, those years ago back at Cambridge. You were supposed to find OS1. Everything that comes to pass is preordained by God.' Helen was weary now, and her head hurt, but she clung to the theatrical energy she had learnt from Margaret. 'It was now, in these portentous times, the times of Rapture, that God chose you to find the gene for sin. What it means, the way it manifested itself, we don't know yet. There is much to do. But you are the disciples of Shepherd, and I believe the devil is tempting you right now. Jason and Chelsea were martyrs. They will become anointed saints. And Stuart too. Everything will be OK, Mary.'

Mary had stopped moving and held the baby more gently now, tears rolling down her face as she nodded in proud recognition of her own divine part in this sacred story. But Clancy was not convinced and Helen could see the baby was still in danger; they were all in danger.

The baby's screams had made inaudible the commotion that had been going on outside, as the Total Depravity tour bus, which had dropped Mikko at his insistence at the end of the lane, now ploughed up to the cottage gate, spewing up mud and decimating hedgerows on either side as it went. There were deep voices and shrieks of laughter as the contents of the bus spilled out, having decided to try to retrieve their leader. The freezing torrential rain had subsided now, but there were muddy potholes everywhere, invisible in the pitch black once the coach's headlights had been turned off, and bodies fell occasionally to the sounds of squelching following by laughter. Some tottered in high heels and miniskirts, others staggered in boots and chains, and in their inebriation, they gingerly approached the dark cottage like zombies, yelling 'Mikko,' accompanied by various insults in Norwegian.

But now there was another commotion. Flashing police lights, sirens. Swift and Quinn finally pulled into the lane, followed by two local police cars called in as back-up, but they found their path blocked by the Total Depravity tour bus.

'What the fuck is going on? Are they all in on this?' said Swift as they exited the car. They waded through the freezing mud and past the Scandinavian zombies in the garden, and found the cottage door open.

Just as Clancy was about to lunge forward and take the baby from Mary, there was a clattering down the wooden stairs, and

Swift burst into the basement, closely followed by Quinn. They attempted to take in the bizarre scene.

'Jesus Christ.'

For a brief moment, there was a silence and a stillness. Like one of the sixteenth century woodcuts that illustrated the harsh Reformation texts in Argarmeols Hall library, the ones that Helen had studied for so long, each figure in the room was frozen in their own personal, timeless battle. Everyone waited in silent anticipation while Swift ran back to the Shepherd case in his mind from the beginning. Matthew Clancy, Sister Mary, Sister Helen, Mikko Kristensen, Stuart Killy, a baby, a garden full of drunk Scandinavians. And in the time it took for his heart to miss a beat, Darren saw everything. It had been there all along, what Andrew Shepherd had been trying to do, and who had wanted to stop him. He remembered what Sister Helen had told him on the beach. *Sometimes belief is more important than truth.* All the detective training in the world - forensics, statements, records, procedures - that would only ever get him so far. He needed to get outside his own head and into the minds of others, and he was finally in Shepherd's head, where he should have been from the beginning.

Quinn approached Mary cautiously, her arms outstretched. 'Give me the baby, Sister Mary. Easy now.' Clancy grimaced and squirmed with frustration as Quinn took the baby gently in her arms, and then he and Mary held each other's hands and began to pray quickly. But then Clancy stopped mid-prayer and, as if having just had an idea, he began an attempt to talk himself out of it. 'Detectives, I'm so glad you're here. We managed to apprehend these two suspects for you.' He motioned to Helen and Mikko in the corner, where she was slumped against the wall, drained, while he was still unconscious. 'And goodness knows what might have become of this poor child if we hadn't got here in time.'

But Swift wasn't listening. He was looking over at the hospital bed on the far side of the room, where the rotting stump of a leg was clearly visible.

'What the fuck... Is that Stuart Killy? Jesus. Colette, call an ambulance.'

By now, two back-up officers from Lancaster police had clattered down the stairs and blocked the doorway.

'Matthew Clancy, Mary Jones,' said Darren, 'I am arresting you both on suspicion of the murders of Jason Hardman and Chelsea McAllister, and for the kidnapping of Stuart Killy and Helen Hope, and... of this baby. And... is that?' He looked over at Mikko's body, lying face down on the floor. 'Is he dead?'

'I don't think so, but he needs help quickly. He must have terrible internal injuries,' said Helen, who was trying to manoeuvre herself closer to Mikko. Swift was still confused by Helen's and Mikko's parts in all of this, but he was starting to suspect that they had simply been one step ahead of him on the same journey the whole time. 'So whose side is he on, then?' he asked Helen.

'Ours. Ours,' she said.

Clancy was led away protesting, with a calm incredulity, that it was all a misunderstanding and would be resolved by morning. Mary was overcome by her spiritual agitation, and as her handcuffed body was manoeuvred towards the doorway, she twisted around.

'Look to the child, Helen! Look to the child!'

In a blur of sirens, radios, bodies, paramedics and police lines, Helen was eventually released from her ankle cuff, shook out her stiff leg and shuffled over to Mikko's body. He was beginning to stir and groan.

'Mikko,' she said. 'I'm sorry, I'm so sorry. Listen, I don't believe it. I don't believe any of it.'

He tried to open his eyes.

'It's OK, I don't think I'm dying, dude. Everything just fucking hurts. And don't ask me if I saw the hooded guy and the gate while I was under. Because I didn't see shit. Actually, I did. I saw you.'

Chapter Twenty

'Aye, aye.'

Detective Constable Colette Quinn smiled as the automatic doors slid open and she strolled into the reception area of Halton Hospital, where Detective Inspector Darren Swift was waiting.

'Hello, stranger,' he said warmly, and they sat down side by side on plastic chairs. 'How's it going, back in Crosby?'

'Same old. But never mind that, fill me in on the case. I heard Canter let you back in on the case. Didn't do too badly in the end, did you, boss?'

'Would you believe it was all thanks to Dave? And you, of course. We're a good team.' They gave each other a look that brought all the tension to the surface and then washed it away.

'So, anyway, yeah.' he continued, 'Canter let me handle the questioning for both Clancy and the nun.'

'And?'

'He's denying everything, still smooth, still blaming the heavy metal band. She… is a fucking nutter. Refuses to even mount a defence, just keep spouting the Bible. But now we've got the van, they'll go down, no problem. Forensic evidence all over it. The only place where they weren't careful. It's just a matter of building the case now.'

'And what about our heroic heavy metal team?'

'The amateur detectives? They properly beat us to it, didn't they? Completely innocent, both him and Sister Helen. He's probably been discharged from hospital now. As for her - I hope she takes the opportunity to leave that convent.'

'Detective?'

Darren stood up as a woman pushing a pram came towards him, having been directed over there by the receptionist.

'Kirsty Long, social services. And this gorgeous little one is baby Elizabeth. We're calling her that for now because it was Chelsea McAllister's middle name.'

Darren and Colette peered into the pram, where a baby girl slept peacefully, wrapped up in pink blankets against the cold outside.

'Ah, she's dead cute, isn't she?' said Colette. Darren nodded in absent-minded agreement as they began walking down the hospital corridor, but he found it hard to tear his eyes away from the sleeping baby. Since Christmas, his dreams had been tormented by confused images of Andrew Shepherd's project, of what this baby was supposed to represent. It was nothing he could ever discuss with anyone; not with Matt, or Colette, or even with that Sister Helen Hope. It was madness, madness. But he couldn't get rid of that nagging feeling somewhere deep within him. *What if?*

As they approached the intensive care ward, the baby squirmed, struggled and cried, so the social worker plucked her from the pram, shushing and murmuring capably. She motioned to Darren to take the pram, and he pushed the empty vehicle inexpertly down the shiny corridor, the multi-axle wheels veering from side to side and making Colette laugh as she dodged out of the way.

'So if and when Shepherd wakes up, what's he going to be charged with, then?' she asked.

'Well, that's the weird thing. I'm not sure he can be charged with very much at all. Spiritual grooming is not a crime. Voluntary IVF is not a crime. His hard drive was completely unrecoverable after he smashed it, and there was nothing specifically criminal amongst the rantings on his apartment walls. The people he manipulated were vulnerable, but they weren't underage. No kidnapping, no violence, no assault. He genuinely believed he was helping them. Saving their immortal souls, in fact. A Shepherd of souls.' Darren was embarrassed at himself for even saying this out loud, and continued quickly,

'I mean, we'd have to meet this guy and see what he's actually like, but I imagine that the fact he indirectly caused these people's deaths would be punishment enough for him.'

'In any case,' added the social worker, 'there's no question of him gaining custody of this child following his behaviour. But access - possibly. And seeing the baby might help him recover, might help him talk. That's what the police think, right?'

They reached the private room where Shepherd was being held.

'I suppose,' said Colette, 'if he recovers, he'll be released into psychiatric care. I mean, he is completely insane.'

Darren was still looking at the baby, who was now fully awake, and stared back at him from the social worker's shoulder. 'Insane, yeah.'

The uniformed police officer stationed outside Shepherd's door knocked gently and opened it for them. Inside, the prostrate figure of Andrew Shepherd lay surrounded by machines that beeped and flashed as his bare torso gently rose and fell, his arms above the bedcover with palms open. His beard had been trimmed, his hair washed, but it was still long and unkempt, and fell around him on his pillow. An immense calm filled the room, and Darren couldn't help but be reminded of a church altarpiece. A nurse was tending to his intravenous drip, and she looked up and smiled brightly.

'He's showing signs of stirring, actually. Rapid eye movements, fast heart rate, audible breaths. We think it might be today...'

Dr Andrew Shepherd is standing at the Strait Gate. He has been walking for what seemed like an eternity, heaving one foot in front of the other as if they were made of lead. The golden sky has been weighing on him, but as he walks, it has gradually been resolving itself into two distinct and immiscible welkins.

Reprobation

One a dark red, thick with black storm clouds; the other a very pale yellow, almost white. The line that divides them gradually becomes clear. A wrought-iron gate, silhouetted black, with nothing before it, and nothing after it. Atop the gate sits a cockerel weathervane. Next to the gate stands a hooded figure, faceless, who instils neither fear nor hope, but simply a stillness, an acceptance. It is not yet time. Andrew Shepherd turns away and opens his eyes.

* * *

Lilith Taylor is taking her final breaths. She is alone, and she is not afraid. The rhythmic, throaty sounds that she makes become gradually fainter, and the monitor beeps slow down at the same pace, in a descending cadence of mortality. She thinks about her life, and the terrible things that she has done. She killed her own child, yes, she killed her, and eventually she killed her husband too. Those were the big things, and she had never confessed them to anyone, especially not to Shepherd, to Him. Because why would she? And who knows, perhaps they were necessary. But there were the small things too; the little cruelties that she meted out. The lies, betrayals, the petty meanness. She was not a good daughter, or a good mother, or a good wife, or a good friend or neighbour. She doesn't really know why she did any of it, or why she doesn't feel bad. In any case, she got away with it, perhaps because she believed. Because Andrew came, He came to save her, and then she knew that she had been right to believe.

As the heart monitor slows further, Mrs Taylor's body twitches occasionally, involuntarily. Her wasted arms are pock-marked with brown and purple age spots, so much so that nobody would have spotted the extra needle marks in the crook of her left elbow. Or at least, not the young care assistants who diligently washed her every day. It has only been four weeks since He was last here, and the virus has held, she knows that somehow. Her eyelids flutter, and behind them the world narrows to a tunnel, and she moves along it with ease, not like the last times, when she had been terrified and had battled one foot in front of the other as if through treacle. This time she almost skips like a carefree young woman again. The way begins to construct itself into a path, with a vast sky that splits into two distinct halves, and she is approaching a gate. The hooded figure is there; she knows him now; she has been here before, and she imagines that his face, if she could see it, would now be the face of Shepherd. As she approaches, she is not afraid, because this time she knows she will pass through the gate, and she also knows which way she will turn.

Outside, it is a bright, crisp January morning; a low sun in a cloudless sky, reflecting off the frosted grass. The nurse who visited earlier had flung open the curtains so that the quality of the light in Mrs Taylor's upstairs hospital room is almost blinding. It shines on to her pale face, hair, nightgown and bed linen, so that she almost radiates white light and a visitor would have had to shield their eyes. The light catches dust particles in the air that seemed to glitter around her. With an almost imperceptible gasp, she takes her final breath and the monitor flat lines into one continuous beeping sound. Soon a nurse will appear, take the time of death, and Father Anthony will come and say a prayer. On the counter next to her bed is a Bible, open at *Corinthians 11: 13-15. And no wonder, because Satan himself is transformed into an angel of light.*

Thanks for reading *Reprobation* by Catherine Fearns. Keep reading for an exclusive extract of *Consuming Fire*, where DI Darren Swift and Sister Helen Hope's story continues.

Acknowlegements

Thank you to everyone who has helped me on my writing journey and made the Reprobation series possible:

Laurence & Steph Patterson, Jeff Gardiner, Mark Angel Brandt, John Campos, David & Maureen Meldrum, Bob Stone at Write Blend, Jerome Pellegrini, Alex Skolnick, Geva, Zoe Green, Louise Braddock & Paul Tod, Lisa Brunner, Claire Coombes, Alice Cullerne Brown, Dorothy Roussen, Pritchards Books, Cassandra Thompson, Stephen Black, Writing Magazine, Rachel's Random Resources, Zooloo's Book Tours, UK Crime Bookclub, La Citadelle, Radio Merseyside, Geneva Writers' Group… and to James and Ted at Northodox Press – thank you for this wonderful opportunity.

CONSUMING FIRE

CATHERINE FEARNS

Preface to the 1879 translation of the Ars Adrammelechum

It is with far more trepidation than pride that I present, to whomsoever it may concern, this modern English translation of the Ars Adrammelechum. In full awareness that I denigrate the words of this strange, majestic and terrifying text by adding my inferior contribution, I am convinced it would be remiss of me not to prepare the reader for what follows. And, moreover, to entreat the reader to resist going beyond this introduction. Be faint of heart; do not succumb to the bombast that afflicted me and which can only end in hubris. For while it was my mortal duty to commit this work to posterity, my task has also been my destruction. Further mortal warnings are to be found below, but it is perhaps easiest in the beginning if I provide the reader with a faithful delineation of how this mysterious tome came into my hands.

In 1875, I took up a position as lecturer in the History Department at the University of Geneva, my first appointment after graduating in theology from Oxford. My remit was to conduct research on how the communities of the Jura region, on the border between France and Switzerland, had maintained their Catholic traditions in the face of post-Reformation persecution. As Protestant severity swept across parts of Europe in the sixteenth and seventeenth centuries, enclaves of devotees clung to the magic of the Catholic faith. Their practices were conducted in secret, shrouded in mysticism, hostile to outsiders, and consequently little had been done before now to document this particular consequence of the Reformation. For months I endeavoured in my task, visiting churches and burying myself in libraries, but I confess that my initial alacrity was soon oppressed by a debilitating ennui. Whilst my subject was not in itself tedious, quite the contrary, I was consumed by loneliness in this foreign country, where I struggled with the French language. Worse still, I was becoming increasingly aware that I myself was a tedious subject, as it were. I was utterly unloved by my students, a rowdy rabble far more interested in frequenting the opium dens and brothel houses of the Old Town of Geneva than attending my tutorials. One evening, I found myself drowning my sorrows at the bar of La Clémence when I overheard a group of young people in uproarious laughter over the tiresome dreariness of their tutor, Le Pré Anglais. I must own that I spent some minutes trying to convince myself otherwise, but this insufferable Pré they were mocking was none other than myself. I daresay it was at this moment I took the decision to make something of my researches that these frivolous young people could not possibly accuse of dreariness.

On the fringes of my study had always been the knowledge that the Jura border communities had maintained their Catholicism by blending it with ancient Celtic traditions. In a region famed for witchcraft, this paganism would seem to border on the occult, and so, until now, I had felt it anathema to my theological work. But I now wondered if I might use it to entice my students; even the word itself – 'occult' – is so deliciously forbidden. Through whispers and gossip in the churches I visited, I heard of one village in particular, an isolated hamlet near to Geneva on the French border, where there had long been rumours of strange occurrences; healings, miracles, cures; but also, of disappearances and unexplained fires. The name of this village was Les Paons. I reproached myself for the unnamed fears that had kept me from this study before, and yet it was with many misgivings that I, one morning in the autumn of 1876, travelled to Les Paons. The coach journey into the Jura took five hours and was all winding, treacherous tracks that caused the horses to struggle and inflicted upon me an unpleasant nausea.

When I finally arrived, I found the village to be traditional in style, with clusters of wooden chalets centred around a cobbled square. It was silent and strangely devoid of beauty, lacking the charm that one would expect from such whimsical architecture. Notwithstanding my weak constitution, awkward manner and poor French, still I found the villagers to be hostile and resistant. Not a single person would talk to me about local practices, religious or otherwise. At the time, I wondered if their obtuseness was simply due to my being unconversant with local customs, but as I look back now, in the terror of hindsight, I know it was something far more sinister.

Having manifestly failed to engage anyone in conversation, I made my way to the village church, parts of which dated back to the twelfth century. My reasoning was that if the architecture and contents of this church gave me no clues, I could at least pray to God for some inspiration. St Beatus' church stood on a hill at the top of the village, and as I mounted the stepped path towards it, I felt eyes, many pairs of eyes, boring into my back, as if the entire village was observing. I knew from my studies that St Beatus had remained a Catholic church, this village having successfully fended off the Reformation. However, on closer inspection, it appeared to have undergone no less iconoclasm than the Protestant churches that had been so cruelly whitewashed. The medieval gravestones that filled the grassy churchyard surrounding the main building had been left to seed. Many were partially covered by weeds, their engravings obscured by lichen. Any that were cross-shaped had fallen to the ground. A statue of the Virgin Mary had been decapitated and dismembered, while along the church wall, gargoyles and stone reliefs of biblical figures had been similarly mutilated.

The heavy wooden church door was bolted with an iron padlock which was coated in cobwebs, suggesting that the place had not even been opened, less still attended by a congregation, for a very long time. As I turned away from the church in disappointment, I jumped in fright and clutched at my chest, for in front of me on the pathway stood a huge blue bird with myriad emerald eyes in the tail that it shook at me. A peacock. We stared at each other for some moments before it strutted away.

By now it was late afternoon and, eager to leave this ominous place, I gave up my quest and return to Geneva. Before enduring that winding journey again, which would no doubt be even more treacherous downhill and in darkness, I decided to steel myself with a drink in the village inn. Almost inevitably, the establishment emptied of its few customers when I entered, but I remained steadfast, emboldened by the thought I would soon leave this place never to return. I ordered a mug of ale and when I looked across the bar; I noticed I was not, after all, the only remaining patron in this establishment. A fellow drinker was propping up the other side of the bar – old, drunk, haggard and unkempt – and whom I strongly believe now to have been a former cleric of the village, hounded from his role. He was staring at me, so I slunk away to find a booth, but he immediately followed and joined me, causing me almost to retch from the stench; surely, he was a beggar. But he did not ask for money. In a hushed voice so deep as to be almost a growl, he began to tell me a tale. Struggling to follow his accented French, I listened with the strange assertion that all my miserable life had been leading up to this moment; that it was my destiny to hear this tale. The man told me that in the vault of the village church I would find one of two copies that exist of a mysterious book he called the 'Ars Adrammelechum.' From the words alone, I knew this to be a grimoire, and I also knew the chthonic evil to which it referred. *The Art of Adrammelech: a spell book to conjure the fire demon Adrammelech,* and perhaps the key to all the strange events that were reported to have happened in this place.

I noticed that the man could hardly bear to say these words out loud, and after he told me the name of the book, he was consumed by a violent coughing, so much so that I feared he may be breathing his last. But he regained his strength and stared at me for a disconcerting length of time, and he quivered as if agonising over what to do next. Finally, he opened his coat to reveal an iron key which hung on a rope around his neck, telling me it would open a tiny wooden door at the back of the church's nave. He then described to me the sepulchre beneath the church, accessed by moving a stone behind the altar, where I would find the book inside an old chest. He told me never to go to the church, and never to open the book. And then he changed his mind; afflicted by a sudden panic, he gripped me by arm and urged me to take the book, and to destroy it. He took the iron key on its rope from around his neck and pressed it into my hands, looking about him as he did so lest the innkeeper or anyone else should see. Well, dear reader, we all know the perversity of human nature – since Eve took a bite from the apple, since Pandora opened the dreaded box – and from that moment my destiny was set.

My whole life I have been oppressed by a certain timidity of nature, and yet tonight I felt uncommonly courageous. Partly, I own, by liquor, since I had imbibed a not insignificant quantity; but, also by some unknown force of temerity that compelled me, that told me nay, I simply must.

I ordered my coachman quietly to return forthwith to Geneva with an empty carriage, uncoupling one horse for myself, which I tied up behind the inn. I waited until nightfall, *lurking in the woods outside the village, then crept up to the church, where with much struggling and creaking I was able to use the iron key to open the wooden wicket door into the narthex, exactly as the old man had described. There was just enough moonlight coming through the stained-glass windows and the hole in the damaged roof for me to feel my way past the pews to the altar and behind, where the stone moved for me, again, just as had been described. At this point, I cursed myself for having no oil lamp. I was forced to light a match in order to safely navigate the stone steps that were revealed to me; as one match was extinguished, I lit another and finally reached the floor of a sepulchral chamber beneath the church. It was littered with more broken and dismembered statues; a mass grave of iconoclasm over which I had to clamber, feeling more blasphemous with every step. I was down to my last few matches by the time I found a dust-covered wooden chest. With much heaving and creaking it opened, and there inside lay an object, also covered in dust and cobwebs, but unmistakeably book-shaped. I cleared away some of the debris that covered it, coughing and spluttering as clouds of grey surrounded me. Down to my last match now, I hid the filthy book inside my clothing and stole back to Geneva with much celerity, my precious treasure clutched against my person, my exhausted horse arriving in the early hours.*

Of course, I had no intention of either sleeping or obeying the old man's instructions to destroy the book. I immediately lit the lamps in my bedroom and began poring over it. The first thing I noticed was its cold, deathly smooth texture, its familiar and yet unfamiliar colour. Yes, it was bound in human skin! I had heard of this custom of anthropodermic bibliopegy, a macabre yet common practice in the seventeenth century. I shuddered at its touch. The second thing I noticed, with some dismay, was that this would be a tedious reading exercise, as the text was written in old French. In the end, though, this difficulty in reading led me to linger over every word with even more morbid fascination as I struggled with the meaning of this terrible book.

Although the author offered no clear introduction such as I have done, I was able to deduce – from the signature, date and place, and from textual study – that he was a Catholic priest who around 1650, as the Reformation spread, had been hounded from his parish and fled to the continent, where he travelled for many years. On reaching as far as Damascus, he discovered an ancient Samarian or Phoenician text of unknown authorship but written in Aramaic. He then spent many years studying and translating it. Unable to use the newly invented printing presses for such a blasphemous book, he wrote it out by hand in old French, making only two copies. He brought them back to his village, which at the time was called Guerillot but was at some point renamed Les Paons (the significance of this will send a chill down the spine of readers who venture further into the text), and where he was re-installed and became something of a cult leader. His name was Pré Jérome Hugonnet.

As I read on, my eyes grew wider and wider, my heart beat faster and I shuddered continually; never have such terrible words been committed to the page! I should have believed it a hoax, a fiction – a cruel trick by a depraved mind. How could something so appalling be created in the conscience of a mere human?! And yet many of the details, as a theologian I know, can be confirmed by other ancient texts. The Old Testament itself – the Book of Kings no less – tells of a god who demanded the fire sacrifice of children by his people, the Sepharvites. Further still, the perfidious contents of this tome, vile as they were, amounted to no less than an oracle into other worlds. What knowledge! Knowledge that opens vast chasms in the

mind that leaves you teetering on the brink of your sanity!
The Lord God rebuke me if it is not the truth. I ask you again,
dear reader, how could something so appalling be created in
the mind of a mere human? It could not! For these were the
words of demons! Worse than demons – these were words from
a place beyond Hell itself!

And so, in this way, it was my great misfortune to discover one
of these books (the whereabouts of the other is unknown) and
to make the first English translation. Here it is consecrated to
the reader without partiality, without abridgements, without
explanatory notes, other than this here faithful rendition of
how it all came to pass. I have tried as much as possible to
retain the spirit and character of the old French, but the reader
must forgive any errors or discrepancies in tone, for it is most
difficult to translate into our modern vernacular.

Finally, dear reader, a warning. A most serious and dire
warning. While this work was undertaken in the spirit
of academic endeavour and research, I must counsel great
caution in the reader's choices beyond this point. I would
indeed question the purpose of any reader who takes it upon
themselves to turn these pages. My life is now in shadow, and,
as the first chapter of the grimoire will point out so presciently,
what has been seen cannot be unseen. Everywhere I go, I sense
that strangers are lurking, following; my personal effects have
often been moved during my absence; I hear noises at night.
Several times, the charred carcasses of animals, cruelly burned
to death, have been left on my doorstep; several times birds
have come crashing into my window or down my chimney.
My dreams are plagued by unspeakable terrors, so much so that
I dread going to sleep and I am by consequence so exhausted I
am unable to teach. I have taken to opium to dull my terrors,
to whorehouses to avoid the loneliness of my bed. As my
rowdy students give up their frivolities and become pillars

of society, husbands and fathers, I outstrip them in vice and descend towards my personal place of annihilation. My sense is decaying, my body ravaged by syphilis and alcohol. And yet I fear less for my mind and body than for my soul, which is wrought upon by the demons whose words I dared to read. I suspect my end is nigh, in one way or another, and so by sending this text away to England, I hope that I may leave some small mark on this world, whether for good or ill.

I realise that my entreaties will be in vain, because I too was counselled, as the reader will be, by the first chapter of this book, not to look any further. And of course, I could not resist. I did indeed question the morality of my translation, and after much soul-searching I decided that it must be kept for posterity, that to destroy such an ancient and powerful text, no matter how terrible its contents, would be a crime in itself. Choose ye well, exhorts one of the ghastly verses within, and I can but choose the way of truth. And so, dear reader, you must now decide for yourself whether to continue on this journey, or should I say, this descent.

I bid you farewell and shall remain, eternally, your most humble and obedient servant,

Reverend Doctor William Lovett
Geneva, November 2nd 1879

Keep reading at Northodox.co.uk

CONSUMING
FIRE

CATHERINE
FEARNS

Printed in Great Britain
by Amazon